SWORDBOND

"The Fanged Horse Folk will raid us for what little we have left," Kor told his people. "But we will withstand them all, and Mahela's hell, and whatever evils may befall us. Together." Kor spoke so fiercely, I knew he held back tears.

He raised his sword high above his head. Tassida and I raised ours and touched them to his. And where the three swords crossed there blazed a light fit to dim the rising sun, white as starlight. The stones in the pommels shone as well, red and sun-yellow and amaranthine. Faces gaped, pallid.

"We three together make a multitude," Kor said.

Swordlight flared so brightly that people hid their faces in their hands.

Tor Books by Nancy Springer

MADBOND
MINDBOND

WINGS OF FLAME

NANCY SPRINGER

MINDBOND

TOR®

A TOM DOHERTY ASSOCIATES BOOK

MINDBOND

Copyright © 1987 by Nancy Springer

First printing: November 1987

A TOR Book

Published by Tom Doherty Associates, Inc.
49 West 24 Street
New York, N.Y. 10010

Cover art by Tom Kidd

ISBN: 0-812-55492-2
CAN. ED.: 0-812-55293-0

Printed in the United States of America

0 9 8 7 6 5 4 3 2 1

Two there were who came before
To brave the deep for three:
The rider who flees,
The seeker who yearns,
And he who is king by the sea.

Two there were who came before
To forge the swords for three:
The warrior who heals,
The hunter who dreams,
And he who is master of mercy,
He who has captured the heart of hell,
He who is king by the sea.

—TASSIDA'S SONG

Chapter One

I was dreaming of Tassida, her startling dark eyes and willful brows, her strong warrior's body, her small, tan, pink-tipped breasts. Well remembered, those breasts. Kor and I had torn her clothes off, frantic, searching for a wound, and found instead a young woman where we had expected a boy. . . . Much as I ached to, I had never touched Tassida's breasts, never courted her in any way, not by so much as a kiss. But sleeping on soft grass under a midsummer moon, I dreamed that she came to me. For some reason it was all right, now, for me to love her. She came in her proud way and laid herself atop me, and I caressed her breasts, kissed them, nuzzled them with my face—

Cold. That could not be true of Tass. She was all warmth, blazing heat even, passion's fire within her.

Cold as icy seawater! She stared down at me ghoulishly, teeth bared, her handsome head turning to bone, as if she were long dead and rotting—

I awoke with a panicky jolt to find that I could not move. A cold and heavy presence lay on me, holding me helpless with its weight, enveloping me in fishy folds, pinning my arms where it had found them. One hand lay trapped at the breasts. Yes, by Sakeema, the thing had breasts, huge ones, hard and chill, and my face was wedged between them so firmly that I could scarcely breathe. And the smell—Kor had not mentioned the smell. It was subtle, but fearsome, the very smell of horror, a womanly smell gone evil. And slime, threatening to choke my nostrils. But slime was the least of my peril. Down in the area of my chest and belly I could feel speartip teeth and a strong sucking force. Like a starfish on an oyster, the monster had its maw wide open, and it was working to devour me.

It was worse than any demon dream. I struggled, trying to thrash about, trying to kick away six feet of breasted body and fleshy, rippling wing atop me, and the thick, snakelike tail that wound tightly around my legs. But even in strength of desperation I could not move, fainting, there was not enough air—could not remember who I was, the devourer was turning me into—otherness, taking me within. I would no longer be—be—

I was Dannoc, Dannoc, Dannoc.

I was horse tamer, skilled archer, storyteller—Dannoc, son of Tyonoc, who had been king of the Red Hart Tribe. My father had been bested, but, Mahela be cursed, I would not be taken by any minion of hers! Hatred of what had been done to Tyonoc made me suddenly rock hard and calm. My breathing quieted, became shallow as I willed myself into a sort of trance. Merely enduring was the worst of tasks to me, for I far preferred to strike. But I had to endure until dawn, when the devourer would be forced to loosen its grip—and perhaps then I would have a blow at it.

Bowels of Mahela!

Even as I learned how to withstand the demon, it lifted off me and attacked in a different way.

Furling itself—those hard, swollen dugs shot out streams of cold liquid and collapsed. I caught a glimpse of a single great eye in the moonlight, and then the thing stood head down and upright, folded into a shape like a stubby arrow with the maw at the fore, fastened just below my ribs like a huge leech. It thrashed its flattened tail, swimming in air as an eel would in water, boring into me, mindlessly set on possessing me one way or another.

"No!" At least I could cry out, for all the good it did me. None at all.

I struggled to rise, to throw it off, and only gave myself more sickening pain, for the monster held me pinned to the ground with its great weight crushing into my gut.

Who was I? I could not remember my name!

Dannoc. Strong and tall. Dannoc, son of Tyonoc. A devourer had done this same thing to my father and turned him into a living, walking shell, demon-possessed by the evil thing hiding within. If that should happen to me, if I should then betray Kor as my father had betrayed me—

I could see Kor, my comrade. It had to be him, lying by my side, though another of the swaddling gray-skinned monsters hid him from head to foot. Only one hand lay free, curled on the grass.

He would be well enough. He was a king among his own people, Korridun, son of Kela, a wise king with many powers, and he had survived the devourers before. For me, it was the first time, and I was failing—I felt self slipping again. The thing was besting me, and I would kill my body before I let a devourer take it and turn it against those I loved.

Sakeema be thanked, at least I could move my arms. Sword and knife lay in the grass beside me, and I reached for the knife, groaning with the agony of the movement, which forced teeth yet deeper into me. Such weapons were of no use against devourers, I had been told, slicing through them as if through water, leaving no mark. Therefore I meant the knife for myself. Made of sharpest obsidian, it would find its way quickly to my heart, I hoped. . . . Kor's hand, lying near the weapons. He had made me this same promise, to kill himself before he let himself be possessed. Kor, my friend like no other . . . Hardly thinking anymore, hardly knowing who I was or what I was doing, I reached beyond knife and sword and gripped his hand, just to say farewell.

His fingers curled around mine, and strength surged through me.

Strength as of four warriors, ourselves and two out of the past. A high courage, so joyful, so effortless it could sing. I sat up, shouting out loud, and aimed a hard blow at the devourer with my fist—but already it had let go of me, had unfurled, was flying away. The other joined it, the two of them rippling away like the flat, stinging fish that live on the sandy bottom of the sea. For a moment the capelike shapes of them shadowed the moon, and then they were gone, and Kor was sitting up, blinking at me.

"Thanks," he said.

He thought I had handbonded to help him. I snorted, spraying slime, scraping slime from my face with my fingers, and his dark eyes widened.

"There was one on you, too? Dan, are you all right?"

"Of course," I said. "I just reached over to lend you a hand, weakling that you are." He had been fighting off foes both human and monstrous since he was a boy.

By then he was kneeling by me, staring—there was blood all over my chest and belly. "Great Sakeema," he whispered, and without ceremony he emptied a skinful of water on me. I sputtered, but he was intent only on washing away the blood, seeing the wound. "Great Sakeema, Dan," he whispered again.

"It very nearly had me," I admitted.

"You will not be riding for a while." He brought bandaging, passed the lambswool strips tightly around my body. I sagged against the binding, for my surge of strength had passed and I was beginning to feel weak and sick. "What happened?" Kor demanded. "I would have thought, pigheaded as you are—"

I was not too weak to glare at him in protest, and he grinned.

"Stubborn as you are, you should be proof against devourers."

I flushed—perhaps he did not see it in the moonlight, but he must have known, for he was Kor. "I was dreaming," I mumbled. I would not say of Tassida, for he loved her, she was his by a bond I scarcely understood, part of his kingship. He was the reason I would not court her.

"Oh." He smiled, though not to mock me. "A dream of the sort in which the cock lifts his head."

I merely grimaced, mortified, remembering how I had been pinned with my right hand at the breasts, the left one down by my bird.

"So the creature had a goodly hold on you before you awoke." He wadded a blanket by way of pillow, eased me down onto it. I lay there and let him wash my head and hands. A smell as of death still lingered on me, and I shivered. Kor brought another blanket to cover me.

"I keep telling you, Dan, tunics have their uses. Leather vests, even." He was trying to rouse me by teasing. Red Hart born, I went bare-chested nearly always, even in the wintertime, and on this fine summer's night I had not been covered by so much as a fawnskin. But Kor, being of the Seal Kindred, had the sense, as he put it, to keep himself warm. I reached out with one hand and pulled up the woolen shirt the Herders had given him.

"Not a mark on you," I said, and his smile faded.

"Luck was with me. I had the blanket up. The monsters are mindless."

Being of the Seal, he slept under blankets and furs. Being of the Seal, again, he had a skin of seashell tan and dark hair cropped like fur, as dark as mine was sunbleached bright. My eyes were sky blue, his the deep gray-green-brown of vast water. He was nearly as tall as I, and nearly

as strong, but deft, so controlled and contained as to make
me feel oafish.

None of it mattered. We were brothers.

We had done it with swordcuts and a handbond beside a
visionary pool, only a few days before. The cuts on our
fingers were but half-healed, and the handbond had been
tested for the first time this night, and had saved me.

Kor brought wood for the fire, blew embers ablaze.
King he might be, but I knew he would nurse me like a
mother until I was well. I knew without words that he
would stand guard over me for the rest of the night.
Yellow light of flames made me shut my eyes, and I
dozed.

I awoke after sunrise, blinking up at tall pines and
snowpeaks and the heady blue of mountain sky. My fanged
mare, Talu, was ogling down at me and breathing a vile
reek, stench of carrion meat, into my face. Her flaccid
nose seemed uncouth, huge. Peevishly I reached up to
push it away, groaning with even that slight effort. Talu
gave a snort of scorn and walked off, tail swishing, to
hunt a nest of asps up among the rocks. There was nothing
she liked better to eat than snakes.

Kor came over, laid a hand on my forehead. "How do
you feel?"

"Why do you ask?" I retorted, querulous. He knew well
enough that I was wretched, for he felt it himself. He felt
the passions of all whom he knew well when he was
waking and near them. My sorrows, my joys, my suffer-
ings were all his as well as mine while we traveled together. A mixed blessing, for my illness made him miserable
as well.

"I ask to annoy you," he snapped.

"Well, how do you think I feel?"

"Rather less strong than thin soup." He sighed, giving
up spleen. "There must be some sort of venom in the bite
of the devourers."

"Lovely," I muttered.

"Something to make the victim weaken. I always felt weak and sick for days afterward, and maybe not just from self-pity." He pulled down the blanket and had a look at me. My wound was still oozing.

"Sit up," he directed, helping me.

Unsteadily I sat while Kor undid the bandaging—he wanted to look at the injury in the light. He made me lie flat as he pulled apart the lips of the puncture to see how deep it was. He was gentle, as always, and I had thought I would be strong and silent—a pox on silence. I screamed with pain.

"Sedna's bones, Dan," Kor whispered, his face grave.

He bound me up again.

"If it were not for those mighty muscles of yours, the creature would have struck through to your innards. Perhaps it has, even so. Perhaps you had better not eat for a while."

I did not much feel like eating.

How he sustained himself the next few days I scarcely know. I was reared a hunter, but he was not. His people lived mostly on fish. He knew the ways of netting birds, so perhaps he did that, or caught something in a snare. We had a little maslin flour he made into thin gruels for me, I remember. But I do not remember much. I was far away with fever.

To sustain myself, I dreamed of Sakeema.

Once in a vision I had traveled with him, with Sakeema, that king above all kings, who had lived in my grandfather's grandfather's time. King without a tribe, born in a mountain cave, suckled by a deer, king who had never called himself a king, much less a god. . . . He who ruled all men and all creatures, yet did not rule, but merely lived. Power of healing in his hands. Power of new life—marvelous and beautiful creatures sprang from his touch. Blue deer with antlers the clear color of ice, white eagles, butterflies bright as fire. Few of the many wondrous creatures were seen anymore, for all had dwindled and decayed since Sakeema had left us.

Sakeema, who had promised that he would come to us again. Who in my vision had given me a friend's promise that he would come again, in the way we least expected, in the time when we needed him most.

Dreaming, I yearned for him, inwardly chanting a song of longing and love.

> The hart wears a crown but Sakeema wore none.
> Sakeema the king, where have you gone?
> Badgers have setts and the bears have their dens.
> Sakeema the king, where is your throne?
> What wantwits we are, what wanhopes all!
> We did not know you truly until
> The deer had taken you back to your dwelling.
> How will you come to us, beloved king?
> Perhaps even now you are walking among us,
> And dolts that we are, still we do not know you.
> Dear king of the creatures, prithee come back to us,
> Bring back the stags of wonder, we beg you.
> Our hearts ache with thinking of the small spotted
>   deer,
> Our hearts ache with thinking of the great maned
>   deer,
> Of the brown and yellow deer, our hearts ache with
>   dreaming.
> Bring them back to us, Sakeema the deer king.
> Bring back the stags of splendor, we beg you.
> Bring back the wolves of wonder, we beg you.

I awoke in the night, perhaps the second or third night, seeing the shadows of the looming pines, seeing wan moonlight, hearing a goshawk scream, and I felt an awful dread. I was very ill, and it frightened me, for I was not accustomed to being so sick. Wounded, yes, but not sick. Kor lay asleep beside me. I could reach over to rouse him if need be, but if I were to die I would be truly alone.

Sakeema, I silently begged the night, *please come to me, please help me.*

Awakened from my vision, I had been unable to remember his face, and I had despaired. But lying in the wound-fever and dreaming of Sakeema, I deemed that I saw him truly, for I saw Kor. No one could have done what Korridun had done for me and not be Sakeema.

Even in my right mind, I thought the same. Though at the time of which I speak I was nearly senseless. A day or two passed of which I remember little except wretchedness. A night came, moon on the wane, and I slipped in and out of nightmare. The devourer had indeed taken me, I was worse than dead, and utterly alone—no, I was waking, and the shadows lay long.

"Kor," I begged.

He was sitting by me in the night, and he reached over and gave me the handbond, not for the first time. It strengthened me with the will and courage of ourselves plus the two kings whom we had seen in the swordpool, heroes of old whose names we did not know. It strengthened me, but it could not avert what faced me.

"I am dying," I whispered.

He did not deny it. I could not see his face in the darkness, but I felt his taut distress as he gathered me up so that my head lay in his arms. His hand clutched mine tightly.

"I, who have faced Pajlat in battle and survived," I complained, trying to make light of it, "I, who have brought up a sword out of the pool of vision—I, who have survived eversnow and Cragsmen and hotwind wildfire, I lie dying of a wet dream and Mahela's ill will? It is unthinkable."

I would not have had strength to hold forth at such

length had he not been handbonding me. The peril to my body remained the same, and he knew it. A sort of warm salt rain was falling on my face.

"Sakeema," I begged him, "know yourself. Heal me."

I had called him Sakeema once before, and he had laughed at me. This time he was in no fit fettle to laugh or argue. He spoke only four words, and his voice was choked.

"I am not Sakeema."

"You, who died in torment for my sake, not Sakeema?"

"It was you—who brought me back, Dan."

He could barely speak. Shamed, I kept silence.

"There is no—power of healing in me. I wish I were— who you say I am—for your sake."

I had sensed for a certainty that he was. No one could have loved me as he had, showed me the mercy he had shown me, given self as he had given for me, without being more than man, more than king. But if he did not know it himself—and it was the custom of the Seal Kindred to humble their kings—perhaps he felt as helpless as I did.

Helpless, sinking down to death.

I felt as if I were drowning, but too weak to struggle, too weary to feel much pain. A heartsick longing for life was in me, but not much pain. Sinking, sinking down into the black water, swept along by its flow . . . flow turned to flight, black water turned to night sky. I seemed to drift in it without effort, looking down at my own bandaged body with an odd leave-taking tenderness, looking down on Kor where he held me in the glow of dying embers, his tears falling onto me. . . . I did not want to leave Kor. Above all things, I wanted to stay with him. But a tug like the current of a strong stream pulled at me—I strove against it, and still it carried me away, no matter how hard I struggled. I cried out to Kor, but he could not hear me, and soon I could no longer see him . . . then all was black, as if I were dreamlessly sleeping.

And then someone was roughly shaking me.

Indignant, I muttered reproach and opened my eyes, blinking in bright daylight. But my indignation left me when I saw Kor, his head drooping over my shoulder as he held me, asleep or swooning, exhausted, the marks of tears on his face. And by my side knelt Tassida, scowling down on me.

"What ails you two?" she barked with that proud lift of her chin that I loved. "Kor!" She gave him a shove to rouse him.

He raised his head as if it were almost too heavy for him to bear. Then I sat up to face him, stretching my arms, feeling as well as I ever had in my life. He stared, his mouth opened wordlessly, and joy lighted his eyes like sunrise over mountaintops. I hugged him.

"Kor, you rascal, you did it!"

"Did what?" demanded Tass.

"He brought me back from Mahela's grasp! I was nearly dead— "

"Dan," Kor interrupted, "I did nothing." He had hold of me by one shoulder, as if I might somehow float away from him.

"You must have! Without knowing, as you held me. I was as good as gone—"

"Perhaps we only thought that." He was smiling, but he looked abashed. "Perhaps we're a pair of jackasses, Dan."

"You certainly look it," Tass snapped, and she turned away, stabbing kindling into the embers at the heart of our firepit.

"How could we say for a certainty that you were dying? Perhaps you were just about to take a turn for the better."

"You know as well as I—"

"He was bright-eyed enough when I woke him," Tass put in, busy with the fire.

I lost patience, lunged up and started ripping at my bindings. "What are you doing?" Kor exclaimed.

The bandages were stiff with old blood. "Get these filthy rags off me," I raged. In my haste I could not manage the accursed knots tied behind my back. Kor got up and complied, to humor me. And as the swaddlings fell away, I turned to face him.

"Now," I challenged him, "say you have done nothing."

He gaped, turning so pale I thought he would faint. For my wound was gone as if it had never been.

"No," he whispered, swaying where he stood. I went to him to steady him, but once by his side I could not help but embrace him again.

"No!" he declared more loudly, forestalling me. "I am not—who you say I am!"

"Why do you fight it so?" I asked him, astonished. To be Sakeema and bring life and healing to an ailing world— what could be more splendid?

He straightened and met my gaze, his strength somewhat regained. "Dan," he stated, "I am overjoyed to see you well. But I tell you plainly, put that notion out of your head or I will knock it out."

Behind me, Tassida laughed. I puffed my cheeks in exasperation.

"You're tired," I said to Kor. "Rest. I will bring in meat." I threw a wadded blanket at him. But when I bent for my arrows and bow, a dizziness overtook me and I had to brace one hand against the ground to keep from falling on my head. It was Kor who laughed that time, warm and low.

"Healing or no healing, you have not eaten in too long a time, brother."

"Sit down, both of you," Tass ordered. "I have a few ends of old meat."

Strips of bison dried for traveling, she meant. She brought water, then washed stones and put them in the fire for boiling with. She made a three-legged stand nearby, slung a deer gut from it to cook in, squirted water into the gut from a goatskin, and put in the meat.

I sat and watched her, trying to calm the pounding of my heart when her movements brought her near me. Tassida. She was not many men's dream of womanly beauty, perhaps. Not dainty, she. Limbs long and strong, scarred from hardship and battle, a face somewhat like a comely youth's, firmer yet more fine. Her clothing was a wanderer's rough clothing, deerskin leggings, a patched tunic of brown wool. I had loved many women more soft and sweet. . . . Gazing at Tass, I could not think of their names.

The stones had heated. She moved them from the fire to the cooking water with loops made of green willow.

"Brother?" she inquired when she was done, as if Kor had just spoken.

We lifted our right hands to her, smiling, and showed her our matching marks—all my wounds had been healed except this one that I cherished. Then Kor showed her his sword—stone flashing red in the pommel—and we told her all that had happened since we had seen her last.

After a time she gave us warmed and softened meat to eat. "I am not hungry," she said abruptly. Her manner was odd, but it did not matter to me. She had always been distant with us, her past a mystery, a fargazing look in her eyes.

I ate and stole glances at her, utterly content, joy of living filling me so that I knew Kor had to feel it as well—I sensed his smile even when I was not seeing it. Even when I was looking at Tassida, her handsome face, the way the light brown lovelocks of her hair stirred in the mountain breeze, the soft sheen of her doeskins. Or at the wide-spaced pines with trunks nearly as orange as flame, the lush grass of the parks between them, or at the horses roaming there, my ill-tempered dun mare, Kor's yellow Sora, Tassida's beautiful, grass-eating Calimir. Or at the sky, so close, so blue I could scarcely bear it in my happiness. These were the uplands my people loved to roam, and I could not have chosen a better place to awaken in. My belly was being filled. Who could want for more?

Red deer came out of the distance, appearing like visions to graze at Calimir's side. And suddenly I felt the pang of an old longing, so old most folk knew it only as legend. There had once been eleven sorts of deer besides the red. Where had they all gone? We were few, we tribesmen, and the Demesne we hunted was vast. We had not eaten them all. Not even a tithe had we eaten.

The red deer sufficed to feed us, but the longing of the spirit went unfulfilled.

I felt Kor's wry gaze on me, and shrugged, and reached for my arrows and bow. Leaving him and Tass by the fire, I went off to down us a deer for our supper.

Chapter Two

Truly, Kor was weary, after nursing me more nights and days than I have fingers on one hand. I had thought he would be talking with Tass when I returned with a yearling hart, but he lay soundly asleep. Tass and I skinned and butchered the young deer ourselves. It did not surprise me that she was expert. She had been on her own, hunting and warring and carrying on some nameless quest, for years, maybe her lifetime of years, for all I knew. She had told us little, Kor and I.

"You hunt with mercy," she commented, severing the neck.

I nodded. The spine was broken cleanly by my arrowhead of chipped flint, so that the deer had died within an eyeblink. The Fanged Horse Folk, and even some of my own Red Hart Tribe, said that meat tasted sweeter when it had leaped in fright and pain, but I did not care. Venison downed by my bow might be cooked the longer, to my way of thinking, for the red deer were like tribesfolk to me, and I wanted never to make them suffer. I had practiced long to learn the skill of killing them instantly.

"If I cannot slay with the single bolt," I said, "I do not shoot."

"You should have so much mercy on Kor," said Tass.

"What do you mean?" I demanded, though I knew well enough.

"Calling him Sakeema."

I glowered at her. "Can you say it is not true?" I argued, lowering my voice so as not to awaken him.

"I hope it *is* true." Dark fire in her voice, for no one knew more of the legendary past than Tass. She traveled plains and mountains and seacoast in search of it. With a jolt I realized that her longing was perhaps greater than my own.

"Why does he deny it?" I muttered.

"You know what they did to Sakeema, Dan."

Ai, yes. Torments—and Kor had already withstood torments enough for any ten heroes. Shamed, I kept silence.

"Also, you know Kor, that he does not speak untruth or lack for courage. But you cannot know Sakeema for certain. So stop badgering Korridun. You are hurting him."

I retorted the more sharply because she spoke truth. "You dare speak of hurting Kor?" I whispered furiously. "You, who spurned his proffered pledge?"

I should have known those waters were too deep for me. She looked me levelly in my eyes. All powers, but she was strange and beautiful, her dark-browed face as startling as a dream.

"I spurned him for your sake," she said, "and if you should be fool enough to ask me the same, I would spurn you for his."

I stood up, reeling a little as if I had been struck, and took the offal away upon the deer hide to feed it to the fanged mares up on the slope. And there I stayed watching them, though their rendings made no very pleasant sight.

"Bring mushrooms for stew!" Tass shouted up the mountainside at me, and her shout woke Kor.

I gathered mushrooms and crowberries in a fold of birch bark. By the time I had enough I felt ready to face Tass again. She and Kor scarcely glanced at me when I came back to the fire, for they were quarreling. Or rather, Tass sounded vexed, and I sighed. Our Tassida had been the best of comrades when she was a boy: steady, courageous, ardent in a quiet way. But since we had found her to be a maiden, she seemed always to be on her mettle.

"I can't get any sense out of her," Kor appealed to me. "She says she just happened to find us here."

"It is true!" Tass dumped mushrooms and berries into the stew, stirred it savagely. "Wind of chance pushed me this way. Whatever urgings govern me, I always obey them."

Kor quirked his eyebrows at me, as if to say, See? But I was in no fit mood to dispute with her, and kept silence. She crouched with the stirring paddle in her hand, her lips slightly parted—they were of the shape of a noble bow, double bent. My mistake, to notice those lips. I felt a warm tide rising in me and battled it, ashamed, knowing Kor would feel both the warmth and the shame. No matter. He knew far worse of me.

"And you, Korridun King," Tass added more quietly after a moment, "you will be bound homeward now?"

"No. I mean, yes, but only for a little while." How his head lifted at the mention of his home along the western sea.

"Only for a little while? But where, then?"

"To go with Dannoc, to find his father."

It took the best wits of both of us to explain to her that Tyonoc had been gone for years, only the shell of his body left, possessed by a devourer that made him, seemingly, into a monster. When, maddened beyond bearing at last, I had struck with my sword, the devourer had rippled out of the wound and flown away. Tyonoc's body had crumpled like a husk, then disappeared.

"His self and his body are together again, somewhere," I declared, "and I must find him!"

Tass put down the spoon she had been holding. "Dan,"

she said with an odd gentleness that cut worse than wrath, "you are a blockhead."

"So I have often been told," I said stiffly.

"And justly so. If—"

Whatever she meant to say, I smothered it in noise. *"You,"* I cried, "who venture alone to the arid plains in search of—nothing, mere smoke puffs, imaginings, you call me blockhead? My father is real!"

I had come close to truth, for I saw her startle as the lash stung. "And you are besotted with him," she retorted. "You have been besotted with him since I have known you."

"It is called love," Kor put in mildly. "Have you a father whose name you know, Tass?"

The soft-spoken question, with not even a tinge of wrath or self will in it, served to stop us both at full career. The look on Tassida's face smote me. Then for the first time she answered us a question about herself.

"No," she said briefly. "I am sorry, Dan. All that I meant to say is, how can you tell me he is—whole, somewhere? When the devourers try to take you, it is as if you are nothing. You no longer exist."

So she knew that much. And the doubt she raised was one I had not wanted to face. I no longer felt like shouting at her.

"If it is so for my father," I said heavily, "then we will find it out."

Silence.

"There is my mother, also," I said after a while.

"And my mother the king," Kor said, his voice low, "and my father, who followed her."

"And where do you expect to find them all?" Tassida asked.

"Westward," said Kor, the single word.

The vast water that lay beyond his headland home. The sea from which the devourers came, to which they returned.

"The ocean?"

Kor nodded. "Mahela's realm is reputed to lie beneath the waves."

"Would you two think with your minds instead of your hind ends?" Tassida's voice rose. "How do you propose to reach Mahela's realm?"

"Getting there is no problem," I quipped, trying to make a jest of death. Tass gave me a glance of such fury it silenced me. But Kor spoke quite serenely.

"I am a king of the Seal Kindred. If my mother's blood runs strongly enough in me, I will be able to find my seal form."

Be a seal, he meant, and swim to Mahela's court, as his mother Kela had once done for his sake. Nor was Tassida very much staggered to hear it, for she had seen many marvels.

"Have you ever done so?" she demanded.

"No. I never wanted to, before."

"Then how—"

"Fasting, vigil." Kor shrugged. "That is as it comes."

"And Dan? Do you propose to go out in a coracle and drown yourself?"

Kor winced, for such was very nearly the way in which his own father had died.

"That also is as it comes," I said.

"Meaning, you have no plan," said Tass acidly.

Kor smiled. "Are you thinking of coming with us, that we must answer so many questions?"

"That is as it comes," she retorted, mocking us. "Once you are at Mahela's court, supposing you should ever reach it, what then? She is the goddess. You will not be able to take from her anything she does not wish to give you."

"We will see," Kor said quietly.

Tass snorted like a horse. "You are a cockproud ass! If—"

Kor interrupted, though without heat. "I meant what I said just as I said it. We will see. If we gain nothing else, we will gain knowledge."

"Much good it will do if it dies with you at the bottom of the ocean."

"Be of better hope, Tass!" he protested.

"Dolt," stated Tass, and she got up and strode off between the trunks of the great yellow pines until we could no longer see her. Kor sighed with exasperation.

"Do you want her to come with us?" he asked me, not turning to look at me.

I grimaced, for it was a vexed question. Being without her was perhaps less of a torment than being with her. "She plans to have neither of us," I said.

"Truly?"

"Yes. It is perhaps a mercy. If anything could turn us against each other, it would be she."

"I think nothing can. And I wonder what is her reason for refusing us." Kor was still staring straight ahead. "Do you want her with us? In some ways she is wise. And she will never betray us."

"Blast it. . . ." My thoughts floundered helplessly. I took joy in seeing Tass, in hearing her, in being near her. Not joy enough to ease my thwarted desire, but still . . . "How am I to say I do not want her with us," I burst out, "when I long for her?"

"I have seen you looking at her. Well, we still make a matched pair of fools, then, Dan." Kor smiled and stretched as if waking from sleep. "I will ask her when she comes back."

He and I sat companionably, stirring the stew from time to time, heating the stones to cook it, dropping them in with the willow loops. Afternoon passed. Sometimes he dozed in the warm sunlight. Sometimes we talked. Evening drew near, and the sun sank, heart red, toward the snowpeaks. Silently we sat, side by side, and watched it.

Color flamed through the sky. By Kor's side, the stone in the pommel of his sword blazed red, seeming to answer the sinking sun.

As if something had spoken to him, he picked up the sword and with both hands held it before him by the cross of the hilt, blade down so that the tip rested on earth. Like a young shaman taking vigil he sat holding it thus, his face uplifted to it and to the sunset light and to the blood-red light of the jewel. His dark eyes seemed to see far, forever, and his look was rapt.

"Zaneb," he said.

The name of the sword. And I knew it was not a name he had made for the weapon, but a name he had found. Sundown, it meant, and sun sank behind the eversnow as he said it. But as it vanished a glory went up, as if to crown the mountainpeaks, a splendor of the purest glowing amaranthine light, a half-circle flash of that unheard-of color, and then gone. . . . The blessing of Sakeema in the sunset, his greeting, gone. Long shadow of evening fell over us, and out of that sudden dusk strode Tassida.

And the heart-red jewel in the hilt of the sword in Kor's hands gave forth light like a bubble of blood that burst skyward, as if yearning for the lost sun. And Tassida stopped in her tracks.

But Kor was not looking at her. Softly he laid his sword down on the ground. "Zaneb," he hailed it, and lightly she rose and presented her hilt to his hand.

"How did you know her name?" I breathed.

"It came to me, as the sword came to me in the tarn."

"You would have known Alar's in like wise," said Tass, "had you not been so afraid." By the scorn that roughened her voice I knew that she was herself afraid. But some nameless sadness was on me so that I did not answer her. Zaneb. Sundown. . . . I sat gazing at Kor as he held the sword, I felt the touch of something beautiful, yet—fated. . . .

"Dan," Kor said to me easily, quietly, as if I had spoken to him, "there's a notion I want out of your head."

"I cannot help what I see as truth," I told him just as quietly, "but if it distresses you, I will say no more of it." All powers be thanked, not even Kor could read thoughts. Or so I believed.

"Well enough," he said.

We ate in silence, watching the snowpeaks turn dusky purple and disappear into nighttime sky. The stew was thick and fragrant. Kor and I used the last of the millet to make flatbread, which we toasted on the hot stones. We all ate ravenously. Only after every scrap was gone, except the chunks of cooked meat meant for the morrow, did Kor break silence.

"Ready to ride on the morrow?" he asked me.

"Yes."

"Truly? You feel strong and well?"

"As well as I ever have. You?"

"The same." He turned to Tassida. "Tass," he proposed calmly, formally, "travel with us, be our comrade again."

She seemed taken aback, and edged away from the fire. "I—I don't know."

"I promise you, I will not importune you in any other way." He turned to me. "Dan?"

It was a promise not lightly to be given, but I nodded. "As a comrade, Tass," I told her. "Just as we were before."

"You know that is not possible," she said.

"As close as we can make it, then. Tass?"

"I don't know," she muttered. "I must think. Or listen. To whatever it is that guides me." She walked off into the darkness.

She was gone all night, though I awoke from time to time and fed the fire to keep it blazing, making of it a beacon to guide her back to us. I daresay she knew the way well enough without it. Kor poked at the fire from time to time also, and prowled about, and he was up before the dawn, waiting. Which was well thought of, because it was not long after first light that Tassida came back and began gathering her gear stealthily, as if she did not wish to awaken us, though in fact we were awake already.

Kor stood up and faced her, his eyes grave. Only then did she speak in answer to his mute question.

"I must go my own way," she said softly.

"And what way is that?" he asked just as softly.

"For the time, back the way you have just come. I wish to see this pool of vision."

I had come stumbling to my feet. "We could show you."

"No. I will find it." She turned away, whistling for her gelding.

"Why off so early, Tass?" I was honestly puzzled—my wits are not at their best when I am half-asleep. "It is not yet sunrise! Stay awhile, eat with us."

"No. My thanks, but no. I am going now." The handsome black Calimir appeared at her side, his white legs and mane and white-spotted belly glowing eerily bright in the dim light.

"Let me get you a packet of meat, then."

I started rooting about for something to wrap it with. But Kor stood motionless where he was, and his voice when he spoke was low.

"You are frightened of us."

I listened for a snort, a scornful reply, but they did not come. There was nothing from Tass but silence.

"Frightened of us, since we know you for a maiden! Tass, why? What have we ever done to you but honor you?"

I straightened to look at her, food forgotten. She was

strapping on her wolfskin riding pelt, tying her pouches to it, fastening the cordgrass bridle, all in haste, as if she were fleeing from a real danger, and her eyes in the dim light looked haunted.

Kor took a step forward, and she froze as if he had rendered her too terrified to move. But his gaze caught hers, and she answered him.

"Nothing," she said, her voice so struggling we could scarcely hear it. "You have done nothing to hurt me. You just—are."

"Are what?"

She jerked her head away from his glance and vaulted to the horse's back. Kor caught hold of her reins, and I stepped to his side. "Careful," I warned, trying to ease what was happening with a jest. "She'll have her knife out in a moment."

"No!" Tass seemed jolted into speech at my words. Protests spilled out of her, and tears started from her eyes. "Dan, that was an accident—I thought you knew! I wanted only to cut the reins and get away—"

"I know, I know!" I hastened to reassure her.

"I never meant to hurt you." But she brushed away the tears impatiently with the back of one hand.

Kor stood beside me, holding the reins so hard that his knuckles whitened, and abruptly he asked a strange question.

"Tassida. Who gelded Calimir?"

She stared dumbly at him, and I turned to stare too. His changeable eyes were dark, purple-gray and stormy, and as deep as the stormy sea.

"You have told us there are no other tribes but the six I know. No person of any of them would geld a stallion, not even those slave-keeping Fanged Horse scum. And Calimir is not a fanged steed nor yet a curly-haired Red Hart pony. You have told us that horses of beauty, of the old breed, run wild on the dry plains east of the thunder cones. You must have caught Calimir there. But who gelded him?"

I looked back at her, seeing a trapped fear, seeing a secret too terrible to speak, and I felt a chill.

"Do you not think you owe us some small measure of truth?" Kor demanded.

Slowly, as if she could not help herself, she drew her knife of sharp blackstone. "I deem—you already know. Turn loose my reins."

Neither Kor nor I moved. "She did it herself?" I murmured to him, too stunned to speak louder.

"She must have."

"I saved his life, raised him from a tiny foal!" Tass cried suddenly. "He followed me like a dog, he was as gentle as a dove. But when his neck began to swell, he grew hot and mettlesome, and I didn't—I couldn't—"

"Didn't want him acting like a stud," said Kor, his voice careful, colorless.

"You can see he does not hold it against me." She was weeping, her knife gripped hard in her hand.

"Of course not," said Kor bitterly. "The creatures who befriend us, they are patient, mute, forgiving, they do what we ask of them without needing to understand. The horses, they let us ride them to war, through fire, beyond exhaustion unto death— "

Her head lifted with a snap at his tone, and her dark eyes flashed. She spun her knife briefly and raised it.

"Unhand my reins," she ordered.

Kor let go and stepped back. His compliance seemed to startle her so that she did not ride away at once, but lingered, sheathing her stone blade.

"Do not think too badly of me," she said softly at last, glancing at both of us equally.

"I cannot think too badly of you ever," I said, though an odd sort of weight lay on my chest, hindering my breathing. "Gentle journey."

"Gentle journey," Kor echoed me.

"And the same to you both, and—good fortune of all

sorts. . . ." She seemed about to say more, but then, abruptly, she wheeled Calimir and set off at a canter toward the east. I raised my hand in an awkward salute, and she returned it just as she disappeared between giant pines.

Kor and I kept a numb silence as we went about the business of breaking camp. Nor did we eat. Not until we were mounted and riding westward did we begin to speak.

"I would never have guessed it of her," I said to Kor.

"You are trusting."

"Fool, most folk say."

"Special sort of courage, say I. But I have been a king for too long, and I always wonder, and suspect. . . ."

"She could be killed for it if folk knew. Stoned at the stake. Abomination . . ."

He made no reply except to shrug.

"It's as well she would not lie with you," I said, trying to jest but not truly jesting. "You might have found yourself—altered. In the mid of night."

He grimaced by way of answer. We rode on for a while, edging up the flanks of the mountains, making our way toward the Blackstone Path and the Blue Bear Pass.

"Why did you speak of it?"

"I wish I knew." Kor sounded wry.

"You have more courage than I."

"Less. I think I wanted—to stop loving her."

Sakeema, his honesty. Understanding pierced me.

"It makes no difference," I said softly after a moment. "Loving goes on."

"I know. To my dismay."

Chapter Three

Daily we wound our way higher on the long shoulders of the mountains. Yellow pine gave way to dense spearpine and aspen amid spines of rock. The going was hard, but we saved many miles by slanting our way north and westward toward the Blackstone Path, which would take us over the mountains. The name of it came not from the mountain stones, which were granite gray, but from the knife blades made of obsidian, the black stone, which my tribefellows would chip and carry to the Seal and Otter peoples to trade for fish oil—along the coast even flint was scarce, and folk made their knives of shell and bone. The Blackstone Path snaked steeply up to a high nagsback, scarcely to be called a pass, between the Chital and Shaman peaks. It would be a hard way for the horses, and for us, but we had decided to attempt it this time rather than brave the gentler Shappa Pass, where so much misfortune had befallen us.

Autumn comes early to the high slopes. Aspens were turning yellow by the time we neared the trail.

Kor made the best of traveling companions: steadfast, seldom complaining, dryly amusing at times, at other times content to be silent for half a day or more, giving the mind a chance to rest itself in dreams. What endeared him even more to me, every day's journey gave him fresh cause for wonder. My mountains amazed him at every turn anew, and his eyes sparkled as he looked about him. He gazed days on end at the yellowing of the aspens amid evergreens, and at the alp, the high meadow far above, already touched by frost or an autumn moon, glowing the color of embers beneath gray-blue crags.

Blue sky, white snowpeaks, green pines, and the smaller trees so yellow they seemed to shine as we came within sight of the Blackstone Path. A slate-blue hulk squatted amidst the boulders that marked the way upward to the pass. Kor frowned at the sight of the Cragsman.

"I hope there is no toll to pay this time," he muttered.

But what could the Blue Bear require of us? Pajlat's steppes lay far away—no Fanged Horse raiders could be waiting in ambush. We knew better than to consort with the deer folk. And the Cragsmen had done no more than laugh at us before. Though Cragsmen were stony-hearted, capricious. . . .

And hard as the crags. Folk said they took form from the bones of the mountains themselves. And they could send great shards of mountain down on us, I knew. But an odd sense, something more sure than daring, was growing in me. It was as Kor had said the night we had clasped hands in blood brotherhood: we two together could do anything. Our handbond gave us strength and our swords gave us might. Ventures of any kind held few fears for me.

The Cragsman rose, clambering over the boulders with thick legs the color of granite in shadow, thudding down to bar our way as we rode up to him. As we sat our horses, his head was on a level with ours. I noticed the greenish, lichenlike growth of his hair. I saw his bare, massive chest, gray-blue and mossed with fur, broad as two shields. He stood spraddle-legged and scowling.

"Get down," he said.

I made no move to dismount. "We want but to pass," I said evenly.

"Something about you two displeases me. I smell enmity. Get down."

Kor shrugged and swung down from Sora. More reluctantly, I slid off of Talu. The blue giant scanned us.

"You." He pointed at Kor. "I challenge you. Fight."

Kor's mouth came open, more in astonishment than in fear, though the prospect of single combat with a Cragsman was fearsome enough. "But that is absurd!" he protested. "I am of the Seal Kindred! We deal fairly with all. How can you call me your enemy?"

"You wear my people's bane at your belt. Both of you do. Made of my ancestors' bones and of their blood. I see it, I smell it. I will kill one of you, and then I will kill the other. Fight."

The Cragsman emphasized the challenge with a lift of his knobby club. I got hold of the horses by their bridles, one in each hand, as they reared, lifting me off the ground—my weight constrained them to stay with us yet awhile. Kor sprang back from the Cragsman's blow, not yet drawing his sword.

"I have never done anything to you or your people! Nor do I wish to begin now."

The Cragsman gave forth a roar that seemed to bend the sky and quake the distant peaks. "Take him, Kor!" I shouted at the same moment. "And do not hold back—strike to kill! Nothing less stops these louts."

His sword sprang into his hand. The red stone on the pommel blazed like fire.

"I will pulp you with a single blow!" the Cragsman bellowed, swinging—the club was nearly as long as Kor was tall. But Kor stepped deftly under the stroke. A canny fighter, Kor. He had learned to fight with wit when he was a stripling facing far larger challengers in combat, challengers for his kingship. Still, I trembled as I watched. It was as the Cragsman had said: if he landed but a single blow on Korridun, he could kill him.

Kor did not wait for that mischance. He struck even as the club swung. With all his might, with speed beyond any I had ever seen in him, in anyone, he struck, and the weight of the downswinging club, the might of the Cragsman's blow, only aided him. Even as I blinked he had severed the huge hand that wielded the club, and the Cragsman roared again, a terrible roar of agony.

Kor's sword rose again, faster than I could follow, this time to strike at the giant's throat. Almost before the riven hand had struck the ground the blade swished again. But the Cragsman had fallen backward from the shock of that first stroke, and I had been wrong when I had said that nothing less than death would stop these louts of stone. This one scrambled and staggered away, gulping and roaring, "The bane—the bane—my people's bones and blood. . . ."

Kor stood where he was, staring down at the abandoned hand at his feet, and I came up to stand beside him. A thick, sluggish, yellow-green flow was creeping from the veins of the wrist, and as we watched the stuff changed color, growing at the same time darker and more bright, and hardened into a shining shape as of puddled water. I stooped and picked it up—it flashed in the sun as did our swords, but with a brownsheen glint. Still, it was of the same strange stuff, very smooth, hard and chill—what had Tass called it? Metal. I had never seen such a thing before, or known that the swordstuff came from the Cragsmen. The few times my people had managed to kill one, it had been by sending a rockslide down atop him.

Kor stood woodenly beside me, and, glancing up at him, I saw that he was troubled, though not by the lump of strange stuff in my hand. He seemed scarcely to see it, and I laid it down and stood to peer at him.

"It wasn't me," he said.

"What wasn't you?"

"Zaneb—she has passions of her own. I was content to send him away. She struck to kill him."

Stiffly he raised the sword. Bright shards of brownsheen metal fell off the blade, striking the rocky ground with a faint ringing sound.

"Sheathe her," I said, and he did, and deeply breathed, and looked around him.

So the swords had seen this same sort of combat before—when? And at whose side? For what purpose? To gather blood? To bring back bones of Cragsmen and make weapons of them? There was no time to speak of it.

"Shall we go on?" I asked Kor slowly. "The lot of them might come roaring down on us for revenge."

"Or they might keep well away from us, if they are truly afraid. Perhaps Alar does not like Cragsmen either."

I felt my sword stir in its scabbard as he spoke its name, and that decided me.

"To mount, then, and let us ride quickly."

We rode at the canter when we could, and we rode past dusk and late into the night until moonset, trying to put ourselves in an entirely different place. We rode out of spearpine and into blue pine and spruce. From time to time we heard bellowings far above, among the rocks that pierced the eversnow. They did not comfort us.

With first light the next day we were on our way, pressing the pace all through the day. But by sundown we considered that we had fled far enough. The air was starting to thin, for we had nearly reached the tree line. We would need our strength for what lay before us. And we had heard no more bellowings, nor seen a Cragsman.

We had nothing to eat except foragings, a few nuts, some bundleberries. "What I wouldn't give for a handful of oatmeal," I complained to Kor. "Or even a stinking fish."

I meant to make him smile, and partly succeeded. He quirked a wry half-smile at me.

"Our horses eat meat," I held forth, addressing earth and sky with my plaint. "Would that I could eat grass and leaves!"

"Go stalk us a deer," he said mildly, "and I will make the fire."

I took my stand behind the last stunted spruce at the tree line, looking out over the highmountain meadow that stretched to the eversnow. High meadow had always seemed a magical place to me, and never more so than that evening, when the westering sun set it afire, sedges and hummocks of heather and leaves of stunted shrubs blazing red and orange and again red, so rich a red it seemed black in shadow but bright as blood in light. And there was a white mist also, rising out of the redness, and moving in the mist were the tree-shapes of antlers with the velvet fluttering about them—the harts would soon be in rut. I took the stable-stance, arrow nocked and bow at the ready, and waited for one to graze near me.

It did not take long. A splendid stag drifted out of the mist no more than twenty paces from me and stood, head lifted, as if he were admiring the sunset world very much as I had been. For a moment I held fast to my arrow, telling myself that I would wait for a better shot, though in fact I could have killed him cleanly where he stood. . . . Truth was, his glance seemed so nearly human that my heart misgave me. But my stomach stirred, reminding me of hunger, and I thought of Kor waiting at our campsite, already preparing the cooking fire. I made sure my aim—

Out of the mist bounded a hind, pure white, as white as the mist, and she leaped up to the hart, my quarry, and nuzzled him with her mouth. My bow sagged until my arrow pointed at the ground, and I let it fall limply away, for I felt weak. I had nearly slain an old friend.

"Birc!" I called.

Red hart and white hind gave a startled leap but then

stood still, heads high, looking toward the sound of my voice. I walked out of my cover so that they could see me.

"By all the powers, Birc," I said, my voice shaking, "you should be more careful. I nearly killed you." I had not at all been expecting to see him, for we had left him two mountains away, near the ill-fated Shappa Pass.

The hart trotted up to me, great antlers riding on its stately head, very beautiful, dark brown eyes gazing into mine and glowing with joy. I reached out a hand in greeting, touched it on the neck, and there stood Birc in his human form, brown hair unruly on his forehead as of old. His shy smile broadened almost into a grin when I threw my arms around him and gave him the embrace of a comrade.

"Birc, well met!"

His face flushed with pleasure, and in his excitement he made little bleating, troating noises, such as the deer speak among themselves. Though he had been one of Kor's people of the Seal Kindred, and they were not a hairy folk, I saw that his naked body was covered with a fine, reddish fur.

"You cannot speak?"

He shook his head. Small spike antlers jutted from his forehead just at the browline, revealed by the stirring of his hair.

"No matter," I said. "Come see Kor. He will shout for joy."

The white hind stood by Birc's side, she, the most lovely of hinds, her fearless eyes of a purplish herb green and very human in her dainty head. Her I would not touch. I was afraid of her, for I knew what had happened to Birc through embracing her.

She walked with us back to camp. Kor sat working bow and bore to make a fire. The sticks clattered down forgotten when he saw my companion.

"Birc!" I was right—it was a shout. In two strides Kor

had reached him, embracing him with the hard clasp of a
king. Birc gave a soft, bleating cry of happiness.

"By our ancestor Sedna, but I am glad to see you well!
Sit down, eat with us—oh, blast it to Mahela. Dan, I
suppose there is not anything to eat."

I shook my head. It seemed out of the question now to
shoot a deer. But Birc reached over with casual ease and
touched the white hind along her level back. For a moment
my vision seemed to blur, and then she stood there also in
her human form, a maiden with those eerie green eyes, a
glorious mane of russet hair and white skin covered with
pale fawn-colored fur. My breath tightened at the sight of
her, she was so beautiful and so strange. Still standing
with his hand on her back, Birc spoke softly into her ear,
as deer speak, nuzzling her with his lips. Then she turned
and went away upslope, and Birc sat down by our
fire-yet-to-be.

Kor went back to his plying of bow and bore. "I
suppose I ought to set some snares," I said without much
fervor. Snares took time. A day might go by before a pika
or a whistling marmot chose to hang itself in one, and not
much more than a mouthful when one did. Meanwhile we
were miserable with hunger.

Birc spread his palms at me in a gesture as if to say, Do
not worry.

"Just think," I told him with mock annoyance, "we
could be butchering your haunches right now." I went to
my pack to get the lengths of rawhide I needed—

Without the sound of a single footfall the white hind
came back to our campsite, she in her womanly form, and
with her came a retinue that made me drop snares and
forget hunger: half a twelve of other deer women, their
beauty such that I stared. They were of a richer fawn
brown than she, their manes of glossy hair as red as a red
deer's flanks in springtime, their eyes brown or green or
yellow-brown, like resin, all depth and glow. And of

course they were naked, their breasts brown-tipped, full but not overfull, as dainty as their delicate way of stepping. And the soft swelling beneath their merkins—ai, but I lusted. Their strangeness, the fine fur that covered them, no longer served to put me off. I felt hot and watery with longing.

"Kor," I said hoarsely, clenching my fists, "do not touch them unless you wish to grow antlers."

"Speak for yourself, Dan," he replied with some amusement in his voice. "I feel no desire to touch them."

He had the fire going at last and was feeding it with pine needle and bits of dry rot and deadwood. I looked down at him in amazement, wondering if he might not be jesting, and saw that he spoke, as usual, merest truth. Quite at ease, he rose to greet the deer maidens, gave them a grave and courtly bow of welcome, then gazed at them much as I had gazed on the white-misted meadow, with the same sort of love. Certainly not with any will to possess.

The deer maidens carried rude baskets of willow and were laying out mats of woven willow. On them they placed what looked like the oat cakes Kor's people called jannock, or perhaps a sort of scone.

"Bread!" I exclaimed, all other desires forgotten for the time, and Kor softly laughed at me.

We sat and ate greedily. The cakes were made of wild seed, I decided after a while, coarsely ground and mixed with honey. Only a starving stomach could have thought them good. That, or the tastes of a bark-stripping deer. There were roots of some sort, also, baking like earthapples near the fire, and a basket of late berries, most of them bitter. I ate them anyway. The viands and Kor's demeanor had served to cool my cock somewhat, and while I ate whatever one of the lovely damsels laid before me, I made sure I never touched any of them, even so much as to brush finger against finger when they offered me food.

When dusk had deepened nearly into nighttime, the

white hind and her deer maidens left the roots baking in the embers of our fire, gathered up their willow baskets, and left us as silently as they had come. I looked after them with longing and relief quaintly mingled in me. Birc smiled crookedly at me in what might have been sympathy of a sort and slipped away into twilight like the others. Kor and I were left with fireglow and shadows.

We lay back on our blankets. Somewhere a mallow thrush sang.

"Are you going to be all right?" Kor asked. "Through the night?"

"If not, I will shout."

"Not bolt, like a roused stallion?"

"I give you my word, I will bide." I looked across firelight at him with some annoyance, more wonder. "I cannot believe you do not long for them," I said.

"How can I, since I have seen Tassida?"

I stared. "You are joking," I said, though I knew better.

"No jest. I have never wanted to lie with any woman since I have known her. I think I shall never want any except her."

The hopelessness of his love, and mine . . . I felt hollow, aching. "That's a drawback," I muttered, "in any case except this."

"It is," he admitted, for his faithfulness was nothing to boast of, to a tribesman's way of thinking.

Silence for a while. He shifted his bed so that he lay back against a rounded boulder. Darkness hid our faces, a comforting darkness, letting us speak of secret things.

"Dan, I never told you. The nights we stayed with your tribe, a maiden of your people came to me. Karu, they called her."

The flower of the Red Hart, she. Tall, straight, and fair, skin like a clear sunrise and her yellow braids hanging below her waist. She had gone to Kor, when to my knowledge she had never gone to any other! I sat up and stared at him.

"You should feel honored," I said with more awe than jealousy.

"I felt greatly honored, and I told her so. But I had no heart to lie with her. And I told her that as well, and why."

"But why!" I protested, astonished.

"I have just told you! I—"

"But how can you be so sure? It takes much searching to find a lifelove. Two come together and then, if the bond does not hold, they part to try again with others. How else is one to know but by trying?"

"I know my lifelove," he declared.

"Kor—"

"Were you so willing to hurt and be hurt when Leotie left you?"

She who had taken my brother Tyee as pledgemate. Hurt, yes, it had hurt indeed, as did Kor's thrust. I winced, but before I could parry he cursed between his teeth and rolled over so that he lay facedown, his voice muffled in his blanket.

"Sorry, Dan. Truth is, I—Mahela's bowels, perhaps I am a coward. I think—I could not play this game you describe to me. I have always dreamed of—a special one. . . ."

"We all do," I said softly, forgetting anger.

"And I have thought that once I have given myself to a woman I will be hers forever. I will not be able to help that."

I could not gainsay him. Had I not often sensed something fated in him?

"The maidens of my own people—we were good comrades as children, but often now they seem to me as strange and cold as—as devourers. And less willing." He sat up, shaking his head. "Bah! I am whimpering. Forget it."

"No. Tell me," I said, gazing at him across low flames. "I was starting to understand."

His shoulders sagged, his face turned toward the ground. "Perhaps I am deceiving myself," he muttered. "Perhaps the devourers have made me afraid."

I knew by then, but I blurted it out anyway. "You have not—you've never—"

"I am yet a virgin, Dan." He lifted his face and gifted me with one of his rare smiles, as if he felt suddenly lighthearted, telling me. "The fishy-flapping demons have given me my only bedding."

"Damn them," I breathed, growing angry with a wrath as sudden as his gladness. "Damn the demons, and damn the prick-me-dainty wenches who would not come to you! The birdwits, how could they have been so stupid! Damn it to Mahela, Kor, it's not your fault!"

He shrugged, abashed by my fervor but faintly smiling. "I think it is the pattern of my life," he said.

"Skewed," I grumbled, and did not know how truly I had spoken.

Chapter Four

In the night I heard Kor moving about restlessly without fully awakening to ask him why. The next morning when I spoke to him he answered me with sour silence. It took me a moment to recognize ill humor in him, for I saw it seldom enough. Once in a tenweek, perhaps, and then it often took the form of silence. He would not shout, most times, unless he was prodded.

"What ails you?" I prodded.

Silence, and a sullen frown. I pulled cold cooked roots out of the ashes of the fire for our breakfast, offered him one to eat. He shook his head. But when he turned away his face and coughed as I bit into mine, I knew what the trouble was.

"Mountain sickness," I said, laying the food aside.

He scowled back at me in dismal inquiry.

"There seems to be a live lizard in your stomach and a Cragsman pounding on your head? Cramps in your limbs? A brawling in your chest?"

With a wan look he nodded.

"It is nothing," I explained. "Only a sickness because of the thin air. Already we have climbed higher than you have been before. It is not dangerous—it will pass in a day or two, three at the most. I have seen it in some of the

39

younger members of my tribe, the very young and untraveled.''

''Thanks,'' he said sulkily, the first word he had spoken.

''They suffer worst. They become parlous ill-humored as well,'' I remarked. Because his sour look roused mischief in me, I did not tell him that I was one who had suffered this same ailment, often and noisily. I merely motioned him toward his blanket.

''We should go on,'' he said, his mouth moving stiffly with his misery. But he got up and started gathering gear, though the commotion in his gut bent him like a bowed sapling. I abandoned my know-all air.

''Kor, you ass, lie down!'' I got up and wrestled the things away from him. ''You are not riding today. Lie down, or I will eat in front of you!''

At the very thought he retched, a dry sound without result. But stubbornly he continued his attempts to break camp, and when Birc ambled in I was still struggling with him. I had him by the arms, trying to make him sit and listen to reason, and Birc raised his brows at both of us.

''He's *sick*,'' I complained.

''Birc,'' Kor demanded thickly, ''do Cragsmen come here?''

Brows still arched, Birc nodded.

''Often?'' I put in.

He shook his head.

''Kor ran afoul of a Cragsman two days ago. Have you heard, are they roused?''

Birc shook his head. The stony-hearted louts were not arming for war? Or he had not heard? He looked somber.

''We have to go on,'' Kor said, though he was staggering where he stood.

Birc shook his head and gestured at us with palms down, telling us to stay where we were. Then he set off at a graceful, swinging trot. He had disappeared behind trees within a moment.

"Kor, truly you are in no fit fettle to travel," I told him. "Birc wants us to stay, and these woods feel sheltered—do you not sense it?"

He straightened somewhat and looked about him. We were camped in the hollow of a lee, and spruces ringed it as if to shield us with their thickest needles. As if the place were protected. Even the smoke of our fire seemed to thin before it reached the top of the stunted evergreens, and the horses for some reason seemed content to wander within the woods, pawing for marmots beneath the ledges, though the highmountain meadow with its many voles and lemmings lay scarcely a stone's throw away.

Kor gave me an appraising look. "You are not saying that," he muttered, "just to argue with me?"

"I feel at peril here," I admitted, "from my own lusts. But it is a peril I can withstand. In a larger way I feel safe, as if in a haven."

Yielding, he lay down in his bed again, and I covered him with my blankets as well. I went off into the woods, set snares, ate my wild carrot roots safely out of his sight. When I returned he was dozing, and I did likewise. After halfday I went to check the snares, and gathered far more pika than I expected. I skinned them well away from our campsite, then carried them back and built up the fire to cook them. I would have liked to have boiled broth for Kor, but we had no deer gut to hold the water, nor any cedar box or basket of spruce roots such as his kindred used.

After the fire had made embers, I scraped a pit to one side and pushed some of the coals into it with a green stick. Then I put in the small carcasses wrapped in leaves. Presently they started to roast, and their aroma filled the air.

"Meat!" I breathed. It seemed the greatest of blessings compared to the seedcakes.

Kor awoke, stirred, and groaned. Then, catching a waft

of the good cooking smell, he turned away his face and tried to vomit, though there was nothing in his stomach, not even water. In compunction I went over and knelt beside him, laid my hands on his shoulders as if that could somehow heal him. "You will feel better soon, Kor, truly," I assured him.

"So you say," he muttered.

"But I have had this same malady more than once myself. I know you will soon be well."

He gave me a look fit to turn a knife between my ribs. I could not keep from smiling.

"Handbond," I offered.

He answered only with a fervent curse and a slur on my parentage. I forbore from laughing at him, but only until I was out of his sight and earshot.

Later I ate, burning my fingers on the hot meat—perhaps there is justice of a sort in such small events. Kor lay still and ignored me, and I sat watching the rising moon, round and orange, like a mushroom cap floating in the twilight sky.

After dark the naked deer maidens came again, bringing seedcakes, the fire's glow flashing off their glossy, rippling hair, off their moon-round breasts that swayed softly with their movements. . . . I was less starved for the food this time, and therefore all the more hungry for the damsels—or perhaps it was the moonlight that put foolishness into me, yellow-red light amidst darkness, autumn moon. Though it was not yet the time of witchcraft— hunters' moon came first. On the mountains, perhaps time ran differently. Or witchcraft. Something happened in me, I felt darkness swirl around me, my vision narrowed, my heart grew hot and swollen in my chest, I felt my manhood stand hot and hard beneath my lappet, and my hands were moving as if of their own will—toward doom—

"Kor!" I called hoarsely.

He was up on the instant, even weak as he was, wobbling over to me, almost falling, and he caught my lifting hands in his own. The deer maidens stood gazing at me in innocent wonder, like fawns seen in the thickets. None of them had made any move to seduce me, but if I had embraced one, I felt sure she would have willingly answered the kiss. Or more than one—ai, thinking made it worse.

"Kor," I panted, "tie me."

"What!"

"I mean it! Tie me stoutly, if either of us is to have any peace this night."

"Are you—in thrall?" he asked in a low voice.

'As Birc was? No, I am not yet bleating." I lost patience. "Would you tie my wrists before I lose what small sense is left to me and overpower you?" I clung to a tree while he went to get the rawhide thongs.

He padded my wrists with bandaging before he bound them, and then I began to comprehend his reluctance. Once before he had bound me like this, when I lay in a prison pit, a madman, raving and dangerous. When I had ceased to rave I had been unable to remember even my own name. But that had been my father's doing. Nothing less than his betrayal could have driven me so out of self.

Or it was devoutly to be hoped, that nothing other could do that to me. . . . Kor tied me, and the naked damsels watched curiously, setting out seedcakes on willow mats.

"Behind me," I directed Kor, holding my hands there. "Then you can go back to your bed."

He shook his head. "In front. I've no desire to make you ache. Dan, think better of me!" Fiercely. "How could I sleep? I'll be here."

His hands, forming the knots, were unsteady. "But you are not well. You have no strength," I told him.

"I will find strength."

Knowing him, I could not but believe him. "Handbond, then," I told him.

We passed the grip hastily. I hoped it would help him, but it served only to strengthen the stark longing in me. Then Kor tied my ankles loosely to a treetrunk. Once I felt myself secured I gave in to the dark whirlings that seemed to surround me, the hot yearning within me, the despair. I lunged against my bonds and howled—a long-drawn, wailing sound that I had not known was in me, that shivered in my throat. The deer maidens raised their heads rigidly at that sound and came to their feet, sensing for the first time that something was wrong, that these odd mortals did not always play at games of binding each other to trees. They left the viands but hastily gathered up their willow ware, their lovely bodies poised as if alert for flight. Still, the look on their faces was as much puzzled as frightened.

Kor had his arms around my chest from behind, trying to restrain me and calm me. He had indeed from somewhere found strength. "Dan—"

I howled again, and a third time. And as I drew breath an answering howl floated across the distance of the night from somewhere far off on the flank of the mountain.

The damsels bleated and fled in great leaps, turning to deer in the midst of their leaping. Willow ware lay scattered. I sat still, my passion for white hind and deer women forgotten—that eerie sound seemed still to drift in the darkened air.

"An echo?" Kor whispered.

I howled again, not so strongly this time—my voice quavered. But the answer came across the night promptly. A chill, thin wail the color of moonlight, a sound that reminded me of the call of the wandering wild geese, that sang of the same yearnings. Longings such as I felt when I told the tales of Sakeema. . . . But strength was in this voice, and a warning.

Urgency in his touch, Kor began to undo my bonds. "No," I protested.

"Trust yourself more, Dan." He drew away the thongs

from my legs, started untying those on my wrists. "Something moves in the night. You may need the use of your limbs."

Something that called to me and frightened me. At the same time I felt a reckless daring, perhaps because I was already disgraced by my own passions, with not much pride left to lose. . . . At the reaches of the firelight something stirred. Eyes shone green, regarding us, unblinking. Kor's hands stopped in their movements as he stared.

"Come closer, wild brother," I softly invited. "We cannot see you."

A few slow paces nearer the fire . . . Kingly head lifted to catch our scent on the air. Power, all was power, the great bone of legs and feet, the thick, coarse pelt, the mighty jaws—but beauty too, the smooth brow, short ears, sheen of fur in the firelight, and all that was wild and lonesome in the steady gaze of shadowed eyes.

"A wolf?" Kor breathed, dumbfounded.

I could not believe it either. No wolf had been seen by anyone of my tribe since my grandfather's time, and few then. Bring back the wolves of wonder. . . . I felt a surge of surpassing gratitude. I was blessed, even if our visitor should rend me apart in the next moment.

"Perhaps it is the very last one," murmured Kor.

The wolf whined and shifted its weight from side to side, plainly uncomfortable in the presence of our small fire. The whites showed around its dark eyes, giving it a fearsome look, for a frightened beast is more dangerous than a calm one. Still, it neither attacked nor retreated, but looked from Kor to me in some sort of expectation.

Orange moonlight had touched me—I can explain my boldness no other way. I whimpered at the wolf in greeting, whined aloud, and it lifted its ears, turning its head toward me in eager interest. I wriggled my hands free of their remaining bonds and started toward the wolf, on all fours, soft sounds in my throat.

"Dannoc," Kor called after me, a low, tense call, "what are you doing?"

"There is a human look about his eyes," I said, not raising my voice, not looking back at him. "Perhaps he needs but a touch to be one of us." If the deer had human forms, some of them, why not this visitor?

"How can you tell? Perhaps all wolves have such speaking eyes. We have never seen another."

The wolf trembled and gathered itself into a crouch as I approached, but held its ground. Nearly on my belly, reaching from a distance, I eased my hand toward the tips of the thick fur on its neck. An instant, a finger's span more, and I would touch. . . . But before my fingertips met fur, the wolf flashed away into the darkness. I got up slowly, brushing dirt and wood duff off myself. Kor stood facing the way the wolf had gone, a keen look in his eyes, sickness forgotten.

"He is very old," he said.

I nodded. I, too, had seen the white hairs about the wolf's mouth and muzzle. The rest of the wolf's fur was of a graysheen color, subtle and shimmering. I felt suddenly immensely tired, and sagged back to the ground.

"Are you all right?" asked Kor.

"Yes," I mumbled, though in fact I was not sure. "Go back to your bed, go to sleep."

"You go to sleep. I have slept all day."

"You are feeling better?"

"Feeble yet, but well enough to keep a watch." He sat down by the fire, his back to a stone. "Go to sleep, Dan."

"But . . . you have not eaten. . . ."

I would have said more, but I was already sleeping, and as I wished to think that he was well, I dreamed that I saw him eat. I slept deeply, but sometime in the mid of night I was roused by the sound of Kor's voice.

"Welcome, wild brother," he was saying. "Stay, rest yourself, be easy. It is not on your account that I am keeping guard. It's for the sake of yon half-naked blunder-head and his fondness for deerflesh.''

Insulted, I stirred drowsily, opened my eyes, and blinked them clear. Kor was still sitting at the fire, and on the far side of it, well back in the shadows but facing him, sat the wolf.

In the morning, when Birc came back, the wolf was lying at the roots of the nearest pine.

Birc ran in so swiftly, so silently, deerlike, that we were hardly aware of him before he stood before us. Glistening with sweat all over, as if he had done a long run—and in fact I think he had been running since the day before, for our sakes. Nor had he yet seen the hinds, his companions, or yet heard of the wolf. He stopped short when he scented and saw it, all atremble, so that I expected him to be a hart, and bleat and flee. But he did not. Since I had known him, Birc had always owned a peculiar sort of courage: he quaked, but he stood fast. Even in his human days as Kor's guardsman he had been that way.

The wolf scarcely looked up at him. I dragged myself out of sleep and sat up groggily. But Kor strode over to Birc with reasonable steadiness and gave him once again the embrace of a king.

"I think it is time we were going," Kor said, and Birc nodded.

Chapter Five

I gathered the snares, brought back pika aplenty, walked to within a cautious distance of the wolf, and offered it three brace, leaving them on the ground. With dignity the wolf took them, carried them off one by one, then tore them apart and gulped them in a moment's time.

It took us far more time to find the horses, for they had strayed a goodly distance—or perhaps they had scented wolf and fled. Talu snorted at even the ghost of wolf smell about me, and it required my sternest command to make her stand still and let herself be approached. That, and an offering of cooked meat. We would never have caught her and Sora if the wolf had come with us, but it had melted away into the spruces somewhere. Even so, the sun stood high before we were on our way.

Kor sat straight on Sora as we rode. I glanced at him from time to time, for he had eaten nothing, and the shell-tan skin of his face had gone a shade paler. But water, at least, he had taken, and if he did not speak, his was a strong silence. His eyes, when he caught me looking at him, dared me to pity him.

The pass took us above the tree line, over the high-mountain meadow. All the plants grow small and low there, but very thick, delightful in the ways they nestle together. In summertime that place would have been aflutter with tiny blue and yellow flowers and butterflies of the same hues. But in the mountaintop's early autumn every small leaf had turned red or purple or yellow, achingly bright in the strong mountain sunlight. And the sky a deeper, purer blue than any flower, and the eversnow blazing white—even the gray crags of the alps shone. There was nowhere I could look without a sweet pain. Not even at Kor. He caught my glance, answered it with a slow smile—he felt it, too.

A flash of living white in the distance. The fair white hind, Birc's mate, leaped off toward the eversnow. I saluted her.

But I saw no black eagles, nor any antelope. Great catamounts once lived in the crags, I had been told, but they had been many years gone, since before my grandfather's time.

We kept the horses to the walk, sparing them in the thin air, and after halfday we ourselves got down and walked beside them for a while. We camped early for Kor's sake, and ate what the deer folk had given us, and Kor ate cold pika meat. There was not even a stone for shelter. We kept watch by turns—for what, we were not sure, but we felt very exposed on that open, windy place.

Sheep roamed the crags. They are wary, keeping to the open rock where they can see whatever comes. I could never have gotten near one in daylight, but in the darkness before dawn I crept to the place where they huddled in the chill mountain night. And when the first one stood up at daybreak, I killed it cleanly. So there was meat for Kor and me, and offal for the horses, and we left a portion behind us, lying on the ground, in case a newfound friend should travel that way.

Walking, panting in the thin air, resting often, we crossed the top of the pass to Kor's side of the great mountains, and he lifted his head, looking homeward.

Our path lay downward now. We reached the tree line the next day and breathed more easily. Kor seemed well and strong by then. We slept amid stunted spruces, some of them bent to the ground and crawling along the slope from the blast of winter wind.

The next morning the horses were missing.

"Ungrateful mares," Kor grumbled.

"Perhaps the wolf is somewhere about," I said, scanning the mountainside, more wistful than believing.

"I hope it has eaten horseflesh, then. Pigheaded animals. Can you track them, Dan?"

I tried. The terrain was rocky, the going rough. After an hour in which my mood soured to match Kor's, we sighted Sora's yellow hide near a slide of scree. She was pawing for vipers and rockchucks. But we could not see Talu with her, and the trail seemed to lead the other way. Kor went to get Sora, picking his way over boulders, and I followed Talu's traces around a shoulder of the mountain.

I went silently—it is the custom of the Red Hart to go silently always. Even bisonhide boots need not make noise. So when I heard the clatter of pebble on rock, heavy footfalls on a ledge above me where no horse could have climbed, I froze in the shadow of the crags, sure I had not been heard, and watched as a file of Cragsmen trudged down past me. Two, three, twice three, the hulking, bare stone-colored backs and shoulders loomed over me and passed on, heads stooped and riding those shoulders like mossy rounds of stone. They carried, as always, their massive clubs, and they were taking a twisting way downmountain, a way that might take them to the Blackstone Path, to—

Kor!

Standing exposed as he was near a slope of talus, waiting for me, and they would see him at once if they came anywhere near him. In no way could I reach him in time to warn him—I knew that even as I ran. And certainly I could not shout, for the Cragsmen might not yet be aware of either of us. But I was terrified for his sake, as frightened as a stripling once was with his mother gone, no one knew how or where, and his father good as gone, and I too old to weep, or so I thought. . . . I was shouting in my mind. *Kor!* There was nothing in me but panic and his name. *Kor! Kor! Danger!*

Dan! he answered me.

I heard it as plainly as if he had called aloud. So taken aback was I that I staggered and nearly fell, nearly went sliding down a snow gully into the arms of air.

Dan! What is it? Are you all right?

Too stunned to answer him in like wise, to tell him anything of peril or Cragsmen, I made no reply. But I could tell direction and distance by his soundless speaking, just as I could have by a shout. He was not where I had left him, but out of danger, off to one side and beyond a spine of rock. I turned toward him. In a few moments we met. Leading both our horses, he stood staring at me—by the looks of him, confounded. His mouth was moving without words, his eyes wide.

"You hailed me," he managed to say. "Inside my mind."

I nodded. I did not want to speak of what had happened—it harrowed me, thinking back on it, as much as the Cragsmen had. Kor was brave. He had my fear to bear as well as his own. Knowing that, I swallowed the terror that blocked my throat.

"You answered me," I said hoarsely.

"For a certainty! How could I help it? You took hold of me like a flood tide." A wry smile. "Why not? You always have."

"Sorry," I muttered.

"Don't be! Try it again."

Violently I shook my head. I could not venture it ever

again, or so I thought. It had been a happening too eerie, too—inward. Kor felt my fear and did not press me.

"What prompted you?" he asked instead.

"Cragsmen." I gestured vaguely, not yet capable of explaining much further. "I thought certainly they would see you on that scree."

"Talu was hunting in the spruces beyond Sora. After I had caught the worthless pair of them I went after you."

We led our wayward mares back to the faint track that traversed the pass, found our campsite, and loaded the gear. It was quarterday before we mounted and set off westward again.

Downward through twisted spruce and blue pine, winding around crags and rocky ribs, all in silence, for we had much on our minds. But when we came to a point that overlooked the spires of the trees, Kor stopped to gaze, his eyes sparkling. "We are coming near my country," he said.

In fact we had much farther to go, but the land had changed so that he felt near to home. Truly he was on his own side of the mountains again: cascades, cataracts, torrents everywhere, rushing like wind and singing and chiming like voices and clay bells, the many mountain waters, some of them mighty, some as fine as spiderweb, rippling down in shining strands from the high icefields, down over rocks and through forest to feed the Otter River far below and flow with the river to the sea. No arid plains in the distance here, no yellow pines and grassy parks. Instead there stood below us great forests of fir, dense, dripping with moss—the cataracts turned even the gray rock green with fern and moss. Farther down, near the rocky headland where Kor had his Holding, salt mists did the same. I saw him lift his head as he gazed, and his nostrils flared as if to scent the sea air, many days journey away—

Cragsmen struck at us from behind.

We should have been watching for them, listening for them, but there had been too much to think of, the day had thrown us off balance. And I, for one, thought we had outdistanced them, we with our horses. I had forgotten how long of leg Cragsmen can be, and tireless. . . . Only a scrape of stone, very close, warned me, and I swung around just in time to duck the blackwood club. And Alar was out of her scabbard as if of her own will, up and meeting the downcrushing arm before I had time even to shout.

"Kor!" Greenish blood splattered down on me. Club and giant hand fell with a thud by Talu's hooves.

Korridun was already embattled, wielding his sword faster than I could follow.

"By Sedna's bones, Dan, it is Ytan!"

With the Cragsmen, a yellow-braided, bare-chested Red Hart warrior, taller than most men, yet looking small amidst the giants. Still quite powerful enough to strike fear: Ytan, my brother demon-possessed. Blue eyes met mine, and he grinned, a warmthless grimace like that of a skull. He raised his bow, the bolt already nocked to the string.

"Aaa!" I shouted, a wordless cry. I knew Ytan's skill. In a moment I would be wearing his arrow—

From somewhere close at hand a snarling sounded, a roar that rose above the roar of cataracts, and I saw a graysheen flash. The wolf flung itself down from the yet higher rocks, landing like a cat on Ytan's back and shoulders, tearing at his neck with deadly jaws. Ytan's arrow and bow dropped from his hands as he reached up to fend off teeth and claws.

"Get to him, Kor, and slit him open! I—can't. . . ."

Ytan was yet my brother, for all that a devourer held him in thrall. I could not kill him. Kor would have to do it.

"There is a—large lout—in my way, Dan."

He was panting. I risked a glance and saw the enormous granite-gray foe who faced him. The hulks kept coming at us in spite of sword wounds and lopped hands, and there were a number of them, more than the six I had seen, all the stone colors. I faced one of dull red. He was old, his hair like so much frost on his boulder of a head, and he was a wily fighter. There was no thought in me, any longer, of Ytan. It was all I could do, even with the sword, to keep the Cragsmen from forcing me back. Our enemies had the advantage of height, their own great height plus a stance on the rocks. And behind us lay nothing but a sheer drop onto fir spires.

I saw Kor take a whistling blow that glanced off the side of his face. "Alar!" I cried crazily. "Zaneb!"

The swords were already doing all they could. But like an echo of my words there came an uncouth sound, a blast as of a bison horn strongly blown, and a great stag leaped over the rocks and rammed his antlers into a slate-blue chest. At his heels came two more nearly as mighty. The Cragsmen saw them and shrank from them, unnerved by the strangeness of it, I think, for Cragsmen are no cowards when it comes to blows. But that the deer of the forest should take battle against them, and in company with a wolf . . .

Ytan had torn the wolf off his shoulders at last, hurled it onto the rocks. Clubs struck—but it was quick, a shining flash, they had not yet hit it—

"Forward!" I bellowed, and Talu took me straight up the rocks with a surge. She could not wait to sink her fangs into the nearest Cragsman's throat. The fellow toppled before her like a downed tree. I made for another, sword upraised and the green-tinged blood dripping off it and rattling on the stones.

"Dan, you hotheaded fool!" I heard Kor cursing behind me. Then he was beside me, Sora bearing down on every foe before her, their blood streaking her yellow hide before it fell away in shards. Zaneb darted, a deadly raptor to meet—Ytan, the one who stood before him was Ytan. . . .

Battle fire burning in me, I shouted, "Take him, Kor!"

But the sword hovered by Kor's head. A moment of hesitation, and Ytan scrambled away, slipped into forest and vanished, leaving his bow behind him. The Cragsmen were unmanned, and fled in like wise. Three they left behind them, dead or groaning. Stags bounded after them, harrying their backs. Battle clamor echoed away into silence.

I sat, my sword dangling from my lowered hand, staring at Kor.

"You could have had him," I said, for I sensed even then that killing Ytan would have saved a stoup's worth of trouble and peril later on. "Why did you let him go?"

"I could no more strike him than strike you, Dan."

Battle fire cooling, it was as if haze drifted from my eyes. I saw my bond brother clearly, scarcely comprehending what he had said, knowing only that the side of his face was bruised black and streaked with blood, his brow cut open, one eye swollen shut. A thick red smear ran down from his nose and mouth. He was trying to stanch it with his fingers.

"Blood of Mahela," I said numbly, vaulting down from Talu.

"No," Kor retorted, "my own."

With more haste than grace I went to him, slipping on mossy rocks, the mare trailing after me.

"He looks so much like you," Kor said, veering back to the matter of Ytan. I no longer cared about Ytan. A pox on Ytan.

"Get down," I told Kor, "and let me see to those cuts."

I took him over by the nearest small torrent, laved the side of his face with the cold, clear water, eased it on with my hands until the bleeding had stopped and the swelling had come down somewhat. Kor sat and leaned against stone. I crouched beside him. The wolf came and stared at us for a moment, then trotted away with a liquid gait that flowed more gracefully than the cascades.

"But for the mien, you and Ytan might be twins," Kor said.

That troubled me strangely. My hands faltered as I washed his wounds.

"Let them be, Dan." He gently pushed me away, got up. "They're scarcely more than scratches."

"Lucky to be alive, you are," I grumbled at him.

"I! Who was it that blundered up here? Mahela take your cock, Dan, what a leap! You must be mad."

It was a touchy business, getting the horses down to the trail again. Boulders give poor purchase for hooves. After we had accomplished it, with some swearing, I went back and found Ytan's bow, broke it, took his arrows for my own. The dead Cragsmen wore nothing worth looting. Kor and I rode on, shaken, alert for danger.

"Look," I whispered once. Off to one side I had seen a flash of swift, bright gray. The wolf journeyed with us.

In my vision of Sakeema, months past, I had seen him ride a great stag into battle while the wolves followed at his heels. Now wolf and harts had fought side by side to aid us. It was of all things most wonderful, most unaccountable. There had been too many unaccountable happenings in the day. . . . A prickling feeling took hold of me, and I looked at Kor, his bruised face, his changing, sea-colored eyes. Sakeema, I thought, nearly shivering.

"Stop that," Kor snapped.

I believe my heart held still, and I stared at him.

"You're the one who summoned up yon wolf! And I daresay Birc sent the deer."

"And you're the one who has taken to hearing thoughts," I said, my voice shaking.

He drew Sora to a halt and looked at me, his irritation gone. "Dan, you are so much a part of me . . ." His voice trailed away helplessly. "It frightens you," he muttered at last. "Well, this 'Sakeema' nonsense frightens me."

I kept silence. We went on in silence.

"It began only today, the mindspeak," Kor said after a while. "It fills me with wonder. Does it trouble you so much?"

The thought of Sakeema filled me with wonder. I had to smile. "We seem fated to be always at odds over something," I said.

"Yes." His voice, low, told me he was thinking of Tassida, as was I.

"And it has served only to make us stronger. I daresay I shall get used to it, Kor."

We camped that night in an island of fir trees amid cascades. The place smelled of green, even in autumn, but the ferns made a yellow blanket under the trees, and the night was freezing cold—we built a fire. We spoke of keeping watch by turns, against Ytan, and decided against it, for every night has its dangers, perils of enemies, perils of wild beasts, perils of devourers. There would be no proper sleeping for anyone who thought always of the dangers. Moreover, we had journeyed far enough so that we judged he could not have followed us. We both lay down, and I slept soundly, under furs.

Sometime after the fire had burned down to embers I was awakened out of dreamless slumber with a jolt. Something was crushing down on me and encasing me, taking me into a smothering embrace before I could so much as shout an alarm. The night was all darkness, cold paplike swellings against my face and the feel of slime. A devourer had me in its clutch. Once again my arms were pinned, though this time less shamefully, against my chest. And the skins under which I slept protected me from its teeth, at least for a time. If only I could wriggle my fists

up toward my face, even just a little, to make a space near
my mouth—

The thing tightened on me when it felt my struggles. I
truly could not breathe.

Kor! I shouted within my mind. Surely one of the
monsters lay on him as well, so I expected nothing of
him—it was my terror that spoke. I called upon him as one
might call upon the god, Sakeema, when in trouble. But at
once I heard his drowsy reply.

What is it?

Confounded anew, I could not answer him. But even
half-awake as he was, he felt my fear.

"Dan!" he cried aloud in horror. I heard him faintly.
And then I caught a blessed breath of pure, chill night air.
He was straddling me, wrestling the monster back from
my face. In half a moment it had slipped out of his grasp
and came down on me again with a fishy slap. But I felt a
surge of strength, knowing that Kor was with me, and my
hand crawled upward.

Again he was striving to pull the devourer away. I felt
the rippling of all its muscles as it opposed him. He could
not move it, but it could not utterly smother me, either.

"The thing is parlous strong," Kor panted aloud.

If I can but get my hand free, I mindspoke him.

"Is it close?"

By my collarbone.

"All right. Ready. Now!"

With a warrior's yell he prized the monster away from
me, and though I could not see, I knew he was giving me
an effort worthy of mortal combat. The devourer struggled, heaved, and threw him off. I heard him thud into the
moss and ferns beside me. But it had been enough—my
hand had shot up by my head, and my elbow levered the
foul breasts away from my face. Kor was winded, the
breath knocked out of him so thoroughly that he could not

speak. But in a moment he had crawled to my side, and his fingers curled around mine.

Now, he mindspoke, *we can wait out the night if need be.*

Struggling up, he sat by my head. I lay in perfect ease, full of warmth and strength. Once we had handbonded, the devourer could no longer dismay me, and I knew it—I would indeed have been content to lie under it all night. But there was no need. Within a few breaths, before Kor had ceased to pant, the monster rippled and slithered off me and took to the air, lashing its snakelike tail in what might have been rage.

Kor gripped my hand hard for a moment, then let go. Dazed, almost disappointed, as if it had been too easy, I sat up.

"Are you all right?" Kor asked me, a catch in his voice as if his breathing still troubled him.

"Not a mark on me," I told him. "You?"

"Blasted cuts open on my face. Nothing more."

We both stank of slime. We washed in an icy cataract, came back and built up the fire, then sat by it, shivering. Kor's face, the bruise shadowed in the light of flames, looked even worse than it would have in day.

"Even Mahela's minions did not want you for bedding tonight," I teased.

He looked up at me from under his brows, gravely. "No jest, Dan. I have been wondering why I was spared. Perhaps you had better beat my face for me, once it starts to heal."

I laughed out loud, but he fell silent, moody.

"Yon was the largest, strongest devourer I have ever encountered," he muttered at last.

"Mindspeaking has its uses," I admitted, and he glanced at me with a flicker of a smile. *Can you hear me?* he asked.

"Yes."

"But I am not privy to your every thought," Kor said. "It is only when you wish me to hear. Yes, it has its uses."

"But—it was not only when I wished you to hear."

"That Sakeema notion of yours? But that is something you wish me to hear, in spite of your promise."

Truth, and though I would not admit it to him, certainly I would not argue with him either. "Go to sleep," I told him. I was weary, but I did not feel that I could sleep again. I settled back against a fir tree to keep watch.

Kor lay by the fire, but he did not sleep, or not deeply. When I finally dozed, he was awake. We both kept watch, for the most part, until dawn.

The next day while we rode, the wolf joined us briefly. The mares squealed and bucked and kicked at him—no small matter, as their temper threatened to pitch us into a chasm. We shouted and cursed, more at the mares than at the wolf, but it was the wolf who turned aside from the trail, tail down, ears half-lowered.

In the days that followed we saw it from time to time, often watching us from a rocky vantage, so beautiful that sometimes we stopped to gaze back. We were reaching the region of sea fogs, where the salt smell hung faintly in the air and the gray mists swirled around the dense green of the firs. Moving in the mists, the wolf shone more like a spirit thing than like a creature of flesh.

The sky had gone mostly gray, sometimes scarrow-bright, sometimes dull, sometimes barred with ragged clouds of a yet darker gray drifting slantwise before storm winds. In the far distance, if mists and trees allowed us, we could sometimes see the glint of the ocean.

"Look!" Kor exclaimed. "Seal Hold!"

Far off at the edge of sight, the rocky headland where he and his people made their home. Lodges looked like no more than jutting edges on it, as weathered as the rock, but we knew the shape of that place well.

"By Sedna," he whispered, looking weak with eagerness. "Do you think we will reach it today?"

Behind us, above us, the wolf lifted its head and suddenly gave forth a piercing howl. The sound shivered through us.

"What is it, friend?" I asked, turning to face the wolf.

It gazed at us across a distance we could scarcely measure, a chasm made of time and failed dreams. We could not see its speaking eyes. Its legs showed thin beneath the dense mass of its fur. In a moment it turned away from us, turned back toward the mountains, and vanished. Old, alone, lonesome, the last of its kind, and we were leaving it there.

Chapter Six

Kor came home at sundown, through the wind-twisted pines and down to the narrow strand between mountains and vast sea, then along the shoreline toward the headland. Rich, blood-red sunset light touched everything, and I felt for a moment an odd desolation, as if the smell of death lay on that place. As if almost I could see the strewn bodies. . . .

I blinked and there was nothing. It must have been the smells— ai, the sea smells. Salt and beached seaweed and fish offal and seal scats. A friendly reek, I knew, but it sent a tremor of memory through me, more feeling than memory, the despair of my first coming to the sea. I, a nameless madman. My beloved father had plotted to kill me, and rage and sorrow had sent me fleeing over the midwinter mountains until I struck like an embodied storm, they later told me, at Korridun and his people. Kor had felt the love and grief behind the attack—his mercy had saved me, and only he had at first befriended me, Dannoc the murderer.

Time gone by, nearly a year gone, and much had happened since. I shook myself, shaking off the sorrow I smelled in the sea. Fish, dead seaweed, black shells, salt . . . water salt as tears . . . Enough. Kor was looking at me, about to say something comforting, and I scowled at him to silence him. Sometimes, even now, his goodness was too much for me to bear. Sometimes I wanted to throttle him.

He grinned. "Pigheaded," he stated. Then with a whoop he kicked Sora into a headlong gallop down the strand.

Startled, delighted, laughing aloud, I sent Talu racing after him. I had never known Kor to ride with such reckless joy. The Seal are not born to be horseback riders—Kor appeared more to fly above Sora than to sit on her. But with her he stayed, and he yelled crazily, keeping her at top speed. Talu's best run could not catch them. We pounded down hard, wet sand, splashed through inlets and breaking waves, jumped rocks with scarcely a catch in the wild rhythm of the race. Coracles ahead, and the fishermen beaching them, and shouts of fear or welcome—

So it was that Rad Korridun, the Seal Kindred's king, came home in a swirl of sand and water and confused noise and sunset glory. Stopping Sora—Talu and I nearly blundered into him—and down in the sand, half-falling, half-jumping, and into the embrace of six or more excited clansmen at once, and the waves washing about their knees, people calling, running down from the lodges on the headland above, slithering down rocks slippery with spray and moss—

"It is the king!"

"Korridun! What has happened to your face?"

"Dan! It is Dannoc!"

Someone caught at my hand, and then I was down as well and part of a mighty hugging, guardsmen and young women, Lumai and Lomasi and Winewa, the one I had chiefly loved for a time. Winewa bearing a tiny babe! I stared, for it seemed to me that the sparse hair on the little one's shell-pink head was nearly as light as mine.

"You've given us a wee girl to break hearts when she's

older, Dannoc,'' Lomasi said, and there were smiles everywhere.

And questions asked of Kor, and sorrow. Tohr, dead. Three other guardsmen who had gone with us, all dead. Birc—gone. . . . A few men stood woodenly, hearing tidings of a son or a brother. Women lifted their faces skyward and keened in formal lament. Two mothers, a pledgemate, a sister wailed in more heartfelt sorrow. Others stood somber. All clamor quieted except the uproar of the heartless sea.

"Istas?" Kor questioned that silence.

"Above!" Istas was too old to manage the rocks, or too dignified to tumble about on them. Clamor broke out again.

"Come, our king, she will be wild with waiting for you."

"You should have seen her when the shout went up. She dropped the bowl she was holding and broke it—''

"—splattered chowder everywhere—''

" 'Slime of Mahela!' she yelled!''

Istas's favorite curse. Except for those who mourned, everyone laughed, chattering and climbing up the steep path.

"She's well, then," Kor said gladly.

"Well! Of course she's well. She's as strong as Dannoc."

More laughter. She, the hunched old woman whose head reached only to my chest. Her strength had once been sufficient to break my foot. She had fully intended to kill me in a most unpleasant way, for I had killed her brother, who had never done any dishonor to me. . . . Bad days gone by, done with. I had taught her the meaning of mercy, Kor said.

"That one," a man added, "she will never die."

At the top she stood awaiting us, a strong old shrew with a deeply lined face and a hump on her back. Knowing her as I did, I expected a blunt comment as we came before her. Istas was honest, though not always honest enough to show her own love and joy. She wore a scowl of irritation like a mask. But the mask shattered when she caught sight of Korridun. Amazement and awe smoothed her face so that for a moment I glimpsed the young maiden she once had been.

"But you have grown!" she exclaimed, gazing up at him, throwing her head back as far as her bent body would allow her.

"Mahela's blood, Istas, I was grown before I went!" He embraced her, and she returned the embrace, but she was not to be put off.

"You have grown!" she insisted. "Not just in body, though there is that, too—you are nearly as tall as Dannoc!" She turned to peer at me accusingly, more herself now, which was as well, for seeing her as other than an old scold had unsettled me. "Something has happened, and don't you two try to tell me otherwise." Her look strayed to the sword that hung by his side, and she stiffened. "Is that one of those great, strange knives?"

"Yes. Quite effective against Cragsmen."

She glanced at his bruised temple and back at the sword. "Where did you get it?"

"Out of a tarn," he said, and she scowled, thinking he was befooling her. But the frown faded into perplexity.

"Rad, you look so much—stronger. What has done it?"

"Mountain air," he told her, and she glared now in earnest.

"Rad Korridun, you young scamp, tell me truly!"

"Truly, then, Istas, there is too much to tell." He was smiling at her with a tenderness that, for once, seemed to disarm her more than annoy her. "Say this: have my cousins come back?" The seals, he meant, returning to the coastal rocks for the winter.

"Yes. Though fewer than we had hoped." Abruptly, possessed by a new thought, Istas whirled and began shouting orders at her people. "Bring in the catch, there, the whole of it! You children, start gathering shellfish, quickly, while the light lasts! To the hearth, you useless girls! We have a feast to prepare! Our king has come home!"

A shout went up, and a cry of joy.

"Istas—" Kor protested.

"Korridun King!" someone shouted, and others took up the chant, lifting arms in a happy salute. A few maidens started a dance.

"Later!" Istas bellowed, and she ran at them, shaking her skirts as if she were herding geese. Giggling, they bolted toward their tasks.

"Istas!" Kor complained.

She did not heed him except to run at him in like wise. "Go on, now, I have a score of things to do! Go wash! You smell of horse. And keep the stinking beast well out of my way or I'll roast it!" She scuttled toward Seal Hold, the deep and many-chambered cave where Kor made his home.

"Blast it," Kor grumbled to the salt-smelling air as much as to me, "how am I to tell them I am leaving again?"

I grinned at him, told him I would tend the horses, and went down to do it. After I had let them loose and stowed the gear in an empty lodge, I bathed myself under a cascade and went looking for a warm hearth to dry myself by. Youngsters and warriors of Kor's tribe would have scorned the hearth. They bathed in the icy sea and rubbed themselves with sticks to awaken their numbed limbs, and these were the people who swaddled themselves in woolens and furs the rest of the time. . . . Twos and threes of them, old friends, hailed me at every turning of Seal Hold, so that by the time I reached the hearth at last I was dry and warmed with talking, and I went to look for Kor instead.

He was in his chamber, beset by a trio of maidens. They were ministering to him with sharp clam shells, cutting his hair short and fur-fashion, as was the custom of his people, and he looked annoyed. He raised his hands in a gesture of despair when he saw me.

"I told Istas, there is no need—"

"Were you going to let it grow yet longer," one of the maidens teased, "and braid it, like Dannoc's when he first came here?"

I felt at my hair, hanging near my shoulders, almost long enough to braid again. In my tribe, braids are the selfhood of a person. A youngster's hair is braided when he or she goes out to keep vigil for a name. All Red Harts but children wear braids. Istas had cut mine off the day she had taken her revenge on me. Sakeema be thanked, mercy had stopped her before she had taken my manhood as well.

"So," I teased Kor in my turn, "you have not yet grown so strong that you can command yon old woman."

"Not without drawing my sword. You must second me at the feast tonight."

I laughed and went off to wait in the hearth hall. The place was full of bustle and good cooking smells. No span of living with Kor's folk could make me truly fond of fish, but that night I was willing to eat whatever they put before me. My stomach was swooning with hunger.

Many were those who came and sat with me awhile and wanted to know the tale of my journey. Even Olpash, a council member and former enemy, came and asked questions. Except for telling them how Kor's retainers had died fighting the Fanged Horse Folk, and something of Birc and the deer people, there was little I could say to them. Our story, Kor's and mine, was all too inward, too uncanny. Though among my own people I was reckoned a great teller of the true tales, this one I could not yet encompass.

Kor's preparations took some time. When he came forth at last, he wore the raiment of a Seal king, the headband beaded with rings of polished shell, each piece tiny and perfectly shaped—years of labor had gone into the making of that band. And armbands of like sort, and a sleeveless tunic of fine, soft leather, and the ornaments of a king, strings of tusk shell, centered on his chest. And over his shoulders there rippled down a short cape of glossy brown sealskin. An odd pang went through me at the sight of him in cape and headband, as if I were losing him to kingship and his own people. He sat by me with a wry look.

What was that? he asked me, mindspeaking.

Pettiness. Pay no heed.

Have less fear, then. I cannot wait to be out of this smother of ceremony and away, Dan.

Some maiden saw me smiling broadly and touched me on the shoulder as she passed me with a basket of bread. I would have a bedmate that night. . . . Istas, the regent, came and took her seat by Kor's other side. Olpash stood, silencing the babble of voices with his chill stare. When all was still enough to suit him, he began a lengthy speech, welcoming the king back to his people.

Pompous old pickthank, Kor mindspoke me. Olpash was a petty seeker after power, a longtime enemy, though seldom openly so, more of an annoyance than a danger. I glanced over at Kor, barely hiding my amusement. Whatever his thoughts might be, he was keeping his face perfectly sober.

Olpash made an end at last. Feasting began.

It was more formal than any feast of my Red Hart Tribe would ever be. These Seal folk had the large hall, a lofty stone chamber within the Hold, which replaced the great lodge I had ruined. And they had planks set up for placing the food on, and logs covered with seal pelts for seating. Still, the chatter and chewing, the greasy fingers and mumbling of bones, were the same. Fish made a pale changeling for venison, but there were strong old mead, and perry, and sour berry wines.

I ate contentedly and drank whatever came my way. Kor kept silence, ate less than I. Istas watched the progress of the feast with a piercing gaze like that of an osprey, and from time to time she shrilled orders at the servers. The time came when everyone was well fed, the noise at a height, and the mess as well.

"Now, Istas," Kor said to her abruptly, "there is nothing to be attended to for a while. Are you free to listen to me?"

His tone of voice alerted her. She turned to him with a searching look.

"Do not put off your regent's cap yet awhile," he told her. "I will not be here for another day before I go away again."

Only the presence of the entire tribe kept her from shouting. Outrage creased her face.

"Rad Korridun, you must be stark mad! Have you no honor? These are your people! You are needed here!"

"What could possibly happen here," Kor retorted, "that you could not tend to?"

"What could happen. . . ." Istas startled us both by beginning to laugh, leaning back against the stone of the hearth, letting her clothes be smudged black with soot. It was not a good laugh, but more like the hoarse baying of a banhound, and Kor frowned, hearing it.

"What?" he repeated.

"Hunger, for one." Istas sat up, wiping her streaming eyes, and there was no merriment in the hard set of her face. "The oat crop is meager. Pajlat will want a share, and so will the Otter River folk."

"This game we have played out many a time before."

"But never so sharply before! The forage is sparse on the high plains, sparser than it has ever been before. Pajlat and his gentle minions will be in a fit mood to take what we do not wish to give them. And if the salmon are less again—and they are always less—"

"The Otter River Clan will request our aid," Kor finished for her, impatient. "What of it? Izu is our friend. We have always given them what we could."

"Izu is no longer very much your friend. . . ." Istas paused, hesitating as to how to go on.

"Out with it," Kor said in a resigned tone, and he turned to me. "This is the ploy Istas uses, Dan, when she has something unpleasant to say and wishes the other to ask her to say it."

"I truly do not wish to speak of it, not before you, Dannoc." Istas's watery old eyes met mine—what matter was this? "The two you killed—besides Rowalt." She sounded sorrowful but calm, for there was no longer any hatred in her for me. "The fosterlings."

"I see," Kor said.

"I don't," I told him.

"They were Otter River Clansmen. My father was an Otter king's younger son, you know, and the Otter sent those youths to me for fostering. I became their adoptive sire, and I chose not to avenge their deaths. The Otter have no recourse, they had given them up to me, but I should have known there would be bitterness."

I did not speak. There was nothing I could say.

"The more so as they must bear with my kindness," Kor added dryly.

It was an understanding I had not expected of him, and it made me smile. Istas scowled and went on.

"Izu and her people are filled with bitterness. There are no thanks in them, anymore, that we try to help feed them. They say that it is our doing that the salmon are less. That the seals eat them, that we let too many seals live. That they will have themselves a feast of seals, that they will club the nursing mothers and the cubs on the Greenstones."

This was abomination, worse than attack against the Hold itself. I saw anger stir Kor's shoulders, but he would not openly rouse, not yet. "Where have you heard this?" he demanded.

"From our people, reporting what has been heard from theirs. They have been here three times since you left, begging aid with surly looks. Nothing goes well with them these days."

"Nor with any of the tribes!" Kor said hotly, as if he had somehow been accused.

"You think I have not seen?" Istas allowed herself to raise her voice—amidst the babble of talk and the clatter of pottery few folk noticed. "All falls to ruin. I am old, I remember when the white whales swam past the coast and the wild swans flew overhead and the sea eagles nested just beyond the Hold. I remember when the salmon ran so thick a child could wade in and catch one in her hands, and there were great bears feasting on them, and wolves, and even wildcats. I remember! Do you think I cannot see how all the world is dwindling and dwindling away like a wretched old woman with a wasting illness? Even the herring swam thin in the surf this year. The Herders grow a little corn, some beans—have you heard, did they do well?"

I snorted aloud, and Kor gave a single bark of laughter. The Herders had grown no crops at all this year, for they had been driven off their lands, chivvied about between my father's greed and Pajlat's.

"Of course they did not, and how could they, on the poor, dying land? And you, Korridun, at this most terrible of times, you speak of going away?"

And he had not yet told her of Ytan, or of the devourers, or of the Cragsmen's anger.

"Off on another—another jaunt?" Istas fairly growled the word, her deep-etched face flushed with passion but hard, controlled. She was like a rock for strength, was

Istas. "When your people need you worst? The Fanged Horse raiders on the one side threatening, and the Otter River folk on the other, and hunger just beneath the horizon—"

"And if that is so, which I deem it is," Kor blazed back with passion that matched hers, "what is the worthiness of my biding here and waiting for the end, as if I were a barnacle on a beached log? When there might yet be time—"

For what, I never heard, for there was the sound of plucked strings and flute notes, and a shout went up. Music was a rare treat, even if it was only the efforts of fellow tribesmen, sometime minstrels, such as we were to hear. Everyone fell silent to listen, even Kor and Istas.

And it was as if the singers had heard of what we had been speaking. Or perhaps the same sadness weighed much on all minds. The first song was a lament for Sakeema, gone over the western sea in a coracle made of moonlight and shadow. The lay told how the strange maidens came out of the sea and took him away, how the seals wept as they watched him go. (For the Seal Kindred say that Sakeema was born in a cave by the sea and suckled by a cow seal, even as the Red Hart say that he was fostered among the deer, and the Fanged Horse Folk, that he was suckled on mare's milk.) The seals still weep for his return, the song said. When times are hard, tracks of tears stain the soft fur below their eyes.

"A weeping seal has been seen on the beaches to northward," Istas muttered darkly to Kor.

There followed a longer story-song about one of Kor's distant ancestors, relating how the seal blood had come to be in the Seal Kindred.

In times long past, it seemed, before there were tribes, a youth was walking the shoreline after a storm, searching for glimmerstones and ivory, when he found a woman of extraordinary beauty lying naked on a brown seal pelt amidst the rocks, bruised and senseless, as if she had been beaten. Yet she was no woman such as he had ever seen. He lifted her up, sealskin and all, and carried her home to his lodge, where he and his mother warmed her before the fire and nursed her anxiously. She soon recovered, and moved about and ate, but she never spoke. She only gazed about her with eyes the color of carrageen. And as she could not tell them her name, they called her simply Sedna, "the seal."

She never smiled. Nor did she care to wear much clothing, though her hands and feet seemed always to be cold. None of this mattered, for the youth had fallen helplessly in love with her, and for her part, she never tried to leave him. Unsmiling but serene, she did the things for him that a woman does for the man whom she loves. She bore him children, two sons and a daughter. The seal pelt lined their cradle. The babies were beautiful, with hair thick as fur and large, dark eyes. She raised them tenderly, and the children were loving and merry, but they spoke only to their father.

A day came of strange storm, when the sky grew green and purple far to the westward, and lightning flared even as snow fell, and ice filled the sky like fog, with hard rainbows glittering in it. Folk cowered within doors, for the air of that day seared the lungs, and those who were frail died of it months afterward. But the strange woman Sedna became restless to the point of frenzy, pacing and whirling within her pledgemate's lodge, whether from fear or some strange ecstasy he could not tell. And snatching the brown seal pelt out of the cradle she ran out into the storm, toward the sea. He ran after her, shouting, but of course she did not answer him, and the storm had reached the height of its fury, so that he could not see. He was battered and knocked down and dragged by wind, nearly killed before he reached his lodge once again and huddled within it, trying to comfort his children.

Nothing more was ever seen of his beautiful lifelove. But the next day, when the storm had abated, he went to the shore, looking for some sign of her. And he found a slender cow seal of a soft brown color lying dead on the rocks, beached and beaten by the storm. Though such a seal was a thing of value, he did not take it home to skin it or butcher it, for a prickling feeling was in him, and he raised a cairn of stone over it so that the gulls would not pick out its eyes. Lovely eyes the color of carrageen.

His children grew tall and strong. His eldest, a son, reached vigil age. And a strange urging took hold of that son, now a stripling, so that he went out and opened the cairn on the shore. There lay the seal, perfectly preserved. And the son took his knife and skinned it and closed the cairn over the remains. He made the pelt into a shortcloak for his shoulders. A year later, when he looked once again in the cairn, the seal's body had rotted completely away.

The name that came to that son in vigil was Korridun: "king by the sea." He was the first Korridun, from whom my friend and bond brother had taken his own name. First Korridun and first king of the Seal Kindred, for his kinsmen and brothers and sisters had many children, the ancestors of the tribe. Strong and tall, though often strange and not always wise, that elsewhen king had ruled them.

Kor sat so still beside me that I glanced at him as if he had spoken, but he did not notice me. Intently he listened to the song, shoulders thrust forward, though he must have heard it many times before. And the cape of brown sealskin lay soft on his back.

Your cloak, Kor—Sedna's skin?

He looked over at me, startled, and nodded. "My mother's pelt," he said aloud, briefly stroking the sleek brown fur. "When she went down to the sea that last time, she left it for me, laid it on my bed. She found her way to Mahela—by other means."

I sat back, letting the song echo in my mind. Ai, but

Kor's people were daring in their settled way! Even the fishermen, venturing far out on the sea in their tiny boats, hunting the cachalot . . . There was a small stirring, a murmur of voices. The harp changed hands—

A minstrel had come for our feasting, after all. Sitting before us, beautiful and uncanny in the firelight, strumming the harp. I half rose from my seat.

"Tass!" I exclaimed hoarsely.

She's being a youth again, Kor mindspoke me, a warning. Tass would take it ill if I revealed her secret in my fervor. I sank back in my place, staring at her numbly. She had not returned my greeting, but sat smiling at Kor or me across the shadows of the firelit hall, picking out chords and song-notes on the harp. A strange melody, strong and surging yet eerie. In a moment she started to sing in her clear voice, low for a woman, not too high for a boy or a young man. It was a new song she sang, one I had never heard.

> "Let me sing you a song of a seeking,
>   Let me sing you a song of a quest,
>   Of Dannoc, the king's son who did not remember,
>   And Korridun Sea King, who could not rest.
>   Which is the leader and which is the led?
>   'I would walk through fire for you, Kor,' Dannoc
>   said."

A stirring of surprise and excitement rippled around the room, as if tall prairie grass had rippled in a sudden wind. And I sat stunned, remembering the vigil night I had spoken those words to Kor, feeling warm with mead and the memory and with love of the singer, but uneasy about the song.

> "Dannoc rode homeward and Kor rode beside him,
>   Braved Cragsmen and sorcery and Fanged Horse
>   raiders,

> With Dannoc the madman who did not remember
> How Tyonoc his sire had betrayed him to slay him.
> Which is the lord, which the afterling?
> 'We're heartbound together,' said Kor Sea King.''

A murmur of wonder rose through the feasting hall—these folk were hearing my tale, mine and Kor's, for the first time. I felt Istas's glance search me, but I would not look at her. My eyes were misting at Kor's remembered words.

> ''And witch wind, Mahela's breath, sparked high
>   plain wildfire.
> As fast as a horse can flee, faster it ran,
> Panting hot, drawing near, as a hound hunts the
>   deer—
> And fire blazed before them! Kor's mare leapt in fear.
> He fell hard, lay senseless. Then afoot back came
>   Dan,
> And took up his comrade and walked through the
>   flames.

> ''Dannoc rode homeward and Kor rode beside him,
> Dannoc his friend who had walked through the fire.
> And coming at dusk to the Red Hart encampment,
> Dannoc faced and embraced there King Tyonoc, his
>   sire.
> And Tyonoc smiled. Then 'Seize them!' he bade.
> And Dannoc was bound, and Kor put to—''

''No!'' I shouted, stumbling to my feet, sending trencher planks and pottery crashing over. I did not care, I could not bear it, for I knew too well what had been done to Kor. ''Tassida, why! Were not the torments of the time terrible enough? Why have you made this song!''

Except for the noise I had made, the hall was as silent as

a hundred spirits waiting. Tassida's answer sounded to the farthest listener.

"Because these people do not know by half how fearsome and how powerful you two have become! Kor died. Tyonoc all but cut him to pieces. And when you broke free you let a demon out of your father's body with your sword. Then you held Kor, cradled him and wept—"

He was standing beside me, one arm around my shoulders, and only his presence kept me from weeping anew or shouting at her again.

Her voice dropped to a husky whisper, but still everyone heard. "—and somehow your passion brought him back to life. Well. Whole. Healed. As we see him."

An uproar broke out. Istas, Olpash, others called to us, demanding to know if it was true. Kor and I did not answer them, but Tassida made her way through the crowd to us, and we spoke with her.

"Is it so horrible?" she asked.

"It is fearsome, as you have said, and too recent for comfort," Kor replied. But he was not angry. Our love for her kept us from anger.

"If you must sing, Tass," I told her shakily, "then give us the song of Chal and Vallart."

She sat close by us, and I saw that she wore a sword, like Kor's, like mine, at her belt, and on its pommel shone a great stone the color of the blessing of Sakeema in the sunset, a color no one can name except by the legendary healing flower of the god, the amaranth. Too red to be called violet, but darkly far from the blood red of Zaneb's stone. It was a color pure, clear, and piercingly sweet, like the fragrance of the amaranth, once known to me in a vision.

Tassida struck the chords of the song. And, so great is the power of music, the babble faded and the crowd grew quiet to hear. Kor and I sat down, and I let my head rest for a moment against his cloaked shoulder, for I felt weak with love and wine and fear, hearing once again Vallart's words to the prince his comrade:

> ". . . I will follow you if you walk into the sea.
> What is a friend? Troth without end.
> A light in the eyes, a touch of the hand—
> I would follow you even to death's cold strand.
> To death's . . . cold . . . strand.''

Chapter Seven

Late the next day, after we had had time to recover somewhat from our welcome, Kor and I left Seal Hold and rode along the ocean again. It was a sunny day with scarcely a haze of fog—rare, along that shore. Tass rode with us, and looked sideways at us, for Kor still wore his sealskin cloak. There were long silences as we rode, and I, for one, felt awkward.

"Did you see anything uncanny at the pool of vision?" Kor asked in the midst of one such silence, glancing at Tassida's sword. The jewel in the pommel flashed in the westering sunlight as he spoke.

"Yes," she replied, only the single word and no more. A quiet, again.

"In your many travels, have you ever seen a wolf, Tass?" I asked after we had ridden onward awhile.

"No," she said. A long pause, so long that I thought we were in the grip of silence still. But she surprised me by speaking. "On my way over the mountains, coming here, I thought I heard one howl. From where, I could not tell. The sound echoed between the peaks."

She had journeyed, we surmised, not far behind us. "The night of the hunters' moon?" Kor asked.

"Yes."

She heard either the wolf or you, Dan, Kor mindspoke me, hiding his amusement.

Hush, I told him. Oddly, I feared that Tassida might overhear us, though certainly I had never feared that Istas might, or any of the others.

Kor must have sensed my doubt. He looked at her askance. "Tass, why are you here?"

Tass had been amiable till then, for her. But the question put her on her mettle at once. I saw her come to warrior alertness on Calimir's back, as if she carried a spear. "Why not?" she retorted.

"No reason. But you say you do not wish to travel with us, yet you seem always to be turning up. What—"

"If you do not want me here," she interrupted hotly, "I will go."

I laughed, feeling more at ease since we were quarreling— our bickering seemed more natural than the silence. "Tass, you have always gone when you wished and come back willy-nilly, like changing weather. What wind blew you here this time?"

She sighed and let go of spleen for a moment, speaking quietly. "I wanted to see if you are still bent on this witless venture."

For answer Kor nodded at the sea. "Greenstone stacks," he said.

Weird spires and crags and hillocks of rock rose from the ocean ahead of us, their shapes sometimes round, sometimes mountainous, but stranger than those of any mountain I had ever seen. The day was nearing sundown, the tide running high, and the great rocks stood darkly shining, wet with spray, looming against an orange sky and water of like hue. The steady clamor in my ears, calling of many seabirds and crashing of surf, made me feel lightheaded, as if I were floating rather than riding along at Talu's jarring trot.

"And look," Kor added, "my cousins."

Portions of the dark and shining rock seemed to move, and I blinked, making out the sleek forms of seals, wet and gleaming. They lay basking in the sunset, some sitting upright as if in salute to the fineness of the day, heads pointing skyward, some nudging each other with whiskered noses, swaying into unlikely curves, some lolling in the spray as the rocks wallowed in the waves: the odd, watersheen shapes of the seals echoed the many shapes of the Greenstones. Or perhaps the rocks echoed seal forms. It was as if the rocks stood there, knee-deep in the sea, for no other purpose than for seals to lie on and frolic upon.

Seals lay at the foot of the cliff to landward, also. Kor dismounted, we all dismounted, and walked softly toward them over the sand of the beach, and they did not flee from us.

"How can the Otter River folk want them killed!" Kor muttered angrily.

Kor's people killed seals sometimes, in need and with reverence, as we of the Red Hart killed deer. But they ate fish so as to spare the seals, and were joyful when they saw that many seals lived.

"Of all creatures, one of the few that has kept the many colors of Sakeema's time. . . ."

The three of us stood looking, the seals nearly at our feet. Indeed, they were of almost every possible creature color, some black, some gray or brown or yellow or russet, and some shone nearly blood-red in the sunset light. Half-grown pups were covered with soft fur as blue as blue fog. Their elders were often mottled and spotted with patches of random color: white ringstreaks, red blankets, brown dapples, yellow specks. I even saw a green tinge on the flanks of some. A grand black bull lifted his head and barked at us—he was as large as I. A gray cow stretched and fanned herself with a flipper. The smallest seal was the size of a small child, but most were middling,

about of a weight with a young woman or a youth of the
Seal Kindred.

"On the plains," Tassida said softly, "horses run in as
many colors as these."

Except for Calimir, the horses I knew were only brown
and dun. All deer were gone except the red, all foxes but
the gray, all wolves . . .

Kor turned to his yellow dun mare with a sigh and
began to strip her of her gear. I turned likewise to Talu.
Whether disturbed by our actions or merely because the
sun was sinking, the seals ambled away or slithered into
the water. Tassida stood watching us with a puzzled frown.

"You are staying here? But you have brought no sleeping robes, no food."

"None needed for a vigil," Kor said.

We walked the horses farther southward along the shore,
beyond the Greenstones, and turned them loose, sending
them away with a shout. Forested mountain slopes rose up
from the sea, rocks full of whistlers and pikas and viper
nests. And there would be leavings on the beach as well,
dead fish—Talu, for one, loved fish, the riper the better.
We hoped the horses would be able to fend for themselves
so as not to take food from Kor's people. We hoped,
perhaps, that they would be waiting for us when we came
back. Though we scarcely dared to expect it. As to the
coming back itself, we scarcely dared to expect.

Tassida watched us, wide-eyed.

"You two—you truly think you can bring back Tyonoc
from the realm of the dead."

The wary look on her face made me think of Istas and
the way she had seen us off, silent, suspicious, half-
fearful after hearing Tassida's song. Whether Tass had
intended the ballad for that purpose, or for whatever purpose, there had been no protests in Istas since. No nattering,
no chewing on the outcome. No talk of safeguards, a
retinue. No protests from any of Kor's kindred, least of all

from Olpash. I had to smile, but the smile washed away as if with the tide, for I was afraid.

"We don't think it," Kor replied, grim. "We go to do whatever task awaits us. Thinking is of no use."

He took off his sword, and I mine. It was dusk, the sun had sunk, the sea washed dim. We carried the swords into a cave beneath the cliffs, not far from another cave I remembered from another time, and the stones in the pommels shone red and yellow, lighting our way with a sundown glow. On a ledge at the farthest indeeps of the cave, out of the reach of tides, we laid them down, blades crossed, and laid our hands on them for a moment, letting our fingers touch in the whisper of light, faint as starlight, and we bade farewell to the weapons we scarcely understood.

Tassida had followed us. "They will be safe there?" she said, more a plaint than a question. I noticed that her voice was shaking.

"They should be," I told her. "Have you ever tried to touch one of these swords not your own?"

"No. Mine—came to me."

"If I tried to take it from you, it would cut me. Slice off my hand, if need be." I smiled, remembering the cut Kor's sword had given me when I had been foolish enough to try to capture it for him, and stepping toward her I raised my hand to show it to her.

She turned and ran out of the cave.

Shrugging, I followed. Kor followed. Tass was swinging up onto Calimir.

"Off again?" Kor called, his voice low.

"Yes. You two terrify me." Nevertheless, she quirked an odd smile at us. "Take your horse gear back to Seal Hold?" she offered.

It would keep better there than in the cave. We handed it up to her, deerskin riding blankets and leather headstalls.

Dusk was darkening. Though I looked intently, I could scarcely see her face.

"Farewell. Gentle journey to you. I—" For a moment her hands touched ours, Kor's and mine, and I felt something for which I had no words. Not even the name of love described it. Perhaps she felt it too, and it made her forget what she wanted to say. She ducked her head, stammering, and pulled her hands away. "Blast it," I heard her mumble, and then she sent Calimir springing landward. We watched him gallop, a dark shape against the pale sand of the beach.

Just as we were about to lose sight of her in the twisted spruces, she reined him in and turned back toward us. Perhaps she raised a hand—I could not tell. But her voice rang out clear and strong through the nightfall. "Come back!" she called. "Be sure you come back to us mortals!" Then she was gone.

I shivered. What had she meant? I felt all too mortal myself.

We put off our boots, our clothing. Naked, we stepped to the edge of the surf, Kor and I. He carried his sealskin cloak in one hand. I had nothing to aid me in making the change, and no thought, either, as to how I was to do it. . . . Cold clutch of seawater at my feet. If the seals were still on the rocks I could not hear them—I could hear nothing but the commotion of surf, or my own heart's pounding, my own fear. I felt adrift, awash, as if already I were drowned and bloating. The nearness of the sea filled me with dread. It was not to me a familiar beauty and sustainer and danger, as it was to Kor. As if entangled in wrack of nightmare, I could think only of black water, chill, deep, and how it had gathered me in to kill me.

And Vallart's words to Chal throbbed like a heartbeat in my head: I will follow you if you walk into the sea. . . .

"Kor," I whispered, echoing the song, "I am not of the stuff of legend."

I do not think he heard me, not above the surf's roar. I would have needed to shout to be heard. But I am sure he felt my fear. He reached over and handbonded me.

Come, he mindspoke, *it is only to go out to the Green-stones, the farthest stack, for now.*

What then, neither of us could say. But how could I hold back, whatever might befall? It was my quest, my father, Tyonoc, whom we sought—was it not? Who was the leader and who was the led?

"Come on," I said fiercely, for the handbond had given me courage. Letting go, but staying close by him, I strode forward to do battle with the surf.

Battering water—it blinded me, burned my lungs, knocked me backward, filled me with terror and rage. I had been reared where the upland streams run knee-deep, and I was not accustomed to the ways of mighty water. It angered me that water should mob, overrun, best me. I strove against it, and it beat on me worse than giant fists, worse than a Cragsman's cudgel. Where was Kor? I could not see—

His grasp closed on my wrist, and he was pulling me downward. Panicked, I fought him too. Was he my betrayer now, like the father and brother who had kicked at my head to drown me in the black tarn?

Dan, stop thrashing. The easing contact of his mind, once so frightening to me, now felt as steadying as handbond. I let him draw me down under the breakers.

No one can fight Mother Sea. She is mighty and larger than the mountains, she always wins. One must slip through her lines.

He brought me up in the quieter water beyond the surf, where I took in air with ragged gasps. Even here waves tossed me and slapped at my face, stinging my nostrils with salt. Disgusted, wanting only to gain the solid footing of the rocks and be out of this foul-tasting smother, I tried to churn my way forward. My hands threw up splashes of green light from the black water. The rocks were black hulks against a sky milky with stars, their verges awash with faint light. At my side, Kor floated at his ease, stretched out on the surface of the ocean, his path limned with dim green, the sealskin swimming like a living thing beside him.

Slip, Dan, slip! Edgewise.

I tried. Sometimes I got on better, but I could not entirely manage it. Kor reached out from time to time and gave me a tug, helping me flounder forward. More often, Mother Sea gave me a hefty blow and threw me back, or I sank, choking, to blunder against the rocky bottom or feel Kor's grasp again on my wrist. Coming up, I gasped or gulped or spat like a cat. It was time past forever before I finally reached the rocky sea stack where we were to keep our vigil, and I had so exhausted myself that I lay flat on the wet rock, scarcely out of the spray.

Kor helped me up to the rounded top after a while, where it was dry and the rock gave back the warmth of the day's sun. He kept silence for some time, until I was done panting.

"You hate it," he said finally.

"Mahela, yes." I was still coughing up salt spume from time to time.

"Go back. The waves will carry you to shore."

"No."

I did not want another dunking, he thought. "I will come with you, and swim out again."

"No! Kor, don't talk like a fool. I'm staying."

"Pigheaded," he muttered.

"Speak for yourself," I retorted.

"But that's just it! Dan, don't you see I am at fault for bringing you here? How can it be right? You are not made for this. If—" He stopped. Something unspeakable lay in his mind, making my own fear anger me.

"I'm past needing a nursemaid," I told him savagely. "You tend to your vigil and your life. I'll tend to mine."

Warmth was leaving the rock. I sat up, shivering in the chill sea breeze. We Red Hart, we go bare-chested into blizzards, but the ocean damp makes us quake. I would be shivering for the most part of the next several days.

Kor sat by me, silent and still, legs folded, hands clasped. But I was not deceived. Not until all was right between us would he be able truly to begin his vigil.

I mindspoke him, but not with words, just a touch, as if I had reached over to touch his arm. Gentle, but he was somewhat startled and turned toward me with a quick intake of breath. Then, delighted, he smiled. Nor were such smiles commonplace in him.

"How did you do that?"

"I—I don't know. I just—" Words would not come, and I puffed my lips in exasperation. "I had to tell you, or show you," I blurted at last. "Kor, pay no attention to my spleen. Our lives are bound, I know that."

"Heartbound, handbound, mindbound," he said softly, moved.

"But, Sakeema be my witness, Kor, I am here of my own will. I seek my father to save him, remember? If I fail, it will be of my own doing, not yours."

Maybe he did not believe me entirely. In my heart I did not believe it myself, deeming of him what I did. But it served, for the time, to free him, and he nodded, reaching over to me. We clasped hands firmly and in silence.

"Look," he said after a while, letting his grip drift away from mine, "the starlight on the whitecaps and the green swirls between, is it not beautiful?"

He was not one to say such things idly. I knew he wanted me to see beauty in the black water so that I would be able to enter it with more ease. But I could not reply to him, and those were the last words he spoke to me for the many days of the vigil.

I shivered through the night, sitting by his side, and saw the morning dawn all too slowly through fog. Nor did the fog burn away, all the next day. I sat bone-chilled and cramped with cold, longing for the sun, but I suppose it was as well that the haze hid it, or our naked skin would have been scorched—sun rays fall strongly at sea. Though at the time I scarcely considered myself blessed. Alone in gray brume, Kor and I sat without eating or speaking or sleeping, as is the custom for the keeping of vigil. We moved only to relieve ourselves into the sea on the far side of the stack or to drink the fogwater that gathered in small pools atop the rock, water that tasted rank and was never enough. I sucked the dew that dripped from the ends of my hair. Other than that, we sat. Kor sat atop his sealskin cloak. I had nothing but the hard rock under me, but I did not complain, not even to myself, for I knew he had not brought the pelt along for his comfort.

Even the second night neither of us slept, though I for one would sorely have liked to, if it were not for the wintry cold. Kor, I think, had already gone into a sort of trance. Alert and tranquil, he faced the sea as if he were only waiting for a beckoning, a sign.

We saw seals from time to time. Some came and lay at the base of the very sea stack on which we sat. We saw many things: cormorants flying, low to the water and as silent as the mist, and some sort of large fish leaping in the distance, and fulmars on the rocks, and the third night, when the mist cleared, a skein of geese across the moon, their piping very faint—the sound of that faraway flock wrenched my heart with a sorrow and longing I could not explain. And the cries of birds, gulls, sanderlings, whimbrels, kittiwakes, every day, as constant as the soughing of the water, and the vigil had taken its course as a vigil should, for I had passed beyond impatience and hunger and cold into something other, and time had ceased to hold meaning for me. The trance was in a way better than

sleeping. I suppose I dozed from time to time, still upright, but I do not recall doing so—I remember only that
everything seemed very clear and bright, as if in a mist
made of sunshine, in which there were no shadows. I saw
every tan leaf of the kelp that swam by the knees of the
rocks, every bladder and stem. I saw a small feather that
dropped from the breast of a passing bird. My breathing,
so it seemed, was as slow and steady as the rhythm of the
tides. I do not know how long we sat, Kor and I, after the
skein of wild geese crossed the moon with a sound as of a
distant clay flute.

But I remember that it was nighttime, and the seals were
dancing. In the sea, where they were graceful as they
could never be on land, in a great circle they danced the fire
dance and whipped the waves to green flame with their
treading, their leaping. How lovely were their scoonings
and swayings, their circle of green shimmering fire. How
lovely the sinuous movements of their heads when they
raised them. One of the seals, moon-colored, seemed to
glow, left a bright trail in the water. I had seen seals of
many colors, so I took no pause that one was white. How
lovely, the white seal, as one after another they leaped
entirely free of the sea and sank again in great waterflames,
green, touched white with foam and moonlight. . . .

Kor got up stiffly, fumble-footed, and made his way
down the stack to where the water lapped. Swaying, he
walked slowly, intently, without turning, the sealskin trailing from one hand. I watched him without moving or
speaking, for it was only right, fitting, that he should go to
join the dance.

He waded into the sea until it reached his thighs, placed
the seal cloak around his shoulders, and dove cleanly,
vanished, leaving a swirl of green on the surface of the
black water.

I watched as if in a dream, accepting. Then suddenly, as
the watcher in the mind decides to wake from a dream, I

no longer sat, but struggled up as if arising from nightmare, as if I were thrashing my way out of dark water. I was Dannoc, weak from cold and hunger, and Kor was gone. I wanted him, and I feared for him, even worse than I had longed for him and feared for him on the mountainside when the Cragsmen had walked past. *Kor!* I called.

No answer. Had another seal joined the bright, shadowy dance? I could not tell.

I staggered where I stood. "Kor!" I shouted out loud.

Every seal splashed beneath the surface of the sea and dove. Green flame turned into a shining blackness with specks of waterglow in it, glinting like hard eyes.

I shouted until I was hoarse, sent my mind searching and calling to no avail. Kor was gone as if he had never been.

Chapter Eight

Wyonet, my mother, had left me without warning, without a word or a trace, never to be seen again. Tyonoc, my father, had been taken by a demon, gone years before I knew. Kor . . . I would not think it. He had to come back to me. Sakeema, beloved king, prithee come back to us. . . . No. Not generations hence. *Kor, soon. Come soon.*

Thirsty pain in my throat . . . I could not call any longer, not even with my mind. My feet had brought me down the stack, closer to the sea, almost within reach of the tide, but I did not care. I sank down where I was and sat with and ache in my throat, not all thirst, with a harsh pain spreading through my chest and shoulders and a hurtful dryness about my eyes so that I had to close them against the dim and hazy dawn as if it were snowglare. I needed the flow of tears, but to weep would have meant defeat, the end of hope. Or perhaps I was merely too proud. A pox on vigils, I decided, and I lay down where I was, on the cold, wet stone, weary beyond shivering, to sleep. But whenever I dozed a spasm took hold of me, a silent, dry sobbing that tore at my throat, awakening me. When I slept at last, it was more as if I had fainted.

Splash of cold seawater startled me awake. The tide was

coming in. I edged up the rock a small distance, not bothering to rise, up to a ledge just out of tide's reach, and I lay there, indifferent to the grasping water that groped so near me. Except for the slapping of the water, the day seemed very silent, and after a while I sat up and looked around. The whitish patch of haze that hid the sun stood overhead. No seals anywhere in sight, none swimming, none hauled out along the rocks to bask or rest—with a pang I wondered where they were. Not even many birds about. I was alone with my shivering self and the vastness of sea and sky.

I sat, not thinking, too tired and dismayed to think. Whatever tides flowed in my mind were too slow and wordless to be called thought. After what might have been half the halfday I turned, as slowly and stupidly as a great turtle, and peered toward the shore. It was the first time since the beginning of the vigil that I had looked landward. Beyond seal-form spires and humps, beyond a white blur of surf, I could make out a wavering band of dark green through the mist—spruce forest on steep, rocky slopes that jutted toward snowpeaks. But the peaks themselves, my beloved mountains, I could not see.

Just as oafishly I turned back toward the ocean.

Let the waves carry you back to shore, he had said. You do not belong here. But something sullen and stubborn was stirring in me. Here I was, and here I would stay, and I would wait for Kor until I died, which happy event might not be long in coming. And Mahela take him, the ingrate. Likely I would die anyway, in the surf, should I venture toward shore. I would be drowned or smashed against a rock, weak as I had become, starving myself for his sake. So let me rot where he could find my bleached bones and weep. I sat scowling and blinking my dry, stinging eyes against the shell-gray day—

A glint of brighter, fishy-flashing gray, far off near the hidden edge of sea. I had seen such a flash once before over the far sea, rising above the water, too large at the distance to be any fish or even a bird. And much too high. But that time there had been only the one, and this time there were—three, seven, ten, more. A full twelve less one, rippling and shimmering and drawing nearer, wingtip to tip of capelike wing. Devourers.

"Mahela's twelve," I breathed, suddenly absurdly sure of it. Kings of our tribes kept each a twelve of retainers. Why not, then, the ruler of death, she who held court beneath the endless water?

A twelve of devourers, less only the one that possessed Ytan . . . The size of them, the weight and swiftness, the gleaming sheen as they parted the fog—I shrank back against the rock, holding my breath in awe and fear, feeling very exposed and no longer nearly so ready to die. As I surely would, die or worse, should one of them choose to take me. I was weak from fasting, no match for a devourer in body or will, lying on a rock far out in the ocean, with not even so much as a flint knife by me— nothing to kill myself with should one of them best me to make a demon out of me. Sick with terror, my gaze frozen on the monsters, I groped about me with both hands, searching for a rock, a driftwood stick by way of weapon, but I could find nothing. The sea carried all such oddments away. One is meant to be helpless, like a newborn babe, on vigil. I was helpless.

Perhaps Sakeema was with me after all. The devourers' errand was not with me, and, mindless things, they did not see me with their single eyes. They veered off and flew by me at some distance, bound landward, north toward Seal Hold.

All my anger had left me with a rush like that of retreating water. Sitting upright once again, shaking with a sense of danger, I began calling again, with my hoarse, choking voice and with my mind, *Kor!* Until nightfall I called. But there was no answer.

Somehow, soon after, the tide in me turned, and instead of yearning for Kor to come back to me, I began to long to go to him. Sometime during that same night, perhaps. I remember that I got up unsteadily and walked to the sea, wading into it until the water had me as far as my waist. Tide was rising, calm and chill. There I stood, aching and waiting, whispering to Sakeema, pleading for something, somehow, to happen so that I might enter the sea and search for my bond brother without drowning. Calling to Sakeema—for still, hidden in my secret thoughts, was the belief that Kor was he. But there was no change, no answer, nothing gained—and when the icy water had crept up to my chest and turned my legs and feet to dead wood, I gave it up with a curse and stumbled again onto the rock. There I lay on my clammy ledge, and there was no hope left in me. I deemed myself bereft, betrayed, defeated.

There is no telling how long I lay there. That time on the Greenstone is a blur of wretchedness to me. But when I sat up again it was no longer night.

Haze of vigil was on me, all those days, like the bright sea-haze that hid the sun yet let me see without shadow every leaf of the tangleweed, every small wriggling creature in the shallow pools the tide left on the rocks. So I remember the passing of time only as a haze and a flow, but some moments, dropping through time like a feather from the sky, I remember with a clearness that pierces me like an arrow. The fire dance in the night had been one such span.

The coming of the white seal was another.

It was twilight. The sea seemed very silent, the reaches of it purple and gray, the sky like the inside of a shell, like abalone, streaked the color of lavender. With scarcely a ripple she raised her head above the surface of the violet water and looked at me, and even at the distance I was caught by her glance. As I watched, she swam to the Greenstone stack where I sat, clambered onto it, crawling toward me. With no hurry, but no pause either, she dragged herself up to me over the wave-smoothed rock and did not stop until she had reached my side. There she stood on the heels of her hands, her flippers, with her face turned toward mine, and below her great, seeking eyes I saw the tracks of tears, dark in the white fur. And her eyes wrenched my heart, for they reminded me of Kor's. Like his they were a nameless dusky color made up of all the colors of the sea.

No sooner had she come to me than I reached out to touch her—she was alive, warm, she was there by me, and I had been so alone. I thought nothing more of it than that, but even had I thought to wonder why she had come to me, even had I known, I think still I would have done the same. It was not merely to pat her, as one would pat a dog, stroke her fur. I wanted comfort, and perhaps she did also. Trembling with the vigil weakness, I put my arms around her shoulders and laid my head against the round curve of her neck.

I felt rather than saw the change, for my eyes had closed. . . . A slight shifting. Bone under the skin. Wet fur, gone. I lifted my head and looked.

She still balanced on the heels of her hands, her feet stretched out behind her. Sea maiden, a face of eerie beauty, delicate as a thin seashell, unsmiling, intent. The salt water still on her—no, there truly were tears clinging below her eyes. A slender body, very pale in the twilight, as naked as mine except for her long, fair hair, which rippled down like water to partly cover her. She made a supple movement and came to her knees—her body was all a graceful flow, her breasts very small but very beautiful. She reached out toward me—if her hands were cold, like Sedna's, I did not feel it. All the love-longing that was in me turned like a spear point toward her. As I moved to meet her embrace I felt no longer weak and chilled, but strong, hot, full.

We lay—not furred like a deer maiden, she, for the fur lay beneath us, her white-furred seal pelt lay beneath us, somehow dry and warm. Her skin, soft, smooth, cool to my touch. Her arms took me in. We kissed. Teeth pointed and sharp beneath her lips, but I was not afraid, not even when she nibbled at the skin of my neck and shoulder, bit gently at my cheekbone.

"What is your name?" I asked her tenderly. "Can you speak to me?"

Her face, great-eyed and beautiful in the twilight, gave me no sign.

"Why do you weep?" I murmured.

She did not answer, but nipped me, as if to say, Do not dally. Her long hands urged my mouth toward her breasts. Then lower. . . . Ai, the hot tide goes through me to think of that lovemaking. She was as lithe as a seal in water, and hungry. I was all ardor. Once was not enough for either of us. . . . I hope I pleased her as greatly as she did me. I know that I remember her with longing and awe, for she left me slack and nearly weeping with pleasure, my eyes awash in mist. Or perhaps I was at last warm enough to weep for Kor. . . . I slept warm afterward, and soundly, with her nestled by my side, her arm over me and her breath stirring the hairs of my chest, nor did I mind the fishy reek of it, or the way she twitched while she slumbered.

When I awoke, she was still lying next to me, her flipper touching mine. I nuzzled her with my snout to rouse her, then rolled over, scrabbling my way with haste toward the sea. Fervidly I wanted to swim in the uplifting salt water, free of the heavy awkwardness my body suffered on land. Also, I had become aware that I was ravenous. I wanted fish.

Crawling, clambering down over the rock, thinking I would never reach the water, wondering why I had climbed so high on the Greenstone . . .

Home at last, I dove with force, leaving a splash and a swirl behind me, and at once I was in ecstasy.

Swimming. If ever there was another joy to compare with swimming, I could not recall it. Weightless, flying in water as a bird flies in air, streak of bubbles marking my passing, my body so strong, so supple, so graceful, sideward curving. I seemed to remember having been cold and stiff—how could that be? I was warm, my fur so thick that water never touched my skin, and my skin itself was dense against the ocean coldness. Only my flippers felt the chill, and they were leathery, they did not mind it. My ear slots and nostril slots closed of their own doing—seawater could not invade me, but I could make free of it as a deer makes free of meadows. Sinuous but arrow swift, I headed away from the Greenstones, toward the open sea.

Twice I surfaced for air. Below, I encountered currents, the many crossing ocean currents, and on one I tasted the smell of fish. I followed it. A school of herring, countless small, bright bodies swimming as one—I saw the flash of them from yet far away. In a green rush I caught the stragglers and gulped them one after another, swallowing them whole. Struggle and flutter though they might, they could not escape the trap my pointed teeth made for them. Ah, fish, belly-filling fish, food and drink in one! I followed the herring and gulped till I was gorged. Dimly I recalled, or seemed to recall, that I had once been a two-legged upright creature who sputtered in seawater and detested the taste of fish—had I dreamed that? It scarcely seemed possible that it could be true.

There were other seals feeding on the herring. I saw them as distant shadows, no more, for the school was vast, and seals are solitary animals except when they are on land to breed or bask or molt. So I was the more surprised, though well pleased, when the white seal came slipping up to me in a wash of yellow-green waterglow and bumped me with her whiskery nose. We fed side by side for a while, until she nipped me and I chased her. Then she led me shooting to the surface, where she leaped clear of the water. I found that I knew how to do the same. We circled down and leaped again and again, splashing mightily, making our own small fire dance.

My sense of time had left me, even more so than during the vigil. Time made small difference under the sea. I noticed only in passing that it seemed to be night again, that fishes were no longer greenish flashes, but black shadows surrounded by trailing moon-colored streaks. Some of the larger sorts were rising to the upper eddies to prey for their food. Lazing along on my back beneath them, looking up at the surface from underneath, at the wave patterns and the way the crescent moon so crazily spun and jumped, I felt the hunter's urge: how large a fish could I kill? I was no longer very hungry, but I chose one as swift and heavy as a slim fighting cock or a diving hawk, gathered myself, and struck with force. The thing shook itself like a thunderbolt in my mouth, sending up a blaze of waterflame, but it only hastened its own doom. I took it up to the surface, tossed it in the air, and ripped it to bits, gulping them, coughing up the large bones, swallowing the rest. A score of tiny fish gathered around me, feeding on the scraps. The white female rejoined me, stealing a chunk of my kill, speeding away playfully. Utterly delighted, I pursued her, trail of tiny bubbles in my face and the moon-white glow of her soft fur ahead of me—

Dan!

An odd urging, very far away yet warmly within my mind. Something that made my heart leap, though I could not remember why. Featly I bent myself at a slingshot angle and veered off toward it.

Dannoc, you blubberhead, where are you?

Here, I mindcalled.

Now I remembered, my name was Dan, and it was Kor, Kor, my pod brother, my comrade since we had been pups on the Greenstones together. When our mothers had gone off fishing for days on end and left us, so it seemed, to starve, we had lain side by side on the smooth-worn rocks and sucked each other's flippers and soft weanling fur to comfort each other. Other young males had fought, but we had never fought—

There he was, up ahead, swimming toward me at his best speed from the sea stacks. *Pod brother!* I hailed him, and I met him in a swirl of water, bumping flippers, touching noses—his whiskers jutted sharply toward mine. Ai, the goodly smell of him, the goodly sight! He was of a rich brown color, with a curling mane and flippers so dark they were nearly black. His mind was yelping with joy and astonishment. The joy I shared, but why the surprise?

Dan, how—when—where have you been?

I was very hungry, and I caught many many fish.

With a flick of her wrists the white seal drifted to my side, hanging back somewhat, her sea-colored eyes very human in her round face.

A sea maiden. He sounded less baffled now. *You lay with her? Dan, I should have known.*

Having been a seal all my life, I did not yet understand. *Should have known what?*

That if there was a creature of womanly form within a day's journey— Something sharp in his tone of mind, even when he gave up the thought and started another. *So she has made a handsome, sun-colored seal of you. Could you not have waited for me? I called and called—*

I, also, called and called! Memory rushed back into me. I had been myself as I had been born, Dannoc the man on a rock, naked, alone, angry, afraid. I felt it all again, remembering, and I knew Kor felt it as well.

I see. All edge gone. *When the change came, I forgot at first, as you did. I, also, was very hungry and caught many many fish.* Rueful amusement in Kor's tone. If I had been able to, I would have liked to have laughed with him.

But we could not laugh together anymore, not in that human way, and there was cause for fear in me.

Kor, the devourers! Eleven of them passed over, bound inland. Toward the Hold, I thought.

Mahela's minions! It was a statement and a curse.

I hope their errand was not to Istas.

I hope their errand was not to Tassida.

A jolt of jealousy, as always when he spoke of her. No matter. He knew worse of me.

What can we do?

Can you turn to a man again? Wryly. He knew as well as I did the answer.

Not likely.

Neither of us would soon walk in human form. I, perhaps never again. The thought scarcely troubled me. We would be fortunate merely to live.

There is nothing for us but to go onward, then.

Onward, to Mahela's realm. Wherever it might be. And whatever strange perils might meet us on the way.

There were no lengthy preparations to make, no provisioning such as was needed for human journeyings. We rose to breathe, cast a glance toward the land mass that glimmered in moonlight, toward dark fir forest sprinkled with the season's first snowfall. Beyond their forested flanks, just a whisper of my beloved snowpeaks. We looked, and then we sank and swam away westward, the shoreline to our tails, our faces turned toward the open sea.

The white female kept pace with us for a while. But when we had ventured beyond the shoals where the herring schooled, she began to circle in distress and make small noises in her throat.

What is it? I asked her. *Can you mindspeak?* Though I did not expect it of her, and I was not surprised when only silence answered me.

I do not even know her name, I said to Kor.

Likely she has none.

She has human form. She came to me, comforted me when I badly needed her. I am sorry to leave her.

I touched her nose with mine. She gave a watery chirrup and tried to lead us back the way we had come. When we refused to follow but went onward instead, she trailed after us for some time, calling, her reluctance holding her farther and farther behind, until at last we lost sight and sound of her.

Chapter Nine

But it is beautiful, my mind murmured to Kor's in awe, and for his own part he was silent, a hush within him that I could feel. If the wonders that lay beneath the sea were all new to me, to him they must have been a longtime dream seen in waking. Everywhere, marvelous creatures, the many fishes with flanks brighter than our swords, and something that shot by like a blunt spear, trailing long legs, and animals like great floating bubbles of many colors. Odd things. Yellow worms. Gilled sea snails, their shells coiled like a wild ram's horn. Flowers that moved, sea daisies, sea asters, orange and blue and purple. And tiny bright things like snow motes drifting upward as if falling through a shimmering green—sky? It scarcely seemed to matter what was up or what was down. The undersea was vast, and as fluid as my new sense of time, and full of shifting shadowlight, and deep, and green. Wet, chill, and green, as if it were always springtime there, greener than any mountain springtime, any aspen grove, any grassland . . . We saw a swimming snake and caught its musky odor as it flickered past, gone in an eyeblink. We saw a shell lash out with a whip and stun a small fish. Shells shaped like swans' wings, open and probing with something that looked like a tongue. Something all in spines, like a hedgehog.

We saw strange plants swaying like dancers in the currents. We saw the prickly orange moss on the rocks. We saw sea butterflies with pink wings flying through the water.

The land is dying, Kor thought to me, *and the sea is full of life*.

Heartache in that. But I felt giddy with wonder. Yellow legs, webbed feet dangled below the surface: a gull was resting on the waves. I darted up beneath it and butted its tail with my nose so that it disappeared with a satisfying squawk. Gleeful, I hurtled back toward Kor, angled my flippers, rolled and nipped his back.

Race! I challenged, and shot off, streaking through the green world—it was hard to remember that ocean had ever been an enemy to me. I could not laugh aloud for joy, but my body did—I flicked my wrists and twisted, spinning in the water. Kor sped after me, bathed in the bubbles of my passing, his nose straining somewhere at the level of my midriff. It was an even match, and he could not gain on me any more than that. But in a moment he veered away toward the surface to breathe.

Enough! You are larger and stronger, as always.

I popped up beside him, head out of the water, and looked at him in daylight that seemed stark and strange to me now, light filtered only by cloud and mist and air. I half expected to see his human face. His whiskered seal visage told me nothing.

Why do you say that? I asked.

Simple truth. He sounded peevish. Something ailed him.

It is not! You are as strong, and most often more deft. I am an oaf next to you.

Women of all sorts must prefer oafs, then.

So it irked him, the matter of the sea maiden. Had he somehow sensed how great my pleasure in her had been? *Is it my fault*, I demanded, *if you want only Tassida?*

At the mention of her name he ducked under the water

and began swimming again. If he had been thinking, he would have taken satisfaction in the fact that I was hard put to catch up with him.

Kor—

Let me be.

Kor, you fool, you are jealous of me! I cannot believe it.

That slowed his headlong pace. We swam side by side, flipper by flipper, slipping through the greendeep with scarcely a ripple.

Why should I not be? he asked at last. Vexation was gone, but the heaviness in him was worse. For my own part, I could scarcely grapple with the question. He, the king whose mercy had saved me, he, who had died and come back to me . . .

You know what I deem of you, I mindspoke him at last, *which you have forbidden me to say.*

That's your folly. Harsh.

I lost my patience. *And it is your folly that you are yet a virgin!*

Curse you, Dannoc, it is not my choice! It is—fated on me.

Then you are more than man, as I have told you many a time.

He lunged at me and bit me in earnest. His teeth tore through the skin of my shoulder. Blood stained the water and salt burned the cut, but such a cold anger was in me that I did not strike back at him. The wound was not great—I would let him writhe for the giving of it.

Ai, Dan . . . Already he was sorry.

I kept silence.

Forgive me. I am full of spleen. Anguish in his tone.

So the sea is salt with the tears of a seal king. Mahela's venom must have been in me already, that I should speak to him so cruelly. But the words stung him to truth.

Ai, why not? Think what life will be mine. No lover will ever come to me. Even Tassida prefers you.

The statement hurtled me out of anger into joy, and I hated the joy, for I knew he would feel it. And I hated him for feeling it, his gift to me, my joy which I would have hidden from him if I could. . . . Then came doubt, and joy faded. Kor would not lie, but jealousy might have nudged him astray.

Don't draw the long bow, Kor, I told him roughly.

No long bow. Mere truth. You do not believe me? But I sense what is in her, as plainly as I sense what is in you. And I have felt her heart turn to you many a time. His tone was bleak, hard. *Never more so than this time past.*

My vexation was lost in astonishment. *But she as much as told me she would never have me, up there amidst the yellow pines.*

And you have looked on me with envy because she speaks with me easily but flees when you come near. The more fool you, Dan. Mahela take your cock, do you not see? She is afraid of you because of—because of . . .

He could not say it, but suddenly I understood him completely. *Because of my cock,* I finished for him dryly, *which Mahela is to take.*

Well, you know what she did to Calimir, Dan.

Comforting thought, I retorted, and felt a smile in his mind—he knew I had forgiven him. When he mindspoke again, he seemed very calm, no spleen or self-pity left in him.

Something has been done to her, sometime, that has made her afraid. But she is not afraid of me.

Because she felt none of the passion of a lover toward him. Joy welled up in me again, then overflowed into sorrow—for him. *Ai, Kor, it is in me to wish you had never been made to know my feelings. Or hers.*

He nuzzled the side of my face wordlessly. We swam on awhile in silence, eating fish as we found them, rising for air from time to time. I no longer wanted to frolic. My head hurt from the quarrel or my own troubled thoughts of

Tass. There were no more birds' legs dangling overhead while we swam, and the vastness that faced me above the surface of the water when we rose to breathe bore down on me like a weight if I let myself take note of it. There was no land in sight anymore, not even a low dark rim, anywhere. Nothing in all directions as far as Kor and I could see but restless water that seemed gray under gray sky—and the sky loomed empty forever. Such endless sea and sky were like nothing I had ever envisioned, nothing I had ever dreamed. They awed me.

Toward evening the sun broke out from behind clouds, making a pattern of pale rays like the fluting of a scallop shell.

It is no use thinking of it, any of it, I told Kor, somber, daunted. *Of Tass, where we stand with her, what she fears, any of it.*

Yes. If we can return alive, then there may be occasion for such thoughts. He understood me, he felt what I felt. *We are very small.* Though no smaller than we had been as men.

I wish we could handbond. Flippers are of no use for that.

Instead I felt the fleeting touch of his nose at my jawbone. *Dan, I had forgotten how weary you must be. It was a long vigil for you. Sleep.*

How?

Lie on the breast of Mother Sea and sleep. She will not take care of you, but your own body will.

So I lay on my back, cradled in the swell, nose above the water, and I found that my flippers twitched and twitched of their own accord to keep me level and floating. It was an odd feeling, giving myself over to the rocking and the washing of the waves. Being so small, I had no choice but to trust the sea as I trusted Kor. Such a vast, cold mother. Yet oddly restful, once I became accustomed to her.

Kor lay by me.

How will we keep from drifting away from each other?
Nightmarish thought, that we might become separated amid
all the vastness.

Our bodies will tend to it.

Our flippers lightly touched, keeping contact. We slept.
Kor drowsed more than slept, I think, for I felt as if in a
dream his watchfulness, his gladness that he had me with
him in this immense and daunting place, his shame when
he thought of the cut on my shoulder—though he knew it
did not pain me, for he would have sensed any pain of
mine. Between waking and sleeping I felt his being, or
dreamed that I did—I told myself I dreamed it. And then I
swam to deeper, dreamless sleep.

Sense of danger awakened us both at the same time. The
sky had gone dark, a wild wind rising, cloudbank hiding
moon and stars to the westward. Waves tossed us high.
Lightning flared.

To the deep, Kor directed, and he dove, swimming
toward the storm to pass under it. We had no choice, for
that way lay Mahela's realm. I followed.

Beneath the vast water, beneath the commotion of the
waves all was calm. But we could not stay there always,
we had to breathe, and when we surfaced we fronted all
the fury of the storm. Rain fell so thickly it seemed to
crowd out the air. Thunder jarred us to our bones, yet we
scarcely heard it amid the roaring of wind and waves.
Whitecaps rose in jagged peaks that made me think crazily
of my mountains, spindrift flying like snow seen in lightning
glare—but there was snow, thunder and lightning and
snow! Ice pelted at my face. Thrashing water hurled me
into the air as if I were no more than a stick of driftwood.
Thrown high, I came down somewhere far from Kor, dove
as if demons were after me. Then worse panic struck me. I
knew I had lost him.

Kor!

No answer. I circled back up toward the stormy surface.

Kor!

Here . . .

My heart thundered in my chest. Something had hurt him, I could tell, but I could not find him to help him in the blackness, the watery chaos.

Kor!

No answer.

Kor! Sakeema, bond brother, pod brother, answer me!

Don't . . . call . . . me . . . Sakeema. . . .

Closer. Lightning flicker showed me a dark form—I sped toward it. I found him by his scent, then, and bore up his weight on my back. He was floundering, stunned, stirring but not much able to help himself. I took him down to the calmer waters below us.

I said it to rouse you. What happened?

Lightning happened. He sounded stronger.

A broad band of the sea before us turned bright yellow-green. I felt a tingle run through the water.

Go deep. Kor started to swim on his own. *It's worse near the surface.*

Even as we dove the sea flashed. We swam in liquid light, a thrill in it that bordered on pain but became ecstasy, a bone-deep excitement. Nevertheless, it frightened me, for if it became stronger it would kill.

We are swimming through lightning! I sensed in Kor the reckless surge I also felt.

Can you go faster?

We had better go faster, or we will have to face the surface again.

We sped onward until strength left us and our eyesight blackened for lack of air. Then we turned and shot up again, close together.

Powers be thanked.

We bobbed about, gulping air. The storm had somewhat

abated, or passed us by, leaving the waves running high but rounded like hills. Snow still fell, melting into the dark water. At a distance lightning flashed.

Mahela's welcome for us, Kor remarked.

It is as well we are in the open sea. If such a storm had caught us near shore, it would have dashed us against the cliffs.

Yes. The seals know when gales are coming. When they leave the rocks, my people know it too.

But the white one, then, the sea maiden—why would she not come with us?

A pause. Then, *The sylkies, the undersea folk,* Kor told me in a quiet tone, *they are fond of land, it seems. They do not care to venture far from the shore.*

And I remembered the tale I had recently heard, of the long-ago sea maid Sedna found battered on the strand after a storm. No comfort in that thought.

We rested again after the storm had passed. The sea, so furious only a little time before, cherished us in her bosom and lulled us. When we awoke, we went on in the direction Kor's inwit chose for us until we scented fish.

A great shoal of smelt, so huge that other seals, feeding on the far fringes, were but greenish shadows to us. The seals had indeed left the rocky shore to take refuge in the open sea. I went closer to look, Kor trailing behind me, but the white seal was not among them, nor had I truly expected her to be. Intent on the smelts, the seals did not greet us, and like them we turned our attention to the fish.

I darted and gorged happily. Many many fish. In a greedy ecstasy I shot towrad the center of the school, shouldering my way through sea that seemed made of fish, frightening them so that they scattered. Kor headed me off and nipped at me, annoyed because I was driving away his dinner.

Dan, you dolt—

His tone changed to one of terror and shock.

Graymaw!

I saw at the same time he did. A great shadow sliding toward us through the greendeep, a huge fish with its terrible jaws agape, rows upon rows of teeth like spearheads. Gray, indeed it was gray, and silent as brume, and the vast maw lay toward the underside of its head, so that it angled toward its prey. One seal, then another, gone before they knew it was there. The rest fled, scattering, making green wildfire of the water—even at the distance we smelled their panic. The graymaw lazily sheared the back flippers off one, swallowed it as a dark tide of blood stained the sea. Then with speed no seal could match it hurtled after the others, struck as I might strike a pollock, tearing a seal to bits, tossing the pieces about the water. Blood billowed with the currents. Kor and I saw no more, for our bodies had taken charge of us and we fled in utmost terror, even though our minds had seen that the brute was veering away from us. It might have been a halfday later when we finally slowed.

Blood of Sedna. Kor sounded shaken still. *It might have been us, Dan, if it weren't for your folly.*

Having nothing sensible to say, I tried to jest. *A pox on graymaws! I was no more than half done eating.*

Hungry, Dan?

A wry inquiry. *Not really,* I admitted. We journeyed on in silence. Gentle journey, Tassida had wished us. It seemed not likely.

Perhaps Mahela knows how long we were on the way, but I do not. Day flowed into day for me, and most often I did not know whether it was day or night above the surface, for it did not much matter to us. We slept in either, swam in either, ate fish of all sorts as we went. Nothing of the human love for routine was left in us. Even the washings of the tides meant little. The sea was so deep we could no longer dive to the bottom, to gauge our way

by what lay there, so we swam as if in a void. Once I
blundered into a sort of spiderweb place under a floating
bubblefish and was stung. My eyes swelled shut, and Kor
had to lead me for a while.

Our sense of time, then, was only "before Dan was
stung" or "after the graymaw struck." And presently I
noticed that the sea fogs were gone, the days fine and
sunny.

A shallow, Kor mindspoke me one such fine day as we
dove, the sunlight filtering down to us.

We could see the bottom again, ocean's landscape billowing up in hills to meet us, seaweed waving on those
prominences like—I blinked. It was more like tall meadow
grass, green and yellow, than any seaweed had right to be,
and through it ran—a deer?

A blue deer with antlers clear as ice.

But that cannot be! Kor, do you see it too, or am I mad?

Look, he answered me, a hush in him. *There are more
ahead.*

The deer ran before us, sharp hooves flashing, grass
swishing around its flanks, high-held antlers glinting in the
light, all beneath the green seawater. And there were more
proud heads raised, dark eyes regarding us. Spotted deer,
and dappled deer of soft hues, and a stately yellow deer
with antlers that spread as wide as its body was long, and
the great-maned elk towering over the others, and a tined
deer, no larger than a middling-small dog, that jumped
clear of the grass and swam a small distance, gazing at us.
And everywhere the does, the hinds, the long-legged fawns
as creamy as rich milk, and the blue stag prancing—I
trembled, feeling something catch in my throat worse than
any fishbone.

Ai, the eagles!

I heard it in Kor, too—the anguish, the wonder. Then I
saw. Birds were flying in the water. The ernes, the white
sea eagles such as I had never seen, but I knew them from

the lore, the campfire tales told since I was a boy. And the black eagles of the mountaintops—them I knew, for it had been but a few years since they had disappeared from over the eversnow. And great swans—the sight of them filled me with such joy and longing that I hurt. And many smaller birds of varied bright colors, the pink doves, yellow wren, bunting, redbird, jay of Sakeema with feathers each of a color more true than the last. And the white owl, long gone from the world of men . . . And, by my grandfather's braids, the peregrine! Soaring with an easy majesty that made me gasp and sputter on salt water. And many, many others, as many as the deer below.

Follow, Kor ordered.

Though they dipped and flocked and eddied and swirled like the sea currents, nevertheless the birds seemed all bound toward one place. We drifted after them, gawking. I saw an undersea hilltop all in a pattern of round trees bearing bright, downhanging fruit. I saw a gliding squirrel slip through the water while small fishes crossed its path. I saw a pair of ringtails questing with their soft paws and curious pointed snouts. Kor and I surfaced for air. The world above the waves, empty sunlit sky, seemed strange and distant now that we had seen what wonders lay below.

The green-lit land beneath us seemed to be rising from hilltop meadowland to steeps and dark crags. I glimpsed a bear rounding a brown spine of rock. Ahead of us, then around us, spires soared in crazy shapes, steeper than any alps on dry land, pitted with caves. On the lip of one of them lay a great tawny cat, stretching.

Ai, Kor, the wolves—

Don't, Dan. I cannot bear it.

The wolves, standing regally to watch us pass, their eyes green and yellow and dusky violet, their pelages red and raven black and buff, milk-white and gray and as orange as the trunk of a drymountain pine. They opened their mouths as if they were panting. Their tongues lolled, their white teeth glinted like stars. One seemed to bark, but we did not hear him. Except for the burble of water swirled by our passing, we heard nothing. All seemed as silent as death.

Black peaks loomed ahead.

Mountains of Doom.

Legendary heroes, Chal and Vallart, had sailed here once. This was Mahela's realm.

She has—she has taken the creatures, Dan, all the creatures of Sakeema, taken them away from the land.

Grim peril in that. We would meet with enmity here.

But why?

Already I knew the answer. Were they not beautiful? I could not hate Mahela too harshly for coveting such beauty. But she had bereft us.

The great glutton, my folk call her, Kor mindspoke me. *She feeds and feeds. Her maw is as wide as the sea.*

We rose for air, cast a glance at the sky, wider yet, wing of the nameless god who cherishes all but sometimes sleeps. . . . In the sunshine we could see on the water the wavering forms of dark peaks, like shadows. The Mountains of Doom reached to within an arrowshot of the surface.

We breathed well, looked at each other, able to tell nothing from the look—two seals, forsooth!—unwilling to mindspeak our fears. Flippers touched, perhaps by chance. Then we dove.

Have you any plan, Kor? It was my quest, but he had been here once before, however briefly.

Only to scout, for now.

Are there guards?

I do not remember any. And why would they stop us? This is ocean, after all, and it is not so strange a thing, two seals swimming in the ocean.

He was querulous, not as sure as he tried to sound. And

I should not have asked, for I knew as well as he that there was nothing for it, when we did not know the ground, but to go on as best we could.

People!

Why should it have surprised me to see humanfolk walking on that undersea land, when I had already seen deer and wolves and creatures of many sorts? But it did, perhaps because some of them were in bright garb such as I had never seen, raiment out of one of Tassida's tales of the old times long past, tunics and baldrics stitched in close broidery, and deep-hued cloaks that floated and flowed, and boots that reached to the thigh. And on some heads circlets of sunstuff, and on some shoulders clasps of sunstuff and jewels. These were goodly men, bearded, dark of wavy hair, of no tribe that I knew, and none of them old. And the women were goodly also, in long, full gowns of cloth that shone. And children! Many beautiful children, almost more than there were men, small children and taller ones, each supremely beautiful, their delicate, clear-skinned faces somber—for they did not act as children ought, but walked quietly in handsome clothing. The birds that flew above them were livelier.

And horses as shapely as Calimir, in all of the splendid colors, blue roan, blood bay, white sometimes spotted like a lily petal, many more colors than I can name. They were not ridden or even led, perhaps because of the steepness of the land, but roamed loose and unconstrained along with the people and creatures of varied sorts. I saw a singing heron walking on stiltlike legs, and gair fowl, and a white weasel running between the rocks, and a family of foxes, white, russet, blue. All were bound, like the birds, toward some single place, all toiling up the black crags.

'Ware, Kor warned, the thought as low as a whisper, as if he feared someone could hear us.

I looked ahead. The highest peak, stark and looming, nearly at a level with us as we swam. On it, aglow with a pearly gleam, a structure I could not understand. If it were a ruler's seat of honor, the largest I had ever seen. A sort of platform, crowded now with people and beasts of every sort, and more stood on the crags round about, the throng of them flowing down the steeps like a mantle. An eminence centered on the platform, something carved into shapes stranger than those of the Greenstones, more fanciful than driftwood, and shimmering even at the distance like a full moon, ten times full. There sat—someone, I could not look. Kor and I drifted off to one side. It was she, Mahela, I felt sure of it. The place was her hold. But what might be the purpose of the bare pines, oddly branched, that towered above her nearly to the ocean's surface? Hangings swayed down from them, banners decorated with many devices. On one I thought I saw the emblem of the Red Hart.

Dolphins, Kor mindspoke gladly. *We are not the only swimmers here.*

Indeed, we had seen no fish since we had come near the peaks. The dolphins came toward us from behind Mahela's platform, a brace of them, somewhat above us and one to either side. We watched the graceful rainbow shapes of them as they swam, not at all afraid of any creatures so surely blessed by Sakeema. Moreover, they came nowhere near us, or even seemed to notice us. But the sunlight slipping down through the green water seemed to lessen slightly, as if a shadow had floated over us, a cloud had happened into the way of the sun.

Of one accord Kor and I started toward the surface. It was time and past time for us to breathe.

And the shadow caught us with fine mesh. We were netted as neatly as Kor in his youth had netted doves, caught like great, flopping fish. The dolphins circled below us and back toward Mahela, closing the trap.

No! Peril made me feel human again. My panic fear of drowning took hold of me, and I could not think.

Tear it with your teeth! Kor thought to me.

I tried, and so did he. But the stuff was as fine as spiderweb, and far tougher, and the pounding of my heart seemed to take up all my strength. We were being towed along farther from the surface, toward the undersea goddess who ruled death. I did not care to think of death. . . . I needed air, my vision was blackening. Everything was going—black as the Mountains of Doom. . . .

Chapter Ten

I remember the spotted wildcat first. It was lying at Mahela's feet. I saw only her feet, dainty feet, shod in slippers that lustered like pearl, draped by the slittered hem of a gown all the colors of abalone—I looked no farther, for I felt weak, and I was lying on the platform.

Kor?

Here.

Somewhere close by me. A low, wary tone in his reply. I centered myself and looked up. Just waking as I was, it did not much surprise me to see him in human form, and I half hoped we were back where we belonged, wandering some woodland. . . . But he was naked, and he stood before Mahela.

A hand stirred before my eyes—it was my own. As human and as naked as he, I stumbled to my feet and stood by my comrade's side, swaying like seaweed for a moment until my head cleared. As if bound in one place my eyes looked only at Mahela's bosom, the white rise of her breasts covered by a ruffle of gown that floated in pink and lavender frills like those of a sea slug. Floated. . . . Green water all around me, and I knew it was chill, but I did not feel it. I was breathing it.

Kor . . . are we dead?

117

If we are, then it is the third time for me, and that is three too many.

"Cover yourself, fool," a cold voice said.

Like a snake through the water the words came, smoothly, eerily, nothing of earth about them, no waft of breath, no mortal warmth. Deity had spoken: I felt the sense of it crawl through my shoulder blades to my spine. With small dignity I layered my hands over my cock. It seemed all too meager a modesty. Kor, I saw, had done the same.

"Not you, Korridun." Something different in the watery voice. "You, I want to regard. All of you."

Startled, I raised my caught eyes and saw—how could it be Mahela who spoke? She was—feathered neck and head of her, a huge cormorant, a glutton-bird, glossy black crest and white throat, hard eye that did not blink, great, hard hooked beak with a dangling pouch like that of a pelican. Her snake-long bird's neck rose erect from just above her half-naked human breasts.

"Come, Korridun, my prize." Yes, it was she who spoke, for I saw the horrible clacking of her beak. "Be more easy."

She sat on a massive sort of cushioned bench with mighty arms and a tall back, the cushions edged with fringe and tassels, the whole of it carved in shapes of all the creatures of Sakeema. Stones glittered where their eyes should be, and their lifeless bodies gleamed with sunstuff and pearl. One of her pale hands draped over a carved eagle's beak. A real eagle—if it could be called real, breathing green salt water as it was—a snow-white eagle perched on the back of her seat above her shoulder. A great moon-gray horse stood beside her, and a mighty maned elk, and bearded men with no expression in their eyes, and by her right shoulder in a pot of carved wood stood—a tree, a small tree, no taller than I, its slender branches bent with the weight of round, blue fruits. That tree was a prisoner like the others, Mahela's most prized captive and shaper of our fate, all of us, though at the time I did not know it. My glance ran past it to the other trees, the strange bare trees, birds clinging to them, long banners hanging down. Devices on them of every tribe I knew, the Herders' six-horned sheep, the fanged stallion of the Fanged Horse Folk, the hook-jawed salmon of the Otter River Clan, snowpeak of the Cragsmen, and Kor's people's emblem and mine, and many more symbols I did not know. The ends of the banners were feathered into sea-weed shapes, and they twisted and floated in the currents—everything was aflutter in the shifting seawater. This place dizzied me, and the sight of Mahela made me feel faint. Her great seat lifted her well above the level of us who stood before her.

"Raise your hands," she ordered Kor.

He had not moved except to stiffen where he stood, but now he complied, saluting her, turning humiliation into an envoy's gesture of greeting. Mahela was not deceived. She lifted her long, bone-colored beak in a gesture of victory. "My people, is he not beautiful?" she cried.

There was a murmur of assent, a muted cheer. The wildcat raised its head and snarled. I had scarcely been conscious of the throng of folk and creatures at my back, but now I felt my nates tighten at the thought of them, and I wished I had hands to place there as well.

"How come you by all these people?" Kor spoke to Mahela with all comity, the courtesy so inborn in him, so that even though he stood naked, heart knew he was one monarch addressing another. But she laughed at him, beak gaping wide.

"How? Why, by taking of them! I am Mahela, I take what I will, tame what is wild, conquer what is strong. That which is beautiful pleases me. I have gathered much of it around me."

Anger gave me courage. "Will you take the mountains, then?" I demanded. "And the sun?" But she did not answer me. She looked only at Kor.

"But nothing so comely as you, young Korridun," she said in a way that might have been gentle were it not so gloating. "Welcome to Tincherel."

I blinked, and had I not felt so daunted I would have bitterly laughed. The haven, the name meant. Tincherel: a sheltered place, a refuge. Mahela so named her deathly realm? But of course she would not call it the Mountains of Doom, as we mortals did.

"Young scoundrel, you have made me wait long for you." Her cormorant eye on Korridun, hard, as a bird's eye is always. Yet, something more than hardness in her voice. . . .

He held his head high and steady, his gaze level. "My comrade and I," he said, "have come to make petition—"

"Since first I caught sight of you," she went on as if she had not heard him, "when you were but a sweet ten-year-old with a gaze wise beyond your years. Ah, the dark, staring eyes of you! I love to have children by me, but for you I made exception. You were not old enough, then, to provide me with what I craved from you. So I acceded to your mother's bargain, and waited until the sap had risen in you, and sent one of my minions to bring you to me after a few years had gone by."

"Devourer," Kor whispered. For the first time he looked shaken. As well he might.

Time, I decided, for me to try my wiles. I bowed, and as I had hoped, the movement brought her gaze to me. "Most gracious lady," I said in as even a voice as I could manage, "King Korridun and I have come here to petition you for the sake of my father, Tyonoc of the Red Hart, and for Korridun's mother, Kela of the Seal Kindred, and for their lifemates, Wyonet and Pavaton, if you hold them here."

"Petition?" She eyed me vaguely, too bored with me even to laugh at me. "But I hear petitions only if it suits my purpose. As it suited me to grant a further span of life to Kela's son here." Her glance darted fondly back to Kor.

"You wanted me to live, and took my mother even so?" he demanded.

"I gave her what she asked, took what she offered."

"You hag," Kor breathed.

Kor, be careful!

"And you, my scamp, you have proved far stronger than I ever would have believed possible of any mortal." She seemed not to have heard him, or had chosen not to hear.

"I will have to be stronger yet, it seems," said Kor between clenched teeth.

"Why? You do not like this visage?" Mahela laughed carelessly, and changed with a watery swirl. She was wholly a woman now, a hard-eyed woman with a white face and hair as glossy black as a cormorant's wings. Her features were fair enough, finer, indeed, than those of any earthly maiden I had ever seen, except perhaps for Tass. But her lineless face was daunting with vast age, as if it had been smoothed by the workings of water and time. It was like a face of white rock, or ice, rising oddly from the floating, tender-colored gown with its many flutings and ruffles, its fringes tipped with pearls. And though her beauty could not be faulted, and though I had never been one to refuse a woman's offer, I think had Mahela been looking at me I would have backed away from her.

She was looking at Kor, and he stood hard-jawed.

"Nearly ten years you have thwarted me," she said, letting her gaze caress his limbs, skim his shoulders. "But you are all the better grown for the delay."

"Look at Dan," said Kor in a grim voice. "He would like it better than I do."

Kor! I protested.

Not so?

No!

"Dannoc is good enough for most women." Mahela glanced at me briefly, and I felt all the peril of her regard. "A bold cock and a ready smile, that is all they want. But you, Korridun . . ."

She paused, and it seemed as if the sea paused with her. Even its washings grew still as she pondered.

"You are very fair, though you smile seldom. And very strong, but there is a gentleness about you. You are full of wisdom and dreaming. All runs deep in you, beneath a still surface. When you make love to me, your mind will touch me, and your soul, and your heart, not merely your body. You will be mine entirely."

Her words chilled me. Ai, but she knew him well! "Bold cock" though I was, I could scarcely have borne what was promised him. How was he to endure it? And it was my folly that had brought him before her.

"Mighty lady, you are mistaken." How could he speak so firmly, with such stark calm? "I can never belong to you."

"No, my prize, you are mistaken." Not even an edge to her voice, just a callous certainty. "I know you are not pledged. I know you are yet virginal. As for Tassida, I have sent my servants to dispose of her."

He staggered as if he would fall. I felt as stricken as he, but also somehow to blame. Forgoing modesty, I reached out to support him, my arms around his shoulders.

"Separate them!" Mahela commanded, jealous, angry.

Handbond, Dan. It may be—the last time. . . .

My right hand found his, gripped, warm. For a single, still moment, Mahela's rage meant nothing, the men swarming toward us were of no consequence. Then they tore us apart.

I flung off the bearded fellow who had hold of me, plunged to my knees by Mahela's feet.

"Take me, mighty lady! I can bear it better. You will destroy him!"

Not so, Dan. Stone hard and strong, Kor's resolve. No heartbreak in him any longer.

"Hence!" And even as she shrieked at me Mahela turned cormorant-headed again, hurling herself forward from her massive seat, her finery wildly swirling, neck snaking, her wicked, hooked bill shooting toward my midriff. Stupid with sorrow, I knelt without moving, meaning to argue further, even though I heard Kor shout. But a hand closed on my shoulder and pulled me back, out of danger.

I—knew—that grip—

Kor stood in the clutches of four stocky men, staring over at me with his mouth half-open, the look on his face wavering between hope and fear. They would take him away now. . . . I struggled, meaning to plead again with Mahela for his sake, but the two-handed grasp on my shoulders tightened.

"No, lad, no!" That voice in my ear, I knew it, but I did not dare to believe. . . . "Do not face her, do not strive against her! She is far stronger, she always wins."

"Get him hence," Mahela raged, "before I tear out his innards and eat them."

Go, Dan, but not too far. Wait for me.

I went, and saved my innards, because I was dazed. Underfoot, sharp black rocks in odd shapes, clinkers, as if from a cinder cone. If they cut my bare feet, I did not care. The touch on my shoulder guided me through the crowd. People stared at me, made way. Children gazed emptily. Women turned to watch after me with more shock than welcome, for I was still naked, and they were gloriously arrayed. I paid no heed. Down steep trails between dark crags . . . Only when we had reached a level, sheltered glen did I dare to stop, and turn, and face him.

Long braids the color of bleached prairie grass in winter, and at the braid tips the blue-gray peregrine feathers of a king. Tall and straight he stood, as tall as I, his lean face browned by weather, scarred by battle, and the scars of hunting and battle showed whitely on his bare, hard chest, his strong arms. The headband of a king lay on his brow, and the armbands did not slip from their place above the muscles of his arm. His lappet and leggings were of finest white doeskin, his boots of white bisonhide. His knife bore a handle of rare elk antler. A short cloak of sable fringed with white weasel tails was flung back proudly from his shoulders. Still, he did not seem entirely a king. A bleakness had made its dwelling in his face, as if something had defeated him.

Tyonoc, my father.

"Yes, I remember," he said with a taut calm, taut as a strung bow. "Dan, my son, I remember all that I did to you and to your comrade. Mahela is not kind. She wishes me to remember."

"But it was not you," I told him.

"In a sense not. But this mind schemed and remembers. These arms struck the blows, these eyes—saw you suffer. . . ."

Eyes the color of a deep sky over eversnow, but now clouded like the ocean skies . . . I went to him and took him into a tight embrace, and then I knew that he was indeed my father, wholly my father, heart and all, for his proud body acceded to the embrace, his arms came up across my back and held me, his head bowed. I felt the tautness go away from him as an arrow flies from the bow, leaving him shaking.

"You do not hate me," he whispered.

"Do you hate me?" I challenged, trying to rouse him to ire or a smile, either one. "Do you not remember how I slew you?"

"Yes. I am grateful to you."

That staggered me, and I dropped my arms from around his shoulders so that he would not feel it in me. He let me go, and we walked on in silence. Too long a silence. After I had regained a noggin's worth of calm, I looked at him and saw that the straight line of his mouth was tugged askew, his eyes nearly closed. He felt my startled stare and pulled half his face into a crooked smile.

"The only thing I like about this place," he said, "is that no one notices weeping. It is all salt water here, and tears do not show." A bitter edge in his voice, almost as if he wanted my pity. He, Tyonoc of the Red Hart!

I stopped where I was, at the foot of a black crag, and stared at him. "You never used to be ashamed to weep," I said slowly.

"I did it more seldom those days. Now it comes too often, it grows wearing."

I wanted to knock courage back into him. "Mahela take it!" I cursed instead.

"Truly, she will, if she wants it." His small jest seemed to cheer him, and he straightened. "Come, this way."

He led me to a place in a hollow of the alps where a skin tent was pitched amid trees, for all the world as if we were back in the Red Hart Demesne except that the trees were of a sort I had never seen and their limp leaves floated in the currents. Also, no cooking fire burned at the entry, and no meat hung nearby. Nor were there any others of my people about. Once within, my father found me a lappet and leggings of yellow buckskin and sat on the ground to watch as I put them on.

"Your hair," he said, "it is long enough to braid again."

I shrugged, feeling at it with the fingers of one hand. Braids were of small concern to me any longer. Somewhere on distant uplands my people thought of hunting food, stitching deerskins into clothing, but I had ridden away from them on a fanged mare, full of a mystic notion, my thoughts not their thoughts anymore, and I would never be entirely a Red Hart again. Standing in the realm of death and breathing green water, I could not have felt farther from them.

"I had thought that you would wear the peregrine feathers, now that I am gone," my father said.

"Tyee does."

"Tyee! Ai, he is a good and gentle man, but he does not have the strength of will to lead our people aright!"

"He does now. He fought Ytan, that—the night you last remember, and drove him away. You did not see?"

"No." His gaze slid down to the cinders by his feet. "I was busy . . . torturing Korridun, and through him, you."

I reached down and shook him by the shoulders until he raised his eyes to me. "Father, that is laid to Mahela's account," I told him fiercely. "And it is past, gone, done with. Think more of what is now."

"Now?" He blinked at me, gave me a wry smile. "But here there is no now. We have nothing but the past. We do not live here, we merely wash with the tides of Mahela's making. The water sustains us. We pay court to her. There is nothing else."

He, my father, who had once ridden a swift pony through the forests and shot the fleet deer, he who had a dozen times fought against Pajlat's raiders, they with their vicious long whips of bisonhide, and driven them off. He who had carried a roused hawk on his hand as he led the magic dancers around the autumn soulfires—that he should sit so limply, so—deadened . . .

"Where is my mother?" I asked him harshly. She

should have been here with him. Her ardor might have stung him to something like manhood again.

He stared at me, rose slowly to his feet, yet he was terribly calm. "Did I not tell you, when I was taunting you? I killed her to stop her from—from pestering me with love."

"Yes, I know! But where is she now?"

He gazed at me as if to say, What does it matter? What could it possibly change? "She was murdered, unavenged," he said. "She roams with the restless spirits, the green-shades."

"I thought all the dead were under Mahela's charge."

"They are, and she makes an indifferent keeper for most of them. We, here, her special pets"—his face quirked again into a half smile—"we are dead in a different way."

"A foul way, and wrong," I told him quietly. "Kor and I have come to take you back to the living land."

His smile faded into horror. "You—but I thought Mahela had summoned you."

"No. We came of our own accord."

"And on my account," he whispered. "Ai, Dan, every sight of you will break my heart." He covered his face with his hands, curled in on himself and sank to the ground.

"We will take you away from this place!" I declared to him. Moaning, his knees pressed tight to his chest, he seemed not to hear me. Tyonoc, my father, king of the Red Hart, he had no right to be so weak! Furious, I got hold of him and pulled him none too gently to his feet.

"Stop feeding on wretchedness!" I raged. "You have let her make a worm of you!"

"Let? But there is no letting about it." He looked back at me with a bleak sureness and no shame. "She will make a worm of you, too, if she so chooses."

"I do not plan to stay so long."

"A foolish plan, Dannoc. No one leaves this place."

I could not answer him. His dead and settled tone chilled me. After a moment he turned away from me, went and sat on the ground again. He had worn a hollow in that spot, from sitting.

"She has been annoyed with me, because she had to wait a few years for my body to take its place in her assemblage here, and because I nearly spoiled Korridun for her by sending him to her maimed. She collects kings, that one. Handsome folk of all sorts, and many pretty children, but her favorites are men, kings and warriors. They, and the comeliest creatures of Sakeema."

Silence. I sat down opposite him, in a rocky place. Over the endless years my rump would smooth and hollow it. . . . No. I would not think the thoughts of despair.

"She has been annoyed with Korridun, also, for she has wanted him badly, and he thwarted her again and again. He is a marvel, that one. She will make a worm of him, too. In a singular way."

The act of love, used as a weapon to enthrall him. How had she come to know him so well, to take such sure aim at the place where he might soonest break and bleed? Or was she wont to enslave by such means, Mahela?

"Does she often take lovers?" I asked.

"Such as Korridun? No." My father sat up with a small show of interest. "She dallies from time to time, as who would not? But this passion for Korridun, unabated over the years, this is ardor such as she shows for none other. And there are those who have been here far longer than I who recall nothing like it of her within their memories."

I rose and went outside.

It was nighttime, as far as I could tell, though the sea was filled always with a faint gleam. The crags loomed stark, for all the folk and creatures had long since gone their ways. I could see only a hard and jagged blackness against fluid green, and atop the dark mountains the form of Mahela's strange dwelling, flat of platform and rounded of base, with the bare trees jutting out of it like narrow spires. Moon-shaped holes had been pierced along the length of it, to let in light, though now light issued out of them instead, as bright as any firelight, but chill, blue-white, like the ghost lights sometimes seen dancing over snow during a hard winter, when folk are starving.

Kor? I mindspoke softly, wondering whether he could hear me from such a distance. I need not have doubted.

Dan! Joy in his tone. *Are you all right?*

Of course. I miss my supper.

My mind did, though my stomach did not. But I meant to amuse him, and I succeeded—I felt the warm mirth stir his mind. *Food, here, is a mark of honor,* he told me mischievously. *They are plying me with great lavishings of it.*

You bastard.

Yes. And I intend to eat quantities of it. Many many fish. Then, surfeited, I shall become very sleepy and unable to perform.

I nearly laughed out loud, but I quickly sobered. *I hope you sleep well. Kor . . . ?*

What?

If you must—to save yourself—will you be able?

Yes. He mindspoke me with a settled certainty, a stone-hard resolve, as when he had silently vowed to me that Mahela would not destroy him. *Fate be damned. Not it, nor any goddess will have the victory over me.*

I felt my spine straighten, my chin lift. *Sakeema be with you,* I told him.

With us both, Dan.

Yes. Fervor deserted me. *Kor . . . ?*

What?

All the many times I wished you would bed a woman—I never dreamed it could be to your peril.

Want to take my place? He was trying to tease.

No. Thought I would if she would let me. Kor, it's no laughing matter.

He knew it. *How is your father?* he asked after a moment.

Ill.

Chapter Eleven

Sleep was deep in that place Mahela called Tincherel, I found, but did no good. Such rest was not needful after a day spent with no purpose, not even the routine of foraging and eating. Sleep served only as a way to pass the dark hours. My father awoke from sleep feeling no abatement of his hopelessness—I could see as much by the clouded glance of his eyes. And I awoke to feel myself slipping into the same despair. We were not much accustomed to being trapped and helpless, we of the Red Hart. Though perhaps all of Mahela's captives greeted despair upon awakening.

We talked for a while of our people, our homeland, the wide sweep of the uplands, the names of the many mountains. I had hoped it would comfort him, having me there to talk to. But the pangs I myself felt told me otherwise. We were a torment to each other, Tyonoc and I. We fell silent.

Kor?

No answer. He was still asleep, I sensed. Startled by how surely I sensed it—startled, and somewhat afraid. Being dead was doing odd things to me. This place, uncanny. Mahela, unloved yet obeyed. If indeed we were dead, what punishment could she threaten that was worse,

what could she do to Kor if he failed to satisfy her? Yet I
sensed surely again, as I seemed to sense too many things
now, that he would be in more than mortal peril.

Thinking of Kor made me wonder whether he had seen
his mother, Kela. Perhaps I could find her. Glad of something to do, I got up and went out of the tent, walking at
random around the crag. Though I had said nothing to him
of coming with me, my father trailed along after me as if
he were afraid I might somehow come to woe—or perhaps
because there was nothing else for him to do. I hated to
think of that. For one like him, idleness was worse than
pitched battle.

He had neighbors closer than I had thought in the silence of the night. Everywhere, set amidst the black rocks
or spreading at their base, were small dwellings, though
none except his in the manner of my people. Some were
built of stone, some of split wood, even a few of brush-
wood in the manner of the Herders, though as of yet I saw
none built of spearpine poles like the lodges of Kor's
people. All were large enough to sleep in, nothing more.
People sat at the low doorways, most of them alone and
silent. There were few families in this place. Even children
sat alone and silent at the doorways of tiny shelters. They
did not gather into groups or play with one another. Nor did
their elders come together for talk, for there was nothing to
be spoken of. No wonder the night had been quiet even
amidst this multitude. As quiet as death.

The place was dismally clean. No cooking fires, no
ashes or smoke, for no one ate or drank—the water we
breathed sustained us. No need, then, for cuckpots. No
stench. No pits for the emptying of cuckpots, no midden
heaps, no offal. And no butchering, either, or skins being
tanned or stitched, or fish being dried. No berry baskets,
no planted fields, no making of spears or arrows. Nothing.
The people I saw stood or sat like so many clay dolls
around a shaman's hand.

I strode up to one of them, a robed and bearded man by a hut of stone. "Kela, daughter of Kebek," I asked him, "she who was Seal king when she lived—where might I find her?"

He stared back at me without answering, almost as if he had not heard, except that his eyes grew hard. Then he turned away. My father came up beside me.

"Bowels of Sakeema, lad! Can you not see that these folk are not in fit humor to chat?"

Dan?

I smiled. My father was speaking, telling me the ways of the place, asking me why I had not taken my query to him. I scarcely knew. Nor did I much care, nor was I listening to him. I heard only my brother, I spoke only with him.

Kor! Were you sleeping?

Yes. I just awoke. So I had been right. *Mahela is being patient with me, for the time.*

May her patience last forever.

Not likely. I heard fear, or despair. So he also was touched by it, even upon awakening. *Dan, you should see this place. It daunts me. The walls writhing with vines and flowers and many creatures, all made of sunstuff, like the throne—*

Throne? I had always wondered, what was a throne. An old song I knew made mention of Sakeema's having no throne.

Mahela's seat of honor. And all staring with those eyes of cut stone. And a smooth substance amid all the sunstuff, to give back the glitter. I have seen myself in it as if in a bowl of still water, but far more clearly. Have you ever seen yourself so truly, Dan? It is fearsome.

Enough to frighten anyone, I agreed.

Are you speaking for yourself? Laughter in his tone of mind for a moment, and I was glad. But then a chill, a horror, came into him again—I heard it. *But the bed, Dan.*

Silence. Sometime my father had stopped speaking and started walking, and I was following him somewhere down the crags. To see Kela, yes, he had said he would take me to her.

The bed. A huge clamshell, it nearly fills the chamber.

A clamshell?

Yes. Thick and fluted, chalk-white striped with Mahela's colors of choice. Pink. Watery purple. Pale blue. Polished stones like a scallop's eyes set around the ruffled edge of it. And within it a great sort of cushion, and mantles and coverings, all the dark pink color of raw flesh.

Lovely.

Yes. And all—perhaps it is the seawater. But there is no warmth to this bed. The coverings slither like snakes, and they are all chill and smooth as slime.

Slime of Mahela. I echoed Istas's favorite curse.

Dan? A small note of panic in his mind. He had not heard me.

Here!

He heard. *Are you walking farther away from me, is that it?*

Yes!

Where are you going? Fear in him, held under control.

Never mind! I'll talk with you later, Kor.

But there was no answer, and I was not sure whether he had heard me.

I walked on, following my father's strong back, shaking off the touch of Kor's fear. Though I did not wish to think of it, I knew that fear, I felt it too: if somehow the mindbond were taken away from us, we would each be truly helpless and utterly alone.

Ahead, on a knee of the crags, I saw a lodge like the lodges of the Seal Kindred, thatched with reeds as theirs were, but far too small. The pines that had been used to build it must have been but saplings. The roofpole rose no higher than my head. I saw no one near.

"Is that Kela's? She must be within."

My father turned his head slightly to answer me. "She? No, she does not stay within. She will be on the far side, watching the course of the sun."

Course of the sun? It was only a spot more shimmering green than the rest of the watery roof over us. Better not to think of the sun, in this place. I followed Tyonoc around the corner of the lodge, and there against the far wall sat a woman with eyes the dark color of waves under autumn clouds—yes, I saw Kor in her face, though she was thinner than he, too thin. Her sleek, dark hair was cut short in the manner of matrons of his people, and she wore a handsome woolen tunic such as they sometimes bartered from the Herders. It was shell brown, and her long skirt was seal brown, and in the fullness of it sat a baby. Other babies sat one to each side of her, the look of the Seal people about their features. I stared, for the little ones sat still and made no sound, no more than others of Mahela's treasures did.

"You." Kela rose to her feet, setting down the child she had been holding. It sat lumpishly where she had put it. A tiny girl with sparse, fair hair. Winewa's baby, and mine—no, I fiercely denied it to myself, Mahela had hold of my mind. It is hard to tell one such mite from another. I had to be mistaken.

Staring at the baby, I had not noticed the hardness of Kela's face until she spoke.

"You witless oaf, you dare to face me! Why in all the names of evil did you bring my son here?"

I must indeed have seemed witless, for I did not answer her. Tyonoc spoke up stiffly in my behalf. "Is your son such a slackard, Kela, that he must be led wherever he goes? Have you not thought that he might be here of his own will?"

She glared at him and raged at me. "Ten years he defied her and all her powers," she stormed, "and then you, cock-proud fool, dolt, ass, you needs must deliver him featly into her hands! Why not kill him more cleanly and have it done with? And you claim youself to be his friend! You—''

"The babies," I interrupted, not hearing much of what she was saying.

"What?"

"The babies."

"Ai, our mighty lady has taken to collecting the little ones now." Kela's voice, though softer, was no more gentle. "These three being of the Seal blood, she was given them to me to care for. Though truly, to care for them is only to dress them grandly and carry them where she may see them, each day. They do not eat, they seldom cry, and they will never grow, any more than the other children here."

"The curse of all honorable folk be on Mahela," I muttered. Then I forced my stare away from the baby, straightened, and faced Kela. "We have come, Kor and I, to take you away from the Mountains of Doom," I told her.

She looked as if she would spit at me. But much as Mahela had brought her low, Kela was still a ruler, with a ruler's dignity. She would not spit or dart her nails at me. "Fool!" she railed instead. "No one returns from here. Wanhope, wantwit fool!"

Accustomed though I was to being called as she had titled me, still it stung somewhat. "You yourself came here as a petitioner on your son's behalf," I reminded her sharply.

"And learned from the mistake," she retorted. Then her voice grew softer. "There is no parleying with Mahela."

"Nor much use, either," Tyonoc said to me aside, "standing here and talking with this one."

The babies had not moved from their places or made a sound. Except that they waved their random hands about in a winsome way, they might as well have been toys, babies of cloth or clay.

Tyonoc nudged at my elbow. "Come. It will soon be time."

I followed him numbly. Soon time for what?

Birds were flying overhead. Flying, not swimming, in the sea, flocking toward the throne place on the upmost crag. A ferret flashed past me, bound that way also. Bearded men in kingly raiment walked up the steep slopes, and women in splendid gowns with trailing overgowns that floated behind them. I began to understand.

"Time to go to Mahela? But, every day does she require it?"

"Every day," my father answered me over his shoulder, his voice flat. "It does not matter, for there is nothing else for us to do. All of us, her human captives, come before her to do her honor, and most of the creatures as well."

We toiled up the steeps with the rest. I kept silence, my eyes on the back cinders under my bare feet.

"But the blue deer of Sakeema," Tyonoc added, "she does not compel."

I looked up at him. There had been a spark, a hint of pride or defiance in him, half-hidden. But as quickly as I looked at him it was gone.

A crowd was forming around the rounded base of Mahela's platform. "Let us get up on one of the crags," I said to Tyonoc, "so we can see."

"It does not matter whether we see Mahela, so long as she sees us and knows we are here."

"A pox on Mahela. I want to see Kor!" I made my way up to a vantage point, pushing to the fore of the people there. Tyonoc hung back.

"There is peril in the fore," he called to me.

"A pox on that as well," I muttered, staying where I was. Curse him, he had never been one to cry danger. One

to reckon the risk, yes, but bold for the sake of his people,
their gain. Ai, what had this mighty one done to him?

The birds perched silently on the bare trees. All of us
had gathered, all stood quiet, waiting. For some time we
waited—that would be Mahela's way, to take pleasure in
how quietly, how tamely all her prisoners waited for her.
Finally a loud music sounded from horns like the bison
horns my people blow at the new moon, but made of a
stuff like my sword, I saw. The horns blared, retainers
bowed, and Mahela came.

With her, Kor.

My heart startled like a deer, seeing him so regal.
Mahela had arrayed him to suit her dreams. Tunic of pearl
gray, of some shimmering cloth, and over that a baldric of
deep sea-storm-purple, and over it a cape of cormorant,
the glossy green-black feathers sheening down his shoulders and back. Cap of purple velvet and cormorant feathers
on his head, soft boots up to his thighs—laden with finery
as he was, he should have looked foppish, but he bore it so
as to seem truly a king. No, more than a king, more even
than a goddess's consort.

Dan?

He did not feel godlike.

Here, Kor.

His glance searched the throng until he found me. The
lines of his face were taut, his gaze troubled, he did not
smile.

The horns blasted again. Mahela was taking her throne.
All her subjects bowed until she had settled herself, all
except Kor and, I suppose, me, for I was not thinking and
in no mood for caution. Even the deer and horses bowed,
curving their necks as did the swans, and the birds on their
perches ducked their heads and spread their wings with a
downward sweep.

Kor stood at Mahela's feet. No wildcat lay there, for he
was her pet of choice that day, and for a moment I thought

that she would make him get down on all fours and crouch
there like a dog. Instead she sat tall and still in her fair
womanly form, her pale hands folded in her lap. Her gown
was dark, and a mantle of moonlike hue flowed over her
shoulders but parted above her breasts so that the white
flesh of them peeped out between mantle and gown, much
like a single eye. At least so I perceived her.

"Dannoc."

Mahela! She had spoken my name! Even at the distance
I saw Kor's eyes widen in consternation.

"Dannoc, son of Tyonoc, come here before me."

Kor, what does she want?

I don't know!

I clambered down from my vantage on the crags, made
my way to the platform, strode up to her with dignity, I
hoped, befitting the son of a Red Hart king, and stood
facing her, knowing I was expected to bow—the murmur
of the crowd told me that. The look on Mahela's face told
me nothing. For some time she kept silence, and, defiant, I
kept my head up and my gaze steady. I was careful not to
look at Kor.

"I have heard," she said at last, "that you think of
leaving my haven."

I sensed that I was not expected to make reply, but I did
so nevertheless. "You have spies, my lady, who hear
thoughts?"

Careful, Dan!

"I have spies who hear what is spoken." Mahela did
not seem to be annoyed, but neither was she amused.
"You, Korridun. You have such thoughts as well?"

Of him she expected an answer, and he gave it in a low
voice. "I would be a fool if I did not, my lady."

At him, she smiled. "You are a fool if you do," she
chided him, not unkindly. "As Dannoc has been told more
than once, no one leaves Tincherel. And I will show you
both why."

Her gaze, on me again, grew hard. She stared me up and down in a way I did not like, as if I were a thing to be used and she were deciding on the usage. I grew afraid, or more afraid, but tried not to show it. Then I grew angry, but, Sakeema be praised, enough wisdom was in me that I tried not to show my anger either.

"You are fair," Mahela said softly, still staring, "in that yellow breechclout, and I would have enjoyed taming you. So fair in your blundering way that I sent my winged servants to take you once or twice. But that is not sufficient reason why I should spare you now. Is there reason? Speak."

I daresay I showed fear, then, for of course I could not think of what to say to her. There had never been cause, before, for me to defend my own being, my worthiness, in speech! But Kor spoke. "Dannoc is a peerless storyteller, my lady."

"Indeed." Her cold gaze on me never wavered, but for some time she did not speak, and I stood motionless as she considered, afraid to so much as shift my glance or stir a finger least it anger her. She had me as she wanted me, Mahela.

"Very well," she said finally, in flat tones. "It would be a shame to cast away a toy so fresh and new. I shall have to dispose of something else. Someone. All the creatures are precious to me."

Her gaze moved away from me at last, searching the crowd—I saw those in the fore shrink back. And I took a deep breath—or draft—feeling dazed and weak, and glad she was not looking at me to see it. Nor would I meet Kor's eyes. Something shameful was about to happen.

She pointed. "You. I cannot remember your name. That is reason enough."

A man somewhat plainer of dress than the other men, plain of face, plainly terrified. He made as if to run, but those who stood on either side of him grasped him by the arms, looking as shaken as I felt—perhaps they had feared that they themselves might be chosen, and they were only too glad to deliver up this other. They dragged him forward.

"No, my lady!" he pleaded. "You remember me now! I am—"

"A very minor noble," she interrupted frostily. "Go. Show our new comrades what happens when someone tries to return to the mortal world, where folk breathe air."

Instead he fell at her feet, sobbing horribly. Mahela changed—she was the cormorant woman, darting her heavy beak at him, hurling him back. He shrieked.

"Go!"

He would have obeyed, I think, but he had lost his strength. Mahela raised her right hand, fluttered the fingers.

"My dolphins, help him."

The two of them came out from somewhere behind her dwelling and nosed the man upward.

Upward through the green seawater, toward where a bright shimmer showed the distant presence of the sun. Upward, toward that shifting surface I remembered so well from my seal days. Up to where the air was . . . The dolphins tossed him the last small distance, themselves staying below the surface. I saw the splash, he had broken through—

With a sound like great hands clapping, the man fell to bits.

He spread like a cloud. Tiny pieces of him floated in the water, drifting downward. Clamoring in excitement, the birds flew from their perch, fighting and jostling each other for the fragments of flesh. Some larger shreds fell slowly toward the platform. Mahela darted out her long neck and gulped them down.

My face, I hope, did not move. But my mind cried to Kor. *She is horrible, beyond all measure horrible!*

He did not answer. I forced myself to find him with my eyes. His face, pale under the tan skin, looked as drawn as if he had been put to torture. His gaze, stark.

Kor! What has she been doing to you?

Nothing but knowing me for what I am.

I did not understand him. I touched him with my thought, urging him to go on. He seemed very weary.

She knows—she knows that I am merciful. She knows—I feel. When I am with her, I cannot help but feel the passions in her. She is cruel, but—there is love in her. Bent awry. Love for beauty, longing for—something that can never leave her. . . . She hopes—I can love her.

Kor, no!

She had taken on her womanly form again, smiling, a not unpleasant smile, and she reached out to stroke Kor's hair.

Kor, beware! She is the great glutton. It is in her to destroy you utterly, to swallow you up.

He did not answer. Mahela was speaking to us.

"You have seen, Korridun and Dannoc?" She sounded almost motherly, almost gentle. "Go away, and you are nothing but orts in the stomachs of birds. Stay, and you live forever. We are immortal here."

It was scarcely to be considered living, to my way of thinking. But I said nothing, for I had seen a doom in Kor's eyes, and I was afraid.

Chapter Twelve

Mahela sent a retainer, one of the dark-bearded nobles in all his splendid array, to summon me before the day was old. The man looked at me with blank eyes as he delivered his message, that I was wanted to amuse the goddess with the storyteller's art. Then he led me off rapidly, taking no pause for my limping footsteps as my unshod feet were cut against the vicious stones of that place.

The entry to Mahela's dwelling was from above, between the bare trees where the banners hung. The servant in splendid array led me up a wooden walkway, past the throne and the tree with blue fruit standing captive in its pot, then down a broad and sturdy ladder. The downward entry reminded me of the pit prison where I had first met Kor. A dark prison, that. This place, not quite as dark but a prison nevertheless. . . . In an oddly shaped chamber full of greenish, rippling shadowlight, Mahela awaited me. It was not, praise be, the bedchamber Kor had described, but a room that was mostly open space. The walls sloped inward toward the floor—I noticed that only dimly at the time, for the mighty froth of sunstuff on them dazzled me, and the bench of sunstuff and blood-red velvet, softer than the velvet of a hart's antlers in springtime, on which Mahela sat, and the swirl of servants around her. She dismissed them with a flick of her hand as I approached, and they backed away from her, bowing, as I came before her.

I stood facing her, awkward, knowing I should bow, not yet able to manage it but ducking my head in a salute of sorts. She motioned at me impatiently.

"Proceed," she commanded.

I stood dumbstruck. Never had I felt less inspired. "What tale would you like to hear, my lady?" I asked after too long a pause.

"How am I to know?" Her voice darted as sharp as her beak had she been in bird form, and she stirred like a hawk rousing. "You are the storyteller. Tell a tale that will please me." Or bear my wrath, her voice said.

"But my lady, how am I to choose?" I swallowed and tried to explain. "I have never done so before. When I tell tales to my people, we sit around the fire at night, camp-fire or cooking fire, and the old true stories seem to spring out of the flames."

"I see," she said slowly, and if her wrath was averted it was because I had given her a new thought, a diversion. "Sit, then."

There was nowhere for me to sit except on the floor, which was covered with a thick red cloth furred like moss, and I did so. Mahela closed her eyes, and the room went dark as night. In another breathspan a fire sprang up out of the floor at my feet, a smokeless, shadowy, yellow-green fire that gave no warmth, though the flames leaped and flickered as if they fed on fatwood—and no logs lay there. My skin prickled at the eeriness of it. Still, the carved sunstuff on the walls cast off dim, shifting shards of light, almost like aspen leaves stirring beneath starlight, and the washing of water sounded nearly like wind through trees. . . . Longing filled me, and the thought of another such night by firelight, Tassida yet a boy, face very fair in the firelight, singing.

"Shall I tell you the tale of Chal and Vallart?" I asked Mahela.

"How droll." She seemed pleased, or amused. "Yes, do."

So I began. "Chal and Vallart were heroes of the time before Sakeema, as long before Sakeema as his time is before ours, a time of wonders, when people and peoples were as many as the stars of the sky, and lived in great dwellings of hewed stone and wore clothing woven of bright fibers. They had many powers, these folk. They wrought great, sharp knives out of a stuff strange to us, and fought with them." (These were swords, such as the ones Kor and Tassida and I bore. But I said nothing more of swords.) "They wrought headbands called crowns out of another strange stuff that shone like the sun, and they strove for the crowns. In peacetime they made themselves walls of air to grow strange fruits within, even in the wintertime, and they made great harps to play music such as folk have never heard since. They built boats great enough to carry the folk of a village in, and they called them ships, and sailed out on the ocean in them, beyond the ocean's edge, and returned."

"I thought your folk would have forgotten about those times by now," Mahela said.

"Most of us have," I admitted. I, for one, had never heard of those times, or of Chal and Vallart, until Tassida had told us of them.

I related the tale.

"Chal was a prince, a ruler greater than a king, for the princes of that time ruled ten times more folk than the kings of this day. Vallart was his comrade and a king in his own right. They had many adventures together, they fought in many battles side by side, and they were steadfast companions. Then in a dream Chal conceived a quest to the dark mountains that lay beyond the sea, the Mountains of Doom. He could not expect Vallart to follow him there. For that journey, it was said, each mortal had to take alone. But Vallart vowed that he would follow his prince even to the shore of death's realm. That he would follow him if he walked into the sea.

"They journeyed to the strand. And there they found a ship awaiting them, a vessel that rode low in the water, though nothing filled it but ghostly voices. It was the ship that carried the dead to the uttermost west.

"Vallart's courage forsook him, and he could not go onward. Chal gave him the embrace of a king and left him, boarded the ship of doom. Bereft, Vallart stood on the shore of his homeland and watched as his prince set sail, the gray ship set sail, gone in the fog as if it had never been, and only the echo of his comrade's farewell remained to him. Then Vallart followed his prince—and walked into the sea.

"He traveled himself the spirit ways to the Mountains of Doom, the place where the king of death made her dwelling. And coming there not long after Chal had, he found that his prince had been taken captive by that ruler and was being put to torture in the prison pit of that place. Vallart in his spirit form slipped through the prison walls and went to him. And embracing the friend who had come to him against all expectation, Chal felt a power fill him that was greater than the power of death herself. It was the power of the oldest deity, the power of love. And by that mighty power he rose up and burst his bonds, and by that power and the sorcery he had learned at the hands of his tormentor, he sank the Moutains of Doom beneath the sea."

I grew aware, by a sense I cannot explain, a sort of presence in my mind, that Kor had drawn near. He was standing just outside the door, listening, as no servant of that place would have dared to stand and listen. I felt as sure of his whereness as if I had turned to see him, and my own sureness frightened me so that I paused in the telling of the tale.

Kor! Stop that!

Stop what?

Never mind. Nothing. Mindspeak had steadied me. I went on.

"Chal and Vallart sailed back to their homeland, back to the land of the living. Many more times they thwarted death, the two of them, and Vallart is said to have brought Chal back from death at least one time more. So many times they refused to die, folk say that in some way they are living yet, and yet together."

Mahela startled me by laughing merrily. "What nonsense!" she cried. "I have no need of ships to bring the dead to me. And the peaks you call the Mountains of Doom have always stood beneath the sea."

"Is there no truth to the tale, then?" I asked her levelly.

"You mortals, how you twist truth to suit your fancies!" Her amusement had not abated. "But yes, some truth. They came here, in a ship of their own. They contested with me. But they never sailed away. You are sitting in the hold of their vessel."

With a shock and a feeling as if the rats of despair gnawed at my gut, I realized what Mahela's dwelling was. The tall, bare trees, masts for sails. The platform where her throne stood, a deck. I, who had never seen these things, only heard Tassida tell of them, I had not guessed before.

"They are here, then?" I asked softly, trying to hold off the despair.

With a careless laugh Mahela said, "Not here. Utterly dead, but not here."

And at once the rats of despair ran away from me as if they had never been, for I knew the truth. If she had been at all able to constrain Chal and Vallart, she would have kept them by her, pets for the gloating over. They had bested her.

"They lived," I said.

Careful, Dan! Do not anger her!

It was Kor, warning me like inwit. But I spoke on, not heeding him, for a thought had hold of me. "In a sense they yet live. I have seen them."

I felt Kor's questioning surprise. And as for Mahela, all laughter left her. "Where?" she demanded.

"On black water. Amid the shadows of stars."

"You fool," she stormed at me, shooting to her feet, and in her fury I sensed a certainty: it was Chal and Vallart whom Kor and I had seen at the pool of vision. Perhaps even their swords that had come to us there. And Kor sensed it as certainly as I did, for I could feel it in him, the sureness, the wonder.

Worth her wrath, I mindspoke him rapidly, *to find out.*

I hope. Dan, tell her no more—we must not betray them!

"They are dead!" Mahela shrieked.

"Truly they must be, my lady, if you say so." Hugging my knowledge to my heart, I no longer cared to contest her. "Who should know better than you? I am indeed a fool, as I have many times been told. I am a dreamer, a teller of tales. It is seldom enough that I know the ways of truth."

Glowering, she slowly seated herself. "Tell another tale," she snapped.

I looked into leaping green flames and spoke. "You have heard the tale of the boyhood of Sakeema?"

"No," she said curtly, "I have not."

So I told it.

"He was reared by the deer, in the mountains, my folk say. And the Herders say by red wolves, on the arid plains. No matter, for the tale is much the same. There came a time, when he was perhaps eight or ten and nearly of an age to take a name, when he had to leave the creatures and learn the ways of men. So he kissed his foster parents on the smooth fur of their cheeks and made his way down the mountains to the place where the trade trail ran.

"Traders, banded together against robbers and Cragsmen, were making their way back from the coast with bladders of fish oil and bags of the dried wickfish that sputter and blaze when a flame sets whem alight. And one night of the new moon, as they camped by the trail, crouched around their fires, a naked boy came out of the forest and set their pack ponies and riding ponies loose by merely touching the hobbles and tethers. For in the experience of Sakeema, creatures had ever been free, not bound.

"The traders, seeing what was happening just as it was too late to prevent it, were filled with fury. The more sensible men and women among them set themselves to catching the straying ponies, but the more muddleheaded seized the boy and commenced to beat him. This also was a new experience to Sakeema. He had known pain enough, learning to leap from crag to crag like the deer without falling, but he had never felt pain inflicted in anger. After musing upon it for a few moments, he decided it was of no worth, and he turned aside the sticks and fists with his small, brown hands.

"After that, though they called him halfwit, not yet ready to admit that he was divine, the traders were afraid of him and gave him blankets and food. Nor was there any difficulty about the ponies, for like all creatures they wished to be with Sakeema, and gathered around him in the night. Within a few days the traders had learned that the ponies would follow him wherever he went, unled. Therefore they were kind to him so that he would lead the ponies rightly. For his own part, seeing that the people he was with wore clothing, Sakeema accepted a gift of a breeching and submitted to having it girded upon him.

"After the traders had returned to the tribe, the half-wild boy they brought with them was given over to the keeping of the king and his household, as was honorable.

For the king, having the most, must therefore give the most, and ought ever to be grateful for occasion to be generous. In the king's tent, Sakeema was made much of, shielded and petted by men and women alike, for he was deemed a wantwit, one to be pitied. Though within a season he learned sensible speech, still no one ever struck him or shouted at him when he did untoward things, for he seemed an innocent.

"But the king's children, when they quarreled or disobeyed, were scolded and sometimes beaten. Among them was a boy of ten summers, perhaps Sakeema's age, and Sakeema thought of him as a brother. And the king was often severe with this boy, for he was a bold lad and likely would someday be king in his turn.

"One day, when the king's son had failed to heed the signals of the hunt and had rushed too soon toward the deer, losing his people much meat by his impatience, the king, his father, took him away into the forest to be lashed, and Sakeema followed. 'How is it,' Sakeema asked the king, 'that you punish my brother, but you never punish me?'

"The king was astonished. 'You complain,' he exclaimed, 'because I treat you kindly? Open up your eyes and be glad you are not punished. Few are so fortunate.' Though the king himself hardly knew why it was that he could not be angry at Sakeema.

" 'It causes me no joy,' Sakeema said, 'to hear my brother's cries.'

" 'Then go where you need not hear,' said the king, and still he could not be angry at Sakeema.

"And still Sakeema did not go away. 'I tell you,' he said to the king, 'far rather would I take those blows upon my own body, than know that they are struck upon my brother.' "

Telling the tale, gazing into the green flames, I seemed to see there the young Sakeema's face, and it was Kor's.

He had once said to me something very much like Sakeema's words. And even as I remembered, I felt the startled leap of his mind.

Dan—where did you get this story? I have never heard it before.

In the flames, I told him. Call it vision, for I felt sure it was true. Even Mahela sat still as the hills of my homeland for the telling.

"The king looked from Sakeema to his son, and from his son to Sakeema, and took many breaths, for he had wisdom enough to sense a fateful moment. But he had not quite sufficient wisdom to accede to the mercy of a god.

" 'My son has done wrong,' the king said finally, 'and he must bear the blows that follow. Such is the rule of my tribe.' Then, as the lash fell, Sakeema went away.

"He went wholly away from the king, the king's tent, and the tribe. For he knew then that he was one whose understanding lay outside the rules of that tribe, and he would not stay there. He wandered, and sojourned with many tribes, learning their speech and their customs, but he never took a name. And he found few folk who understood the freedom of a running deer or the meaning of mercy, even for a moment. Many he found whose thoughts tended only toward war.

"When he grew to be a man, stopping spearflight with the power of his hands, he ended war—for a time. But that is another tale. Folk gave him the name he had never taken for himself, Sakeema, he-whom-all-we-seek, and he taught the tribes a single speech, uniting them for a time, until the kings turned against him—but that is another tale.

"He died taking upon himself the punishment that rightly belonged to the woman who called herself his mother. And because justice unsoftened by mercy begets all that is merciless: one of the kings who watched as he was killed was the one whom he had called brother. Whose back he had wished to save from the lash."

I ended the tale there, sat and stared into the fire Mahela had made me. Behind me I felt Kor's silent protest—why had I not brought Sakeema back from the dead? Beside me, after a silent moment, Mahela stirred, and the green flames leaped lower, then went out. The room filled up with its hard, yellow-green light again. I stood and faced the goddess.

"I am glad you have not said that Sakeema sleeps and shall come again," she told me. "He is dead."

I ducked my head to hide the gleam that needs must come into my eyes, though I stopped my smile before it reached my lips. The matter of Chal and Vallart still warmed my memory, and I would not contest her in this, at this time.

She dismissed me with a gesture that seemed more thoughtful than callous. "Go, storyteller. I will summon you again."

My lowered head, I decided, would serve for bow. Bending it a bit farther, but not backing away in the manner of her lordly retainers, I turned and went. Kor joined me just beyond the doorway.

Blood of Sakeema, Dannoc, what a tale! he mindspoke me with a sort of awe.

Blood of Sakeema, indeed, had colored the tale at the end. I had left out some of what I had seen in the flames. *Did you know they cut off his hands to curb his power? Though he had no thought of resisting them.*

Name of the god, Dan, cease. He sounded shaken. *Surely you do not think Sakeema is truly dead?*

Perhaps, if I was walking beside him. I stopped myself from mindspeaking the thought, stopped my mind from pursuing it in his presence, and Kor must have felt, too, that he had ventured near perilous ground, for he asked nothing further.

"Come," he whispered, leading me toward the farther

end of the hold, "you must see this grotesque bedchamber, if only for a moment."

Like the rest of the ship's innards, the place was lit with a green and wavering sheen that seemed to come from everywhere and nowhere. Kor guarded the door as I went in. But I scarcely looked around me, scarcely noticed the great clamshell bed, for a figure approached me out of a doorway in the opposite wall, and I dodged and crouched, heart pounding, ready to do battle. One hand snatched at my belt for the sword I no longer wore. It was Ytan.

Ytan, in the realm of the dead? Why had my father not said so? And why would he hate me here, with the devourer gone out of him? Yet he crouched and glared at me—

Kor entered the door and walked up beside him, placed a hand on his—my—shoulder.

Plainly, there he stood beside Ytan, his face somehow disturbing, subtly skewed. Yet just as plainly he stood by my side, the warm weight of his hand resting on my shoulder, and I shall love him forever because he did not smile.

I straightened slowly, my mind aghast. Never have I felt confounded in quite the same way. "Ytan," I whispered, and then Kor understood.

"It is your image," he said. "In the shadowing panel."

"I know that now." A tall, strong-looking fellow, straight of nose and jaw and brow. Yellow buckskins, long yellow hair floating about my head—Ytan would have braided his, I should have known that. Still, who looks for braids when the gaze is caught on the face? "Bones of my mother," I muttered, "why do I bother to call myself Dannoc? Why not Ytan. How did I come to look so much like him!"

"More like him in this moonstuff wall than in fact. It shadows you oddly. Leftward."

"You also," I told him, feeling a warm tide of gratitude toward him.

Uneasy in Mahela's dwelling, I left it soon afterward and made my way back to my father's tent. Seeing the dark cast of my face, he greeted me in silence. I sat by his doorflap and tried to tame my thoughts, but they circled like penned ponies, and I could make no sense of them. Nor could I find heart to speak to him of Ytan.

"Did Mahela take your storytelling well?" asked my father at last.

Wearily I said, "I am here, am I not?" He gave me a hard stare, and I smiled to see even so much spirit in him and offered him better answer. "She says she will summon me again."

"The next time you go to her, then, if you please her, petition her for leather to make yourself leggings and boots."

I scowled, for I did not consider that I was going to be in Mahela's realm so long as to need leggings and boots, and plainly Tyonoc deemed differently. But I would not quarrel with him.

"Is Sakeema in this place?" I asked him abruptly.

He shrugged. "How am I to know?"

I checked the fury that threatened to rise in me. How could he speak of Sakeema so indifferently, as if it did not matter? "If Sakeema were here, would he not call himself by the name of Sakeema?" I asked as evenly as I could manage.

"Ah, but there are many here who call themselves by that name. Perhaps half a hundred." Tyonoc smiled in genuine amusement, and I felt very much the fool, but I could no longer feel angry with him. He leaned back against the rise of stone that shadowed his tent and regarded me.

"Dannoc, my son the storyteller, now let me tell you a tale," he said, and I looked at him curiously.

"Not so very long a tale," he added. "Call it the tale of Nicu." And I narrowed my eyes at him, leaning forward to hear, for Nicu had been the foolish name my mother had called me, "little fawn," before I took a name of my own.

"You had not yet lived through even four seasons," my father said with something soft and wry in his voice, "but you were then much as you ever were and yet are: bold, strong, and always rushing headlong into trouble. We joked that your many falls must have thickened your skull. You were standing and trying to walk before you had been with us much more than half a year, and before you well knew how to walk you were trying to run.

"Your mother and I had gone our own way apart from the tribe for a while, for that was a time when everything seemed to go against me, my luck was bad. Tyee and Ytan were sick with the swelling fever. Your mother tended them and you. And when I went out to try to bring in meat for the five of us, my arrow flew awry and I shot a nursing deer."

It was abomination to shoot a hind with a fawn. I winced in sympathy for my father.

"She was not dead, the hind. She staggered away with the arrow in her shoulder, and I could only hope she would yet be well. Then, to try to make things less wrong, I went and found the deer calf—her bleat had drawn it out of the thicket, it stood dazed—a little, long-legged, dappled thing. I took it up in my arms and bore it back to the tent for Wyonet to nurse along with the rest of you.

"And you, less than a year of age, you came stumbling to meet me, with a gait like a duck's, trying to run and falling on your chin and getting up again, and you seized at the fawn as if to embrace it like a brother. I tried to prevent you, but then I saw that the little creature was not afraid of you. Then and thereafter it curled up against you for warmth and comfort, and you treated it more kindly than I would have thought likely of any child so small. And it slept with you at night in your bed.

"Wyonet fed it with her own milk, as she did you, and sometimes the two of you nursed side by side, one at each of her fair white breasts." Tyonoc's voice faltered, and I could see that it cost him something, the telling of the tale, but he kept on. "And sometimes you and your fawn brother gamboled and played together, you in your lumpish baby way and it on its long, slim legs. It stayed with us a cycle of the moon, and then its mother came and took it back.

"Right into the tent at night she came, the hind, stepping over our sleeping bodies, and nuzzled her fawn, and it got up and followed her out. And I lay still and thought nothing of it except that you would be mightily dismayed when you woke in the morning and found it gone. Then I slept again, hoping I had made things right for the deer and my luck would change. But when morning came, you were not in your bed or anywhere to be found.

"I tracked you. Somehow you had followed the deer on those short baby legs of yours, trotting along through the night. But then I lost the trail, and though I searched through the day and far into the night I could not find you.

"Every day I searched, every day for another turning of the moon, and did little else, and Wyonet and I were in despair, and our two remaining sons were sick and hungry, for we scarcely took time even to find food for them. But in a twilight when the moon was rising—and the moon had come round the cycle yet again—I found you standing with the deer herd in a meadow, standing and suckling at the teats of a fair hind, with one arm across the back of the fawn, your foster brother. And I called you by name, and you ran toward me in great excitement, then stood still and started to weep as the deer fled away from you.

"But when I picked you up you embraced me. And I carried you homeward to your mother and brothers, and the next day Wyonet and I broke camp and rode to rejoin our people. For many years after that, all went well for me, and our people made me their king. And if there has always been a softness in your heart toward the deer, I have never thought ill of it.''

Leaning against rock, Tyonoc eyed me in a settled way. The tale was done.

"Why did you never tell me this before?" I demanded.

"Dreamer that you were, and are, there was nonsense in your head enough. We did not wish to add to it.''

I retorted, "Then why do you tell me now?'

"What can it possibly matter now? Call yourself Sakeema, if you wish, like so many of the others here. You have as much reason as they.''

"Give me credit for better sense, Father,'' I told him coldly. "I am not Sakeema.''

But if Sakeema was who I deemed him to be, he was a captive in Tincherel, and he faced Mahela's devouring power.

Chapter Thirteen

Sometime before dark the devourers came back, bellying in with a rush through the greendeep, swooping up with rippling wings each fell servant to a tall crag of its own, and settling, upright, with their snakelike tails coiled around the spires on which they perched and their wings tightly furled around their bodies, so that they looked like looming gray stumps in the undersea twilight, each one with a staring eye that glinted whitely. Eight of them. Three were missing.

I cowered when they came. Many others, I saw, did the same. Then, recovering somewhat, I watched them from as close a vantage as I dared, trying to see all eight of them at the same time, alert for any movement they might make. Mahela came out of her ship-dwelling to look at them, then went back in, walking stormily. I watched until it was too dark to see anything but black forms atop the black crags, and I saw no sign of Tassida. Nor, I surmised, had Mahela.

Nor had Kor, when I mindspoke with him. But he was uneasy on account of the three devourers that had not returned.

They must be yet at large against Tass.

Perhaps. What does Mahela say?

*She says nothing, and I assure you, I am not rash
enough to ask her, Dan! She is in foul humor.*

That, to me, sounded so much the better for Tass, but
all the worse for Kor. I could think of no reply.

I am up against it now, Dan.

She gives you no choice?

Perhaps he laughed, for I sensed a grim amusement.
*She gives me a choice which is no choice. The devourers,
or her.*

Ai, Kor!

She is—she is only a woman, Dan.

I smiled, for it was what I had been about to say to him,
thought I daresay neither of us believed it.

You have decided to risk it, then?

*For a certainty! There are many of them, and only the
one of her.*

And she might yet be the more perilous. . . . I did not
mindspeak the words, though I might as well have.

*Perils we do not yet know seem the more attractive.
Dan, I know I spoke boldly yestereven, but now—I only
hope I can give her what she wants of me.*

I fervently hoped it too, but I made my answer seem
offhand. *Why not? It is easy.*

*When I am forced to be false to myself? When I am
afraid?*

Odd, how heart chooses suddenly to catch hold. I felt the
sting of tears behind my eyes. "Do not be afraid," I
whispered aloud. My hands lifted as if to comfort my
brother with my touch.

Dan?

Here. Kor—it will be all right.

I am summoned. Until later, then.

Later. . . .

The devourers could be seen only as shadows against
the dark. I went down the craggy ways to my father's tent,
to sit with him until he lay down to sleep. Even though I

could not see him, even though we did not speak, I did that. Surely Mahela would not commence with Kor until folk were asleep. . . . As soon as Tyonoc's breathing had steadied into the rhythm of slumber, I left the tent, went outside. The water seemed very heavy, the undersea night very still.

Kor?

No answer. But I somehow knew that he was not sleeping. Afraid of my own sureness in that regard, afraid of—nothing. No time now for fear. He was in peril, or he would be soon.

Feeling my way with bare feet, I walked up the path between crags, toward Mahela's abode. Trying to be silent, though there were no guards I knew of. The fell servants still stood furled on their peaks. Perhaps they slept, I thought hopefuly. No, their single eyes glinted fishy white in the faint sealight. It was not wise, or permitted, to be abroad in the night in this place, that I sensed as surely as if I had been told. But perhaps the powers here had no interest in me.

Kor?

No answer. Mahela, the wretched, ruthless slut, she had started sooner than I had thought. I would not shout within my mind, I would not panic Kor. Hard put to control my own terror—but I knew I must, for he was lost somewhere, cast adrift from self, and I had to find him.

Slipping along between crags or behind them, within the watery shadows that have no edge, I made my way toward Mahela's dwelling. No lights there tonight. Closer . . . as close as I dared, standing in the shelter of the last black jutting rock before the open slope where her subjects gathered.

Kor, brother, it is me, Dan. I am here.

Still no reply. I had to risk.

Forgetting the night, forgetting the devourers, forgetting

that there might be guards. No longer aware of chill water. Reaching out with mind.

As if to touch him without words, as I had done once or twice before . . . It was harder now, everything was harder when I was terrified. The old fear, bone deep, gut deep, of being drowned, and not in ocean, either. Drowned in—in Kor himself, if I came too close. . . . No matter. I searched.

Kor. Bond brother.

I felt—whereness, Kor, he was there, very near but withheld from me. Struggling. He needed me.

Kor, I am here, I am handbonding you. My hand reached toward him through the dark water. My fingers curled.

Dan!

Very faint, as if he were far away. Yet I knew he was just within Mahela's walls.

I hear you, Kor, I am handbonding you, I am mindbonding you.

Dan! The word was like a sob, but closer than before.

I am here.

Dan, don't go away!

I won't, I won't! Take hold of me. We two together are strong.

Handbond. . . .

Heartbond, mindbond. Hang on, Kor.

It is like—being swallowed up.

Like the devourers.

No! Worse. Far Worse. The pleasure, the great joy—I want to do it again, I know I will do it again and be—lost from self. She is warm, can you believe it? Mouth, breasts, belly, all warm and marvelous. I hate her.

I hesitated. *Is it necessary that you do it again?* I asked him at last.

Yes.

Then do not be afraid, Kor.

Silence for a little while. I withdrew my mind from him

sufficiently to look around me and see if I was in any danger. But he felt the difference at once.

Dan!

Here, I am right here. I am outside, by the nearest crag. I was just having a look at the devourers.

And?

They seem to be sleeping now. I no longer see the glimmer of their eyes.

Good. Dan, stay there. Keep hold of me.

Of course.

Even if this takes all night.

Of course, Kor! I knew his fear. *Would I let you drown?*

We were already dead and breathing water—I felt the warm touch of his amusement at the thought of drowning. Mirth even amidst his horror.

I truly felt it. Him. In me. Or had I been taken into him?

Ai, my fear, an odd, inward fear, worse than any fear for the body. Fear of losing self . . . but no, coward though I was, I would not be afraid. No space for fear in that dense night outside Mahela's dwelling, night as black and greenly shining as cormorant sheen. Terror enough where Kor was. Time enough for my own qualms—later.

I mindspoke to him—pain in this as much as comfort, but I mindspoke of the Demesne and of the ways of dry land, of sunshine and warm air, summer breezes, hawks soaring. All the creatures of Sakeema. And the colors, seen beneath sky instead of beneath seawater. Pebble colors, pink lichen, aspen leaf. Sunset color, dawn glow, glow of eversnow. And the smell of blue pines, flash of sunlight on the sea surf, glint of wet seaside rock, soft feel of moss. Seal Hold. Mortal voices, kinfolk—

I should have known that Tyonoc would not sleep soundly through the night, even in the realm of the dead. He had been a king too long for that. I felt his touch, his grasp on my shoulder, knew it without looking at him, vaguely heard his voice in my ears. He began shaking me as if to bring me out of a trance, and I hearkened to him just enough to comprehend what he was saying.

Dan? Kor heard silence, felt the change.

It is nothing, Kor. Tyonoc is badgering me. He wants me to come back to the tent. He says it is not safe here.

Indeed. Dryly. I nearly laughed aloud, but caution stopped me. Tyonoc kept his voice low, though he pleaded with me intensely. I had showed no sign that I heard him, as in fact for the most part I did not. Presently he gave up talking at me, taking a guardsman's stance over me instead.

It seems he plans to stay here with me.

Good. He can watch the devourers for you. Calm, Kor's mindspeaking, but a labor in the words, as if he struggled against great force.

Kor, are you all right?

Just—speak to me.

Our people, his and mine, not so much different. Fire on the hearth, work done, good food, chatter, small quarrels, the boasting of youths, old women scoffing, maidens smiling behind slender hands. Tassida—I dared to speak to him of Tassida. And children, living children who teased and shouted and played. The younger girls, the little ones of six or seven years, so winsome and imperious, always. Boys, mischievous. And very small children gazing with round eyes. Kor loved children, and they seemed always to love him, to cluster around him. All but the children of Mahela's realm.

He answered me from time to time, a single word or a touch, enough to let me know that he was there. Sometimes I felt him struggling and mindspoke him by name, calling on the names of our bonds. I was scarcely aware anymore of the cormorant-colored night—in this place it might go on until world's end. I was no longer aware of Tyonoc's presence, for Kor needed me more, that night, battling, if not for life, for something as precious—for selfhood. . . . At some time I had let myself slide to a seat on the harsh stones at the base of the crag. But when I grew aware of weariness, Kor's as well as my own, I struggled back to my feet to combat it. Weariness might be dangerous.

Remember comrades, Kor? Birc, Tyee, Tohr, others? Remember the wolf, the gray wolf on the mountain, maybe the very last? And how it traveled along with us? The wildness in its eyes. And how its fur—

Warm, he mindspoke. *Again. And again, and again, and again.* Very softly, a thought as much for himself as for me, drowsy, lulling, like a cradle song.

Kor! I warned.

He was gone.

Not asleep. Gone, utterly, as if he had never been. As if he had gripped my hand in farewell, then let go, saluted, and stepped into a pit so deep, so black—I no longer tried to control my panic. It pushed me forward, into the open. Tyonoc snatched me back—I think I threw off his hand.

Korridun! Kor, my brother, where are you!

No answer. Tears choked me so badly that I could not have spoken to him had he stood before me, but my thoughts took their own course.

Sakeema! By all that is beautiful, answer me!

Touch of an odd passion in me, no feeling I could name—though I had felt something like it once before, on a beach at the Greenstones. And, as if out of nowhere, a sense of victory. Then—Kor again, somewhere. Hope and vexation surged through me.

Kor, you ass—

Still he had not answered, but Tyonoc's grasp was on me again, tight with a strong sense of danger. He was trying to pull me back. With a start I scanned the night. A swift shadow was moving toward me downslope from the direction of Mahela's abode.

Kor, are you all right? Something is coming toward me.

Ass, yourself, he retorted. *It is I.*

"Kor!" I whispered aloud, and Tyonoc stared, loosening his grip, and Kor sped up to us, embraced me.

Embrace that lasted not nearly long enough. Arms around him, I swayed, staggered by my own relief and love for him as if by a battering wave. He was naked—pity for him overwhelmed me, as if he were no more than a motherless babe. Something heavy, some sort of furred skin or coverlet, trailed from his left hand, brushing my back. He let his head rest for a moment against my neck and shoulder, and I felt his chest heave once, felt also his urgent thought that there was no time for tears.

"Handbond, quickly," he murmured. "We both need it."

I felt weary enough to fall, faint from the night's ordeal, and for his part he could only have felt worse. But when I gave him the grip, at once a surge of victorious strength filled me.

Tyonoc stood by, gaping.

"Now," said Kor in a low voice, "hold this." And he passed me—a pelt, a seal pelt that felt warm, somehow, even in the chill seawater. He held another like it, except that mine was lighter, glimmering sunnily even in the night.

"Our—our skins?" I could scarcely comprehend.

"Yes. She had spread them on the bed." A grim fury sounded in Kor's voice, but also something of pain. "As if I might not notice. Or to toy with me, to show how consummate is her power over me. She overweens, Mahela does." His tone had grown yet darker. "I have pleasured her into a stupor. Wait here for me, Dan."

"Wait, yourself!" I whispered urgently, for I saw that he had taken his pelt in both hands, ready to put it on. "What if—"

If he fell to bits, like the unfortunate man Mahela had sacrificed to cow us. "Even that is better than this," he said savagely, knowing what protest was in me. "I must risk it.'' He flung the pelt around his shoulders, and at once he was a seal, shooting upward, a black, skimming shadow amid streaks of flashing green.

Kor! Come back!

I have to breathe!

Breathe! Air! It was a thought almost too immense to hold, as vast as sky, if it did not destroy him. With my own watery breath bated, I waited for what seemed far too long a time, though it could not have been more than a few heartbeats. And then in a greenfire swirl he darted before me again. Gladness shouted in me.

Kor! You are all right!

Come on, Dan! he replied with a fierce joy. *We are going home.*

All delight and excitement, I held up my pelt to fling it around me—then looked at Tyonoc and stopped.

"Go on," he urged, his voice alive with his own excitement, his head high, the lines of his body full of ardor. Like the king I had known of old. With a pang I wished I could see his face.

"I have to take you with me," I said, "somehow."

Dan, make haste!

"I cannot leave my father here," I said to Kor aloud.

Mahela's bowels! Dan, if we ourselves escape, it will be—

"But what we came here to do—"

"Blood of Sakeema, lad, go!" Tyonoc was exclaiming at the same time.

What, you wish to see me in torment! An angry, bitter thought, not worthy of Kor, but I had no time to protest it.

"If you truly escape, it will bring me joy forever," Tyonoc told me, full of fervor. "Haste, put it on and go!"

He meant it, he commanded me. I embraced him quickly, then stood and donned the pelt.

There was no change. I stood as before.

"Try again." Tyonoc kept his voice low so as not to rouse Mahela's minions, but I heard uproar in his tone.

Dan, please!

I tried again. Nothing happened. "Wait," I said softly, "perhaps this is not meant for me." And before he could protest I flung the pelt around my father's shoulders. But there was nothing of the seal in Tyonoc, either. He stood as human, dead and immortal as I.

Dan, you must make up your mind to be a seal again. And I tell you—I had never heard Kor speak so harshly, in mind or in voice—*I cannot bear it here, not another moment. You do not know. . . . Come with me now, at once, or I will go without you!*

"We did not come here for your sake!" I flared at him. "Wait a bit longer, if you have any honor left!" And I set off down the dark ways at a reckless run. Tyonoc ran after me, and in a moment the seal that was Kor flashed past me.

What are you about? he asked coldly.

I daresay I know one whom this pelt would change.

One who lay in a small lodge of peeled spearpine. I thumped urgently against the wall, though I dared rouse her only with a whisper. "Kela!"

Kor hovered, moaning within his mind. *Name of the god, Dan, I cannot bear to see her now that I am Mahela's plaything! I*—

"Cannot bear, cannot bear!" I mocked furiously, interrupting. "What you cannot bear, you are bearing."

Kela had crawled out of the low doorway and stood before me, blinking. I held out the pelt to her.

"I am just a stupid Red Hart, and I cannot make the change. Here, be a seal, go." Even though I was angry with him, as I said it I knew I was dooming myself never to be with Kor again, and my voice broke.

A small sound like a whimper came from Kor's whiskered mouth as he looked at his mother. She smiled, reached out, and touched him briefly. Then she turned to me.

"Why, Dannoc, what a generous heart is in you," she marveled. "I am sorry I have called you unkind names."

She took the pelt from me. I stood and bowed my head, trying not to feel the pain, not now when Kor would sense it in me, not now when they would need courage. After they were gone would be time enough to grieve, unto forever. . . . I could not mindspeak, not in any way that would make sense, for only one thought was in me, throbbing like a heartbeat. Kor . . . Kor . . . Kor. . . .

Kela flung the pelt around my shoulders, smoothed it down tenderly with her shell-tan hands.

I was a seal, my buckskin clothing falling away behind me, and I knew only that I must breathe at once or I would die. I shot skyward.

Ai, the night sky powdered with stars! True, crisp, unwavering, airy depths such as I might never again have seen . . . There at the surface, under that sky, as I was drawing in great gulps of sweet air, Kor joined me.

They say, Sakeema speed us. My mother and Tyonoc— they say they will rejoice with us forever. They have their hands at their mouths to keep from shouting. And as if they were in my own body I sensed the muddle of emotions in him, pride and terror and awe and the ache of leaving two loved ones behind us in Tincherel, ache such as I also felt. But mostly terror. *Dan, not another moment, now. Come.*

We sped homeward.

Chapter Fourteen

We swam just beneath the surface so as to take less time about breathing, and we swam at the limit of our speed. Swiftly as I cut through the water—and joy and fear make a mighty goad—Kor swam every whit as swiftly. Sometimes I strained to keep up with him.

Dan, how much is left of this night? Can you tell?

With a seal's fluid sense of time, I could not tell, not even by the stars. Seals are odd folk. I did not know even what season it was, and I had no sure sense of how long we had been journeying or how long we had stayed with Mahela. But a seal's inwit was serving Kor and me, drawing us back toward the Greenstones so that we could never be lost in the vastness of the sea. I could sense those sea stacks so clearly that it almost seemed I could see them, far, far ahead. The sense held the course of our flight arrow straight.

The night seemed all too long, before, I told Kor.

And now it seems all too short. When Mahela awakens and looks for me—

May she sleep well, I petitioned whatever powers mindspeak can reach.

She might sleep well and late. A grim triumph in Kor. *By my body, I believe she might.*

We sped on in silence, scarcely pausing even to breathe. Seawater felt lovely, liquid, uplifting, a goodly substance now that we were using it for swimming in and not to fill our lungs. Starlight, sweet breeze, and the shimmer of seawater—such peace, and the ripple of our passing scarcely broke it. Terrible to think that it would not last another day.

Mahela will be mighty in wrath, I mused.

True for you, Dan. Kor was gently mocking me. I nipped at his neck, surging next to mine.

I hope she does not think to visit it on—

Your father, my mother. Ai, Dan, I hate to think it, too. But—

Yes. I knew, as he did, that they were better off in defiance. My father was a man again, and a king, in his own mind. Kela had acted as befit one who had been king and leader of her people.

Dan—what I said to you—about leaving you—

Never mind that. We are here, are we not? Kor, I am ravenous.

As I had meant it to, that took his mind away from melancholy. *You dolt,* he complained, *do you never think of anything but your belly? There is no time to eat!*

We must eat for strength.

We must make the best distance we can, first, in the time that remains to us!

Easy for you to say. Mahela fed you.

Mahela may keep her food.

We swam on, arguing companionably, gulping a few fish that had risen to the darkened surface to feed—it was not enough, and I said so. After a while I turned the friendly quarrel toward the matter of who was faster, and we turned our flight into a race. It seemed less tiring, so, and we went the faster. I wish I could say truly that I let Kor win, but I cannot. He won despite me.

See? I am weak and starved, I grumbled to amuse him.

Excuses, he retorted with a spirit that gladdened me.

Dawn came. We rushed on, weary but knowing we could not yet rest.

The beauty of daytime sky! Every time we breathed I rejoiced in it as if I had never seen sunsheen on water before, or wind traces on high wisps of cloud, or the way the blue of high sky washed pale toward the horizon. Empty sky, empty surface of the sea no longer felt too large to me, but welcome, cleansing, as if I needed to be purged of something.

There was a sweet taste in the air. Something yellow, like pollen, floated in swirls on the quiet surface of the sea. Odd little purses in strings bobbed in the water from time to time, and moon-colored bubble shapes in masses or strings, or single small globes like floating pearls. It took me a while to understand—the things were eggs, fish eggs or eggs of other undersea creatures, spawn, new life—no wonder the air seemed so sweet! It was spring! Winter had passed while we were gone, and the seasons had come around to a new beginning.

Spring! I told Kor, absurdly happy.

Sometime near halfday I tasted a scent of food in the water. Below us in the undersea twilight, somewhere, nameless numbers of greenling bodies schooled.

Many many fish! I exclaimed, barking aloud, and with a twist of my body I dove. Weary as I was, still I took pleasure in the suppleness of my strong seal form. Also, being a seal brought out the mischief in me, so that I had not waited to confer with Kor. With a yelp of protest he dove after me. The greenlings were a great shimmer off to the southward. I kinked sideward and shot that way, Kor hard after me.

A shadow crossed the sea.

Hunger forgotten for the moment, Kor and I slowed, looking upward and back the way we had come. Eight shadows were speeding over the surface where we had been swimming a moment before. I suddenly felt cold.

Devourers!

We could not see them, for we were well under the water by then, but it had to be the fell servants. I knew of nothing else that flew so large and so swiftly.

Mahela has awakened, I added.

As quickly as they had come upon us, they were gone. They had not seen us.

Sakeema bless your stomach, Dan. Kor sounded shaken. *If we had dived a moment later* . . .

He left the thought unfinished, swam after the small schooling fish again. I caught up to him as we reached the stragglers.

Eat well, he mindspoke me.

We both ate well, following the school until the day was waning, letting ourselves be led far to the southward of where Mahela's minions might expect to find us, staying undersea for as long as we could before cautiously surfacing to breathe. We saw no more of the devourers, but the fear of them clung to us.

How are we ever to sleep? I wondered. Now that my belly was full, it seemed I felt my weariness the more.

By turns. Kor sounded tired as well. *Go ahead, Dan. I will watch*.

No, you. I have not had Mahela to satisfy.

He saw the justice in that, relaxed on the surface of the waves, and slept at once. I watched the clear glow of the sunset, swam circles around him to stay awake, watched dusk deepen and stars appear, caught myself dozing, watched the gray and purple of the west turn black. When I truly could not stay awake any longer I roused Kor and took my turn. But neither of us saw any devourers that night.

We were tired, for small spans of uneasy sleep do not abate weariness very much. Though we pressed the pace the next day, and the days after, as much as we could, we were always tired, one of us always on watch, always feeling pressed, pursued, sometimes snappish with each other, never satisfied with the distance we had come. But we saw no more of the fell servants.

I wonder why they have not found us, Kor mindspoke me uneasily.

The ocean is vast. And we turned aside from the course they expected us to take.

Yes, but . . . Dan, even that first day, when we saw their shadows, they could have been searching for us beneath the water as well. They can fly almost as swiftly undersea as above. And if they had been . . .

We would have been food for their maws, I responded lightly, or as lightly as I could, thinking of a thing so grim. *So rejoice that they were not. The brutes are stupid.*

Kor did not respond to my flippant tone. *Mahela is not stupid,* he said darkly. *She is toying with us. She has some cruel surprise in store for us.*

I did not like hearing this from him, for I felt a need to keep spirits up, courage high. Arrogance, even, seemed better than the despair I remembered from the Mountains of Doom. *I dare say she will search for us yet a while,* I admitted. *But—*

Yet a while! Dan, do not delude yourself. You know she is relentless, and I know it better. She will stalk us until we die.

Perhaps. But . . .

He went on as if he had not heard me, as if a lash drove him. *I half believe she laid those pelts on her bed for no other reason but this, to prolong the game and her pleasure in taming us, to give us a chance to show us all her powers. She plans to break us in her own sweet time.*

It was a danger worse than the threat of death. And he was right, of course, but it was not truth that chilled me so much as his tone. I began to know then that she had laid her touch on him in a way I could not help or understand, and I shut my eyes in a protest too deep for words.

The devourers will be waiting for us at the Greenstones, Kor added starkly.

Are you so sure? I challenged, though not harshly—arrogance had left me.

I am reasonably sure.

Then I think it behooves us to come ashore elsewhere.

It scarcely matters. They will find us wherever we come to shore.

Not fitting speech, Kor. Quakebuttock, some would have called him. Coward. But I knew he was no coward, and though I wanted to rail at him in anger, heartache would not let me. Not yet.

On toward evening of that day, whatever day it was, we both slept and kept no watch—whether more in daring or defiance or despair I scarcely know. And we slept long and deeply. Sakeema be praised for that slumber, for it was our last respite of that journey, and we were sorely to need it.

We awoke to dawn thunder and a glimmer of lightning in the west. On the hunt for fish, we swam off eastward. But before sunrise we had given up thoughts of fish. Thunder cracked more sharply, and lightning flared. Storm had grown closer behind us, as if it were following us.

We scudded eastward, just beneath the waves, as clouds scudded above them, small gray clouds torn ragged and sent slantwise before the force of the wind. Hiss of rain. Waves grew higher. This squall flew faster than we, and gained on us. We could not outrun it.

Let us try to flank it to one side, Kor mindspoke me. *North or south?*

North.

We breathed at the tossing surface, veered to our left, and dove. It was not such a great storm—we could see a lighter gray sky beyond it to either side. When we surfaced again, many minutes later, we expected to be well out of it.

Instead we came up into what might as well have been night, and into the midst of a tempest. Waves that flung us bodily upward into a roar of wind and swell and rain, into a blackness that blotted out the day, blankness shot through with greenish lightning. I took one startled breath and dove, and Kor, praise be, was beside me.

Double back the way we came.

We swam westward, back toward Mahela's realm, for all we were worth. The storm had been traveling eastward, at speed. We should have come up behind it.

Confounded, we came up in the black heart of it once again. Or the black and yawning maw . . . The tempest wanted us, it shrieked, it held us in its clutches and sucked at us hungrily and shook us in great random hands as if it would gnaw and tear us apart. Sea took us to its billowing bosom and tried to drown us. Air was a chill blast that screamed. I fought my way downward at last to the calmer water beneath the swell, but I could not at first find Kor, not until he mindspoke me. He was southeastward somewhere, and I shot toward him.

This way, arrow speed!

We hurtled along with desperate haste, sure that this time, at last, we would outflank the storm. And we stayed under until great clay chimes began to ring in our heads. One moment more and we would surface to breathe—

A blaze of light, a flaring before my eyes—for a moment I thought my sight was failing me. Then I felt the tingle. It had been lightning sending a greenish flame through the seawater.

No!

Kor sounded not so much frightened as furious, aggrieved. I was frightened.

We went up, for we had no choice, and lightning turned the sea to greenfire all around us, nearly stunning us, and hail pounded our heads. Day was gray-black, nearly as gloomy as night beneath heavy cloud, and the waves were raging.

We struggled down and found each other and swam off again, eastward, doggedly.

This accursed squall is following us!

Kor had courage to mindspeak what I had not wanted to think. And events proved him right. The storm battered and dragged at us for what must have been days—I could not tell, at the time, for day and night seemed the same beneath that lowering cloud, and I was long past counting even had I not been a seal, heedless of time. But it must have been days, more than a few days that the tempest chivvied and harried us and drove us before it. It beat us down and tossed us about and slapped at us with a sound like wild laughter. It hurled us apart and, an anguished time later, when I was weeping with despair, a seal's salt tears, it flung us together again. It stunned us with lightning and blows, then rocked us awake, as gently as a mother, before it pounded at us with wind and wave once again. It whirled us in eddies when we tried to swim and rushed us along when we tried to rest. There was very little for us to eat—we grew weak with starvation and with struggling, and the time came when we ceased to struggle. When we ceased even to try to swim, but let the tempest have its way with us, as it had done all along. I thought we would die.

I thought we would drown, we were so weak, wallowing limply in the water, not even trying to surface for breath.

Mindbond, Kor. . . . Mortal danger. Drowning in fact, no time to be afraid of drowning in each other.

I—haven't heart. So he, too, knew that fear, that engulfing closeness. *Dan—is four times too many to be dead?*

Say not so, Kor. We must—mindbond. Up—for air. . . .

I—I can't face that she-squall again.

No more could I. Too weak even to grieve, to say farewell, I let myself drift down through the greendeep. To sleep, to rest, at last . . .

Something lifting, nudging me up. Prodding me toward the surface and into wakefulness. I struggled only when the

storm clawed at me again and screamed in my ears. Then
I drew quick breath between drenchings, opened my eyes,
blinked through spray. Something sleek was bearing me up.

Servants of Mahela! Kor sounded furious. Wrath had
given him new strength.

No, it is not the devourers. A strong, smooth, finned
back, gracefully curved, took me under again even as I
mindspoke. A dolphin. My flippers hooked over its fin in
an awkward grip so as to keep me with it. Kor rode one
much as I did, and many others bobbed all around us.

Minions of Mahela, all the same! Kor raged. *She sent
them to revive us so that she can torment us a while
longer!*

*These dolphins are not Mahela's pets, Kor. They break
the surface, they breathe air.*

A considerable silence. The dolphins bore us eastward
along with the storm, surfacing to breathe from time to
time, or the storm followed along with the dolphins, or
with us, always with us. All the time they conversed with
each other in a way we could not understand, though I
would have liked to, for they sounded cheery and brave.
When Kor mindspoke at last, his thought was quiet with
wonder.

Then there is yet good in the sea, after all.

After all that had happened.

They deserted us as suddenly as they had come, taking
us up to the surface for air, then sinking suddenly away
from under us. leaving us floundering in the raging waves.

Slime of Mahela! I was angry this time.

No, Dan, they brought us as far as they could. Kor
dove, his swimming weary, labored. *Did you not hear it?
Breakers. We are nearly at the Greenstones.*

How could he have heard breakers amid the roaring of
stormwind and the lashing of whitecaps? But my seal's
inwit knew he spoke truth. I, too, sensed that we were
near shore.

Shall we try to skirt it awhile? Stay away from the devourers?

I was nearly blind with exhaustion. Mindspeak helped me to stay with him.

We are as likely to—be smashed against the cliffs—as taken by them, wherever we come to land.

We tried it nevertheless, struggling northward, toward Seal Hold. But we were weak, and I doubt if we made so much as an arrow's flight of headway. The sea had us in a strong grasp, and it hurled us and hurled us and hurled us toward the Greenstones. Above us, the storm shone and flashed and sang. We did not try to dive anymore, and we breathed between blows of the water. Once, flung atop a whitecap, I saw, for a spinning moment I glimpsed, the sea stacks and the distant shore beyond them, seen through a veil of rain. Home . . . and I was not even thinking of forest and mountains, but of a seal's home, birthplace, landfall, solid and sometimes dry, and my throat tightened and my heart ached at the sight of it. Coming home to haul out and die. . . . I did not try to dive out of the pounding waves—I wanted to see it again, but a crushing wall of water fell atop me and buried me.

Flash before my eyes, moon-colored, and it was she, the white seal, my sea-maiden lover, nose to nose greeting me, her flippers beating the water like a bird's wings, faster than heartbeats, fighting against the tide.

For life's sake, lovely one, get away from the shore!

But of course she could not hear me. Kor came up beside me—perhaps he was pleading as well.

Dive, go out to sea, white maiden! I begged. *Body of Sedna, you will be flung against the rocks and killed!*

But of course she could not get away, any more than we could. And even as I thought it a cold grip took hold of us, a fist immense and stronger than ten tens of bison trampling, stronger than a hundred Cragsmen made of mountain stone, roaring, seemingly solid as the mountains, crashing—name of Sakeema, I do not like to think of it. That mighty force pushed and pounded us headlong at the sea stacks: the white seal and Kor and me. And with a rush it took us between the outer ones, toward the shore. But then there was a great tumult of surf, and a feeling as of rearing horses, and we were smashed—the white seal had been swept to the fore, smashed against rock, and I atop her. Crushing her. I heard her shriek as she died.

No time even to cry out in sorrow. A thump—Kor glanced off me, hurtled onward. Thunder sound, or was it surf? Yes, surf. All was harsh whiteness, and the waves carried me in to the shore, as Kor had once told me they would. Flung me, rather. Far more roughly than he had thought at the time, so long ago.

Wet sand. I dragged myself up it a short distance, very short. The sea still washed at my—legs? Something had touched me to change me—I was a man again. I did not care. Naked, I laid my face down in the wet sand. I did not care about anything.

"No, sweet mercy, no!" It was Kor, somewhere not far from me, groaning aloud. "Devourers."

I had to respond to that. "Handbond," I whispered, and I raised my head a little, turned to look for him, opened my eyes. Then I stared, my hand stilled even as it inched toward him.

Devourers, yes. Devourers to the number of twelve less four, I daresay. Gray, rippling flesh swirled to all sides of us, looming and threatening like the tempest, shutting out the sun. Fishily gleaming—the sight of it made me shiver. And the single eyes, whitely flashing. And the strong, snakelike, flattened tails, lashing the sand and the air.

But Tassida was there. Standing straddle-legged over Kor and me, her head high and the color riding in her cheekbones, hair rising in the wind, lightning of the seaward storm flickering behind her as if it were a part of her, as if it were burning in the long cloud of her windblown hair or flying from her brow, her fierce eyes. Fierce, joyous. Sword lifted high, and it shone like the lightning. Tass stood glad and defiant over us, and such was her presence that the fell servants of Mahela did not dare to approach us.

And Kor, my bond brother, lay shivering at her feet, his shoulders hunched as if he had tried to raise himself and could not, his face wintry white, as pale as the spindrift on the waves.

My look caught on him, turned to a stare, stayed. Exhausted, he did not feel my stare or look back at me, and I felt darkly glad of it, for I did not want to meet his eyes. There would be that bleak look in them, I felt sure of it. He was defeated. For all that we had escaped, Mahela had bested him. We had not brought back with us those whom we had gone to save. Those who had befriended us had perished. Even the white seal had been slain.

I did not know then about Istas. But heart sensed that we had been defeated, and there was a bitter taste in my mouth that the sea had left there. We were alive, that should have been cause for joy, but I was not much accustomed to being rescued. We were helpless, and I blamed Kor. He was Sakeema, he should have stood in glory—

He was not Sakeema.

My own utter weariness enabled me to think it, but colored the thought with despair. I laid down my head in the wet sand again and knew nothing more.

Chapter Fifteen

I awoke to a feeling of warmth. A sizable driftwood fire burned not far from me, and I was lying on some sort of warmly furred pelt, with more furs covering me. Sand beyond that, but dry sand—I had been moved up the beach, away from the water, into a sort of dingle of dry, soft sand half-surrounded by tumbled rock. The stones threw back the heat of the fire, and above them the tops of twisted spruces met my sight. An odd, wrenching feeling in me to see them—and it was daylight, gray with brume yet very bright to me, no greenish undersea twilight and no black belly of storm.

A deer gut hung from three crossed stakes near the fire, giving forth the rich odor of stone-boiled fish chowder.

"Mother of my body, no!" I burst out. "Not more fish!"

I heard a low laugh, Kor's, and looked to find him. My own feet were in the way, and I felt nearly too weary to move them. But at last I saw him a small distance around the fire from me. He lay propped up on one elbow, mostly swaddled in furs as I was, but they had fallen away from his shoulders so that I saw the bruises, the color of storm clouds, blue-black and swollen, or older ones fading to sea green. Scarcely a handspan of him had escaped punish-

ment that I could see. And his face, bruised as well, with a
raw scrape across one cheekbone. And his sea-colored
gaze was on me, dark with his memories of Mahela's
realm, yet merry.

"I thought you liked fish now," he teased. "Many
many fish."

I did not answer, for Tassida was sitting near him,
helping him with the eating of some chowder. Tassida. I
had to look at her, and it was no use trying to conceal the
surge of love I felt for her. At once I moved to sit up, talk
with her, perhaps, but I floundered as if I were but a great
fish myself. My body would not obey me.

"Dan, lie still," said Tass as gently as I had ever heard
her speak to either of us. "Wait, I will get you something
to eat. You two, you are so weakened, so beaten! What
has happened?"

Her soft query touched me so that my throat closed, I
could not speak. But Kor spoke. "Mahela happened," he
said.

Bitter undertone to that. I looked at him again. Yes, he
was defeated, but in a different way from my father.
Something hard in him. Sullen. Not . . . Sakeema . . .

"What? She took a blackwood club to you, belabored
you yourself?" Still gentle, Tass was trying to tease some
truth out of him.

"She might as well have."

"Kor. Do I look as beaten as you do?" I asked abruptly.

"Only on the outside." As if his strength had all in a
moment given way, he let his arm fold, his head fall onto
his bed of furs. Tass covered him and came over to me.

Name of love, the warm touch of her hands as she
helped me up. She settled herself beneath and behind me,
she let me lean against her, my head resting in the curve of
her shoulder, her arms around me to hold the bowl. So
stunned was I, and so happy, I ate the reeking fish without
a word to please her. The food would give me strength,

she said. But it was out of her that strength seemed chiefly to come, warmth and comfort and strength flowing to me from her touch.

I ate all the food she gave me, and then she settled me in my bed again as tenderly as a mother might, all but kissed me. She told me to sleep, and I did so instantly, as if I had to obey her or risk breaking the spell of sweetness that seemed to be on us both. Name of love was . . . Tassida. . . .

Kor had once said that she loved—me! That was his honesty, but had he abated his ardor for her since saying it? He was only a man after all, and no god, I reminded myself with an angry pang. So perhaps he had. I should have known better, but I wanted to think he had. It quieted my uneasy sense of honor—for I was dreaming of her.

When I awoke it was nighttime, a night black and soft with fog, and I was feeling the urge that follows food. Thinking of a private place down by the sea, I struggled and sat up—stronger, yes! Started to throw off my coverings, then realized I was naked as a skinned rabbit beneath them, and stopped.

"Go ahead, Dan." Tass spoke from behind me, where she was tending the fire. "Sakeema knows, I have seen you often enough."

Which was true, and many times she must have seen me relieve myself against a rock or tree, those days when she had been a youth and a warrior traveling with us. But I did not move, and she came over to me, offering a hand, as if to help me stand and walk. I refused it, hoping she would not see in the firelight how my face had reddened.

"Everything seems very different now," I mumbled.

"How so?" She sat by me.

I could scarcely say, but I was damned by Mahela if I was going to let her take me to the cuck-pit. "Tass," I burst out, "just bring me some clothes, would you? Please?"

She shrugged and got up. "Bring mine, too," came

Kor's voice from the darkness beyond the fire, and Tass nodded, then went off in the night to get them.

"Her camp must be up in the spruces somewhere," Kor said.

He was awake, he understood what was happening, and he would help me for all he was worth, blast him. Feeling as sure of his aid as if he had spoken, and oddly vexed, I kept silence.

Tassida returned. I took the bundle she gave me, fumbled through it in the firelight, and girded on the lappet before I flung off my blanketing pelts. Finally I wobbled to my feet. There was just strength enough in me to let me unsteadily stand and walk. In breeches tied crookedly, Kor tottered over to stand beside me.

"Handbond," he said. "For strength."

"It is too petty a matter for handbond," I told him coldly.

"Truly? You prefer to fall on the rocks?" He raised his brows at me, then shrugged. "As you will. Just give me your other hand, then. We'll be a horse of four legs—when one end stumbles, the other end stands firm."

Firelight flickered on the pale waves of sand, making them seem to shift and surge like sea billows, or so I thought for a moment. Perhaps it was my own blinking eyes and light head that made it seem so. I gave Kor my left hand, and the two of us swayed off toward the water's edge.

"Your swords are in the cave," Tass called after us, mocking or amused. "Get them, O mighty warriors, if you can lift them. You may have need of them soon."

Kor and I staggered to a stop, nearly falling, and fear sent our right hands flying to bond despite any misgivings of mine. And Kor was yet my bond brother, whatever my dark thoughts, and strength surged through me from his grip. We both stood more steadily, but staring like gudgeons.

For lying at the tide line, lying in a rippling, slitted,

foul-smelling mass was—a devourer. No, it did not move, even though the shadowy night at first made it seem to do so, and plainly its innards were spilled, and its greenish life's blood. It was dead.

"Scum of Mahela!" Kor exclaimed.

"The sword is of good use against them," Tass told us across the night, a note of triumph in her clear voice.

Kor looked back at her across his shoulder. "You have a tale for us."

"The twelve less one are now but seven. That is tale enough."

We passed the felled devourer at a distance, and though we did not speak of it, I for one felt queasy so close to the thing, as if it might somehow poison us or harm us, even dead and dismembered as it was. We made our way down among the rocks of the shore, and I did what I had come to do. Kor stood at a small distance. In the darkness I heard him chuckling, and the sound annoyed me.

"What is it?" I grumbled.

"I have never known you to be modest, Dan."

I blazed at him, "Well, what would you have done?"

"I truly believe I am past caring." Something harsh beneath his amusement. It angered me.

"Well, I am not! You are the more to be pitied, then."

"And you are in parlous ill humor, Dan! Why?"

He was not Sakeema. But he had never claimed to be. . . . Shamed, yet no less sullen, I kept silence.

"Here," he said finally, "take my hand."

I had to, or fall. Presently we found the cave, teetering, trying not to slip on the hard, smooth-worn stone. This was how an old, old man might feel, I mused, afraid of falling, afraid of pain and brittle bones and not being able to get up again. The old are defeated, contemplating the face of Mahela. Well, I was not so old, and breaks would heal, and pain was only pain. . . . A faint light, fainter than starlight, showed us our way to the ledge where the swords lay. The stones in the pommels dimly glowed, showing us the glint of crossed blades lying just as we had left them.

I reached for Alar, and eagerly the sword slid toward me, presenting her pommel to my hand. I gripped it as if gripping the hand of an old friend well met, and I held Alar high awhile, gladly hefting her, letting her blade gather light and send it flashing, before slipping her into the leather scabbard and fastening it to my belt. And Kor still stood looking at Zaneb, and had not yet raised his hand to greet the sword.

I stared at him. He felt the gaze.

It feels—like the taking up of a doom.

"I thought I was the one afraid of my sword," I said. I had been, once. But Kor had never been a madman, with a madman's fears. What ailed him, I could not guess, and I was tired, I had no patience to stand there with him. "Come back when you feel stronger," I told him.

"No. Doom is now." He reached up, fingers open to receive the hilt, and it flew gently to his hand. Whatever doom there might have been, I could not feel it.

But Kor seemed shaken, and stood woodenly. I took his arm, urged him back out of the cave and up the beach. Only when we had nearly reached the fire did he collect himself enough to stop and gird on his sword.

Tass was uncovering something she had roasted in coals. I sank down thankfully on my pile of furs, spent, so weary I was scarcely interested even in supper, until she laid the wooden bowl in my lap.

Meat! Red meat!

"Rabbit!" I blurted aloud, grabbing at it and burning my fingers. She laughed. Kor was staring, not at me but at her.

"You do have a tale to tell us, Tass," he said abruptly.

"A tale? Of the snaring of a coney?" She laughed anew. "Eat, be well and strong."

We all ate. There were oat cakes as well as the rabbit. The fire burned warm—in Mahela's realm, I had scarcely dared to believe that I would ever sit by a fire again, dry and warm, mortal, amidst—friends. . . .

Kor caught my glance and quietly smiled. But his eyes were full of thought, not all of it glad.

When we had eaten and thrown away the bones he spoke. "So, Tass, the tale. Truly, please. Tell us how it is that you are no longer afraid to be with Dannoc."

Was the change in her? I had thought it was the joy of our homecoming gathering her in. But she knew what Kor meant, and there was not much guile in her that night. She sobered and looked down at the sand, denying nothing, saying nothing.

"Will not the morrow be time enough for tales?" she asked at last. "You are both mending, you should rest."

"Sakeema knows what will happen on the morrow," said Kor starkly.

So she told us.

It had seemed a long winter to her while Kor and I were in the sea. She had not gone off on her lifelong wandering quest, as we had assumed she would. As she had always made us think she did when she was not with us. In fact, she had never been far from us since the first day she had met us, never more than three days hard riding away, most often much closer. Near us, yet afraid to be with us, she admitted with her eyes downcast and her hands stroking the sand. Like a moth following a flame. But she had not been able to follow us into the sea.

That being so, she had set herself to watching the sea and our swords and our steeds. Sora and Talu were wandering with Calimir somewhere in the spruce forests, not too far away. Tass had built herself a shelter of poles and skins, setting it up against a cliff and a shallow cave, a short walk from where we were, though it had been too distant for her to drag us there when we were limp weight just washed ashore. (We could go there now if we liked. Not now, we told her, Thank you, but no.) She had spent the winter living there, hunting and fishing for her food. Folk from Seal Hold had discovered she was there, and someone came from time to time, bringing her oats and talk. Nor had it taken them long to comprehend that she was a maiden—perhaps she had not hidden it as fervidly as before. And they had accepted it in her. But most of the time she had been alone. She had never spent so much time in one place and alone. It had seemed a long, gray winter.

Then she had been afraid.

"The jewel lights went out." She raised her dark eyes and looked levelly between us, toward the sea, and her eyes were as dark as the Mountains of Doom, as deep as the sea. "In the hilts of your swords, the stones. One day their light was gone, they lay as dull as pebbles, and I knew you were—dead."

Kor looked down with a small grimace, as of discomfort. I shivered, suddenly feeling the nighttime chill on my bare spine.

"I—I panicked, I grew frantic. I snatched at the swords as if I could warm the life back into the jewels with my hands, or shake them, something—I am not sure what. But they did not let me touch them. They warned me away." Smiling, Tassida raised both her palms toward us in a gesture that made her seem magical, a wise woman, a seeress. And across the four fingers of each hand ran a thin, white scar, very much like the ones Kor and I each bore.

We were stupid with weariness and our own unspoken quarrel, worn down by Mahela's torments, or we would have known, then. Everything.

Or perhaps not. Perhaps the pattern was too vast for us to comprehend so quickly, a vastness like that of sky or sea. Perhaps poison of Mahela was darkening our sight.

Perhaps neither of us had courage to see. Not Kor, who I had thought was a god. Not I, who now felt pain as if I had been betrayed, thinking he was not.

For whatever reason, we said nothing, and Tass went on.

"There was nothing I could do but wait. And then the devourers came, all of them at once, in the daytime. When did they grow bold enough to fly in the daytime? Bowels of my mother, but I was afraid." She hesitated, her head once again bowed, her hands down, fingers tracing in the sand. "You have heard—there is a mode of attack folk do not care to speak of. Shameful in men. All the worse in devourers."

I had heard whispers, nothing more, of something vicious the Fanged Horse Folk did to captured women. Whispers . . . I had not known until I met Mahela that the act of love could be turned into a weapon and an abomination. And suddenly understanding, I sat without speaking, chilled. But Kor, who must have felt it worse than I, nodded briefly and spoke.

"A king must know of such evils. They had done it to you before?"

"Nearly. Not completely, or I would be—I would be like Dannoc's brother. It was but the one, then, and I withstood it, and that was terror enough. But the twelve, less only the one in Ytan . . ."

Alone and exposed on the expanse of beach—too late to hide, for they had long since seen her. No time to take refuge in the cave or her hut, for they were swift, rippling in on a western wind. She had held her sword at the ready as she stood to meet them—not with any hope of defeating them, for she knew, as we did, that knives, even the shining black blades of sharpest obsidian, had no effect on devourers. But she gripped her sword because the feel of the rounded hilt in her clenched hand, the weapon's weight, gave her some small courage. Also, she had resolved, as we had, months past, to use it on herself rather than let them possess her. She raised the blade as the fell servants skimmed around her to gang her, close enough that she smelled their deathly stench—

And the sword of its own accord had darted and pierced a glaring eye. Pale greenish ooze had spurted out, and the devourer had fallen back, thrashing in pain. She had whirled, or the blade had whirled her, to hold off the attack from behind, slicing deeply into a fish-gray body, sending splatters of blood the color of cormorant feathers, green-black, onto the sand. She had severed a thick, eel-like tail. . . . More quickly than she could tell it, she said, three devourers lay dead and the rest were fleeing. And only after it was over had she taken time to think, this sword is no ordinary knife, it is made of different stuff. And she had caressed it, speaking to it softly by name.

"Do you wish to tell us the name?" Kor asked quietly. And I sensed, as he did, that this was no small matter of trust, for Tass.

"Marantha," she replied promptly.

"The amaranth," I murmured. The healing flower of Sakeema's time, gone from the land with his passing, a spire-flower of a color I had never quite seen in any other, the same clear red-purple color as the jewel in Tassida's sword. Of course it was the name of her weapon. But Tass was looking at me curiously.

"Dan, how did you know? I thought all folk had forgotten that flower but me."

"I have seen it in vision."

"Marantha," Tass said again, a different, vibrant tone to her voice, and the sword floated lightly out of the scabbard she wore by her side. Marantha laid herself in the sand, pointing toward us, Kor and me, but between us. As if in a trance we drew our weapons and laid them over Tassida's, blades crossing, so that blades and hilts formed a sort of star of six darts. And the stones blazed out, darting forth their own six-bladed lights, deep yellow, amaranthine, and sunset-red, bright as blood, brighter than the fire.

Eerie, uncanny, unaccountable . . . uneasily my mind built barriers. Perhaps it was not just the three of us, I thought eagerly. Perhaps there were swords for others at the bottom of the pool of vision. Many swords. One for my brother Tyee, one for Leotie, his pledgemate, who had once been my sweetheart. Twelve for his twelve, and as many for Kor's as well. Would it not be overweening to think that such weapons were only for the three of us, Korridun and Tassida and I?

"The day I saw that the glow had come back to your swords," Tass said softly, "I was so happy I wept."

Startled, Kor looked up at her. But her gaze was fixed on the star the swords made.

"So you see," she said softly, "I had time, those long days while you were gone, to think that I had lost you both and to know that I had been a fool to be afraid. We belong together, we three."

Swordlight flared briefly at her words, then subsided to a warm glow.

"Is it fated so?" Kor asked, and if there was fear in him I could not hear it in his voice.

"I do not know the reason. But that we three are to be—comrades—that much I am sure of, now."

"And defeating the devourers did not hurt your courage," said Kor dryly. She caught his meaning at once and looked up at him with a merry smile. Something grew hard inside me, and hurt.

"Indeed it did not. Thought I will never be able to use my sword against either of you two, and I know that."

She had told us once that the weapons with names could not be used against anyone the swordmaster loved. . . .

"I will not leave you again," Tass said.

Both of us, she meant. I was to—share her with him?

Swordlight had faded. I reached for Alar, drew her out of the star, and sheathed her. After a moment the others put their weapons away as well.

"Tired, Dan?" Kor's voice was gentle. I hated him. Without replying I lay and swaddled myself in my furs. One of them was a seal pelt. My pelt. I could be a seal again whenever I wanted, and swim away.

"Sleep with your swords," Tassida told us. "Mahela wants you badly."

I slept restlessly, ill at ease, feeling the hard edge of my own blade by my side, sensing fell shapes moving in shadow at the edge of my own dreams, feeling fear, and not of Mahela's minions. No devourers came that night. There was no need for Mahela to send them. She had only to watch and wait, for yet darker forces were moving in me.

Chapter Sixteen

"We should go to Seal Hold," Kor said in the morning.

Tassida shook her head. "Wait one more day. You are still very weak."

Though mending, both of us, far faster than we should have expected after starvation and Mahela's brutal tempest, so it seemed to me.

"Your people will manage without you another dayspan. The salmon run less, as always, and the Otter beg and the Fanged Horse Folk threaten, and not enough oats are left. Once you go back there, they will want to make a savior of you, there will be no peace."

It was a rarely fine morning. Blue sky, blue doveflower already blooming upon the rocks. Eastward I could see the snowpeaks! Fresh breeze. Greed of Mahela be praised, the high tide had taken the carrion devourer, which had been starting to stink. All was fair now, and clean, as if just washed. I scanned sky, sea, sand. Near the rocks a white shape lay on the beach, left there by the retreating surf. . . .

I stood up, staring, and if Kor or Tass spoke to me I did not hear them.

The white seal. It was she, my gentle lover. I went over, knelt beside her sleek body—she looked as fair as she had in life. I reached out, meaning nothing but to

stroke the glossy fur. But as my hand touched her she
changed. There on a white pelt lay the sea maiden, with
her long, shimmering hair flowing down like tears. Pale,
bruised, dead. I could have stood it better had I not been
so startled, I think. But as it was, I made a choking sound
and reached out to gather her up, as if by holding her I
could somehow help.

Tass and Kor had come to stand beside me, and I looked
up, bursting out, "I—I killed her, great oaf that I am!
When she hit against the rock, I came blundering on top of
her."

"Mahela's doing, not yours," Kor said, sensibly—but I
was in no fit mood to be sensible. "It might as easily have
been you who were killed. The white maiden saved you."

"You—you loved her!" Wonder in Tassida's tone, and
she was staring. "In a—a certain way . . ."

"If I cannot love a woman, I do not lie with her," I
said.

"Dan, I did what I had to!" Kor protested, his voice
sharp with—grief? I stared at him in surprise.

"I have said nothing against you!"

"Not yet."

So he knew, damn him, he sensed—what could have
been decently hidden from any proper friend. . . . Well, if
the cap fit his sore head, let him wear it, then! I gave him
a black look but no answer, and turned back to the sea
maiden.

"We must guard her," I said, thinking hazily of the
legend of Sedna, "so that carrion birds do not pick out her
eyes. We must cover her with a cairn."

She who had floated in the salt eddies to be laid in a bed
of bruising rock—it hardly seemed fitting, yet such a
wrong-headed demon was in me that I could think of
nothing else. I lifted her, carried her up beyond the tide
line to where the dry sand lay in billows. Tassida came
after me with the white pelt.

"Take it," I told her. "We will all three be seals, then, and go swim in the greendeep when Mahela has laid bare the land."

She hesitated, then took the seal pelt back to our campsite, brought other furs instead, a deerskin, a fine cape of otter. We laid the white maiden on the deerskin in soft sand and covered her with the otter cape, fur side next to her, head and all, so as to keep the rocks from her skin.

Then we built the cairn, and what should have been half a morning's labor took us all day, Kor and I, we were yet so feeble. Tass helped us when she could, but she had snares to tend, and foraging to do, and cooking, if we were to eat. Which was of importance, that we should eat and mend. So Kor and I carried stones, small ones, singly, and laid them over the otter cape. Between times we rested, not much speaking to each other. I found ways to busy myself—my body ached and stumbled in protest, but better that than sitting near him, not wanting to meet his eyes. I gathered driftwood and dragged it to the fire—the tide had been high, for the moon was at the full. I hunted in the rock pools for mussels and such, food I had never sought with such fervor. Silent and still, Kor watched me.

If Tassida had not been there, if it had been just the two of us, bond brothers, the silence would have been unbearable after all that we had shared, and perhaps we would have had our trouble out and mended it somehow. But Tass was with us, we talked with her, and she sensed nothing wrong between us—she thought we were tired, which we were. There had not been much need of speech between Kor and me since she had known us. Though time had been when we would have walked under the full moon, Kor and I, and talked for hours while he kept the vigil his kingship demanded of him. . . . I would not think of those times. I had hardened myself to the unspoken quarrel, for it cleared my way to Tassida. Though I would not admit as much, not even to myself.

Sunset, the color of my sword, then bright orange as of highmeadow poppies, sea stacks sleek and dark against it, like great seals. And blood-red sky dimming into purple. Dusk deepening into shining night—stars, full moon rising over the mountains, gleaming off the eversnow. Kor and Tass and I sat amidst it all, eating roast partridge and mussels steamed in eelgrass and the tender spring sprouts of celery and sparrowgrass that grew where soil gathered on ledges near the cascades. It was a blessed twilight. Odd, how such warm and peaceful times come even in the midst of trouble, but it must be so or we would go mad. . . . Pushing aside my dark mood for a while, I ate the shellfish and grinned at Kor, mocking myself. He gave me his grave, quiet smile, and Tassida hummed snatches of song and gazed at the sky, seeing stories there. Times to come, I cherished the memory of that night.

The white maiden lay in her cairn under the moonlight, and the rocks glinted where we had piled them.

Not long after full dark, when stars splattered the sky like foam, there was a splashing in the surf, and we looked. There were seals in the breakers, seals surging up the beach like the waves, seals to the number of half a hundred or more, many-colored under the moonlight. The three of us sat by our dying fire and watched as they left the sea and dragged themselves far up on the sand, much farther than was the custom of seals, up to where the mound of the fresh cairn shone, and in a press of sleek bodies they pooled around it.

Then in a few moments they had undone what it had taken us all day to do. Rocks flew as if out of a thunder cone, flung upward and back by pointed snouts and strong necks. They laid low the cairn, pulled the covering back from the sea maiden with their teeth—

And as soon as one of them touched her he stood by her in human form, and so soon also did the rest. Sea folk, sylkies, Kor's distant kindred, to the number of fifty or more. The white maiden's people, and every one of them as beautiful as she, and as strange. Hair that flowed and shimmered, seal-black or red-brown as wrack or shell-tan or sea-foam white, down to the shoulders of the men, below the waists of the women. They were lissome, the women, but for once my eyes caught on the men, for they were different from any people I had ever seen. Long necks, narrow sloping shoulders, chests of the same breadth as their midriffs, and their long, loose-jointed hands and feet moved at odd angles. Their skins, hairless and sleek, and their cocks, like the breasts of the women, small. But manly and tall they stood, their heads high, their movements graceful, and though their bodies were slight I sensed all the power of the sea in them. And their faces, comely and fearsome. Wonder moved me to mindspeak to Kor.

I would not want to meet any one of them in fair fight!

Nor would I. They look as potent as tide surge, and as mute.

There had been not a sound from any of them. But we sensed a silent uproar—one of the tall men had lifted the white maiden in his arms, and others were holding the pelts, the deerskin, the otter cloak. And there were touchings, fluid movements of quick hands, as if they were speaking in that way. And the pool of them swirling like boiling water.

"I knew it was wrong," Tass muttered, and as she spoke she was on her feet and striding down the beach toward the strangers, looking very much the warrior and a daughter of earth next to their small-boned beauty. She carried the white seal pelt in her hands. "Here it is, people of the sea!" she called aloud.

And Kor, confound him, went after her, holding his own dark, dappled pelt. "Take this one, too," he said roughly. "Never again will any king of the Seal Kindred go to court Mahela. I have sworn it.'' He thrust the pelt toward them.

''Blast it!'' I whispered. Then I found my own sealskin, light brown with a sheen as of sunstuff, as beautiful as any pelt I had ever seen, and I loved it as I did my own body. ''Blast it,'' I grumbled again, and I trailed after the others and offered the limp thing wordlessly to the sylkies.

The white maiden's people had stopped their eddying and stood gazing at us. No fear in them, but much thought—we were envoys from a different world from theirs. They measured us with their stares, then reached a silent agreement among themselves. With slow ceremony three men of their number stepped before us where we stood in an uneasy row. We gave the sealskins back to their long hands, back to the sea. And when my eyes met the eyes of the one who faced me in the moonlight, my breath stopped. It was a glance out of depths beyond my knowing, time before time, like the speechless glance of an animal, full of the ardor that has no voice, but a hundred times wiser, more centered—and utterly, painfully, mute.

Mindspeak? I hazarded, facing that mute gaze. But I knew it could not be, as indeed it was not. The sylkies' minds were of a different nature from ours, their thoughts swam to truth while ours plodded and crawled.

We turned to go back to our fire. But they stopped us, each of us, with a touch. Out of our depth, awkward and awed, we stood with them as they prepared to honor the white maiden.

They placed all the pelts, their own plus the ones we had given them, fifty or more, in a great, soft pile centered on the beach, the white sealskin on top. And there they laid the dead sea maiden, as if on a bed made of all their lives, her head pillowed on their lives. She lay as gracefully as if she only slept. Then they formed a circle around her, us three mortals among them, and began the magic dance that needs no music but the music of the mind.

Like the waves of the sea they wove the dance, cresting and dipping and cresting again, tossing their heads, white-caps beneath stormwind, flowing together as breakers flow an ebb at the strand, circling past and between one another, ocean swell, intermingling in a pattern beyond my comprehension. Like the serpentine of the sea their arms rose and fell. My skill could not begin to match theirs, and after a few rounds of the dance I stood aside, bidding farewell in my own way to the maiden who had been a white seal, who had saved my life. A soundless farewell, while the dance swirled between us—the half a hundred of the sylkies seemed as vast as the world-sundering ocean.

Kor danced this weaving sea-wave dance better than I, for it was in his blood, that wild grace, But he tired soon, and stood beside me. Tassida joined us, and after a while we walked back up the beach to where our fire had died down to embers and ashes, sat there and watched. The sea folk did not see us go, I felt sure. They were well into the trance of the dance, and I drifted into one too, watching them, their hair billowing and flying like spindrift, the white maiden so still in their midst, ingathered, float-ing. . . . I felt as if I were floating with her—I swayed where I sat, my eyelids closed but the dance circled on in my mind, my dreaming.

Sometime before the moon began to set they took her back to the sea. For when I awoke they and all the pelts were gone.

I awoke when the moon stood high, because Tassida's hand lay on my arm.

Danger, I thought at first. I sat up quickly. But the night was still, and the touch of Tassida's hand steady and soft, and her handsome face sober but not alarmed in the moon-light. Kor lay sleeping beside me, quiet, unmoving. I looked at Tass for a moment, and she answered my gaze. Then I got up and followed her away from where Kor lay.

She took me up beyond the edge of the beach, into the wind-bent spruce woods, along a small trail that followed rock ridges to where her shelter stood. A man-shelter shape in the moonshadow, nothing more . . . She guided me in under the leather flap that closed the door, let it fall behind me. I could not yet believe what was happening.

"Tass?" I whispered, questioning.

Touch of her hand showed me the way. The bed was made of spruce boughs. She had brought furs to lay on it. After she had spread them, she sat there and guided me to the space beside her.

"Tass—" My heart was pounding so, it made a roaring as of stormside surf inside my head. I could say nothing more than her name.

"I should never have touched you," she murmured.

"Tassida?"

"I touched you, to bring you out of your seal form. I thought it was you, shining like sunset, Kor lying beside you, the devourers coming from all directions. I touched you to be sure, helped you both to make the change, and now—"

I understood. My way of becoming a seal had been different from Kor's. "You desire me, as Birc once desired a deer maiden."

"It is more than that. I have always wanted you."

My heart, leaping like wildfire.

"Dan, please. Lie with me. Now, before—before my courage fails me."

"Tass," I breathed, and I did not ask her whether she loved me, then or ever. My love for her filled the night and left no room for any want of my own, except that I wished I could see her.

My Tass, my love. Beloved like no other. A warrior's muscles beneath her smooth skin, but she trembled like a

dove under my hand. My Tass, with the brow of a hero
and sweet virgin breasts . . . Not since I had been a callow
young oaf, myself untried, had I taken a girl's maiden-
head, and I had hurt her. This time I must do better, far
better, for Tass.

Ai, that night. Moment by warm pressing moment I led
her along the soft, venturing ways of love, and when she
hung back I waited for her, I coaxed her. I was the salmon
tide, she, the river. I was rainstorm and she the meadow.
And learning not to be afraid she welcomed me, her
quivering ceased, she gave me her trust, her lips moved
against mine, her hands moved to caress me. She was shy,
bold, awkward, passionate. She was all the world, my
Tass. I could have wept. She was amaranth, the flower of
Sakeema, blossoming for me. . . . I think I have never
been so gentle in lovemaking, so careful yet so ardent. I
played upon her as she might have played upon a harp, I
brought her to song's height, hands on her breasts, she
arched her strong back under me, and when I melted into
her any pain she might have felt was magicked into ecstasy—

Kor was there, with us.

His presence, in my mind. The three of us, together. I
laid my face down on Tassida's shoulder, tears and sweat
on my face, her fingers twined into my hair, my chest
heaving against hers. And now that it was over, I wondered if she truly loved me, but I could not ask, for Kor's
sake. I ached.

"Tass . . ." It was a plea, I hardly knew for what.

"I love you, Dan. Since those first days, I always
have." A catch in her voice that caught at my heart. "I
love you . . . because of the way you love Kor."

His presence, there with us, though his body still lay on
the beach where we had left him, I felt sure of it. We did
not speak further of him, Tass and I, because he was a tale
to which we did not know the ending, a song half-
remembered, a face in the dark.

"So much I love you . . . I am afraid."

For the first time I began to understand her.

"And I love you, I am half-mad with fighting my love for you," I whispered to her. "And I also am afraid. Of you. Of Kor. Tass, what are we going to do?"

Her silence gave me the answer, that there was no answer. I withdrew from her gently and found my clothing, wrapped on my lappet and leggings.

"Dan, stay. Where are you going?" A quiet edge came into her voice. "Are you afraid to sleep here with me?"

There had been no thought in me until then of the matter of Calimir, of how Kor and I had once joked that she was likely to alter a lover in the night.

"Do you wish me to give you my knife?" she asked bitterly. "For safekeeping?"

My hands froze in their motions, and more starkly than ever I wished I could see her face, and she mine. Looking at me, she could have seen better truth.

"Tass," I told her softly, "as far as I am able, I must spare Kor."

"But it is no use trying to hide this from him," she said just as softly. "He will know. I think he knows already. Have you not felt it?"

Her words frightened me anew. "Yes," I said, fear or anger roughening my voice. "Yes, blast it, I felt him. But I am not going to flaunt anything before him."

"Dan—"

"Tass, do not quarrel with me, please!" All seemed to be quarreling, those days, quarreling with the others, quarreling within myself. In my own plea I heard the echo of a madman's roar.

"I will quarrel with you all I want!" she retorted. Then, as if she no longer wanted to be close to me, she found her breeches, her ragged tunic, and slipped outside to put them on. By the time I lifted the leather flap to follow her, she was already striding back toward the beach.

The moon had dropped far down the sky. Night was dying, and seemed very chill after the warmth of her bed. In silence I walked back to our campsite. Tassida was sitting by the embers of the fire and would not look at me. Kor lay wrapped in furs as if asleep. But I knew quite surely that he was not asleep, for I felt his waking presence, as I had sometimes felt it in Mahela's realm. I did not speak to him, or mindspeak, but let him think he was deceiving me. I lay in my bed, huddled in my furs, and did not sleep any more than he did.

In the morning we all three moved about as if in a waking dream, breaking camp. Tassida hailed Calimir with a whistle, and our two mares came loping in after him. They were not pleased to see us, wild things that they were, and we had to offer them cooked meat in order to lay hands on them. We ourselves did not eat. We put leather thongs to the mouths of the mares and rode them bareback, and without much talk we made the short journey to Seal Hold, where Istas lay dying.

Chapter Seventeen

Istas lay rotting away even as she lived.

The reek was awful in her small chamber within the rock. I have a steady stomach for most things, but I could scarcely bear it, or bear to look at her. Trying not to retch, I turned away. Tassida had not come in—she was seeing to the horses. As for Kor, he stood stricken by Istas's deathbed, his face chalk white beneath the bruises. This was the old woman who had mothered and badgered him through his youth, counseled him in his kingship, put on the regent's cap for his sake. She was like parent or grandparent to him, and she was the backbone of Seal Hold. Seeing her laid low staggered him so that he bent as if under a blow.

Dan!

The mindcry was jolted out of him. And though I had been ready to flee the stench of sickness, I could not flee that summons. I reached out to him at once, handbonding, putting my other arm around him to support him. I knew that it was not only the sickroom smell that had made me turn away, that I had been ready to flee his heartache as well, and I was ashamed.

I am sorry, I told him, meaning everything that I could say in so few words—that Tass and I had hurt him, and the death of Istas would hurt him, and there was some dark anger in me bent on hurting him yet more, and for all that and whatever pain might ever befall him I sorrowed. But I think he did not hear what I was saying. He was staring at Istas, stunned, struggling for breath.

She looked back at us with blind, whitened eyes. "No fish," she rasped.

Kor made a wordless, panting noise, which she must have taken for protest. Her head rolled from side to side, the sagging muscles of her neck strained as she tried to lift it from its fleece pillow.

"No fish!" she repeated hoarsely. "No fish for the shitbottom Otters. Ten day—storm . . ."

Her old head lolled back, and her eyes closed, as far as they were able. Even the eyelids were eaten away by the disease, as if Mahela were feeding on her, great glutton, could not wait . . .

"Istas!" Kor pleaded in a choked voice, and leaving my handbond, my steadying arm, he went to her and touched her twisted fingers, then her brow. Istas lay fish-belly pale in the dim chamber, and did not seem to feel him near her. Not yet dead, for I could see her labored breathing, but drawing nearer to death. I could not follow Kor to comfort him. I could not bear to stand so close to her, more horrible than any corpse. But he stayed by her until I felt faint from drowning in her stench. When he left her at last and came with me, we walked back to the hearth hall in a sickened stupor.

Most of Kor's people were there, waiting to speak with us, their numbers fewer than they should have been, their faces somber. Our greeting this time had been tearful, an overgrateful gladness mixed with sorrow.

"How is she?" asked a woman, going back to take up the nursing of Istas. Kor stared dumbly, for how could he answer?

"Now that she has seen you, Korridun King, she will

die soon," said another, as if it would be better so. "Now that she knows you have returned, she will let go."

"What has she told you?" someone asked.

Kor sat woodenly in the king's place of honor by the hearth, without answering at once. "She speaks of fish," he said finally, and many voices spoke, vying to tell him what Istas could not.

It had been a hard winter in many ways. Cold—the deadly, ice-laden fog that chills the lungs had moved in from the sea and hung over Seal Hold, killing the weakly young and the old who were infirm. And to add to the burden of grief, three sturdy babies had been taken without a trace, snatched away by demons in the night. My glance found Winewa in the crowd, but she would not meet my eyes. . . . And then Istas had grown weak and taken to her bed.

"And then the storm," said Kor, his voice low.

Yes, had she spoken of the storm? An unaccountable storm, faster than birdflight it had swooped in from the sea, catching the men out fishing in their coracles, drowning many. Every family of the clan had suffered a loss or losses, this grim winter. And the storm had stayed through days and days, tempest of wind and rain, strange green lightning, fearsome noise, hail the size of hand-flung stones. Those within the stone caves of the Hold had been safe, but there had been no fishing done, only oats to eat and those soon gone, for the crop had been poorly. No peace offering of oats for the Fanged Horse Folk this year. No dried fish for the Otter River Clan.

"Have they asked?"

"They will not dare."

Heads nodded, and many voices agreed, grim. The salmon run had been sparse, they told us. As always. For years within living memory the salmon had been each year less than the last, until the days when the salmon had crowded the banks with their red-flashing numbers belonged to the realm of tales and legend. But this year for the first time the Otter River clanspeople had rebelled against their lot. In their long raiding boats made of hollowed logs they had skimmed the rapids of the river and shot down to the sea. And there, daring each other on with shouts of anger, they had taken clubs and killed the seals on the rocks, nursing mothers and pups. A single night they had feasted on the meat, but they had not been able to take much back with them. They had taken the skins, and the carcasses had been left to rot, to draw flies, to draw the wrath of the Seal fishermen who had found them.

"Brave Otters!" It was a young woman I remembered, Lumai, speaking with bitter contempt. "They might as courageously have killed suckling infants and women helpless in childbed."

It was true. Seals were all but helpless on the rocks, unable to run, their slashing teeth easily avoided. And the killing of the white-furred cubs was an abomination.

"You who have been seals, tell us," someone else asked harshly, "do seals kill so many salmon that the Otter clansfolk should kill them?"

Kor seemed stupefied, as if by too many blows. I answered, "No. Seals eat mainly the small fish that school, the large fish seldom, and salmon no more than the others."

"It was us they killed," said Kor in a low voice.

Everyone looked at him.

"It was us, the Seals, that the Otters killed, do you not see? Because for so many years we have fed them. They hate us."

"If they hate us, my king, it is because of the fosterlings who were slain, Voss and Taditu." A deep, strong man's voice. Olpash. The greedy bastard, get of Mahela, would he never give up trying to best Kor? It was like him, to bring back the matter of the guardsmen I had killed when I was not in my right mind. There had been bitter feelings against Kor because he had shown mercy to me. Olpash, playing for power, would have liked to bring back those feelings.

Kor straightened where he sat, and though he did not raise his voice his words struck like stones.

"Already sharpening your knife, Olpash?" He speared the stocky man with his gaze. There was not a sound in the hall, not even from children. Everyone heard. "Can you not wait a few weeks to kill me and take my place? I have only just returned, after all. Istas still lies dying, and she is my regent. If she does not die in time for you, will you feel obliged to kill her too?"

Olpash rose with a showing of stiff dignity and wrath restrained. With a mind, also, I thought, to displaying his bearlike bulk before all present. Standing, he hoped to make the seated king look smaller. "A question not deserving of an answer," he growled. "I—"

"You are a strutting scoundrel. And you are going to be disappointed, Olpash." Kor also got to his feet, and the smoldering fire of his wrath showed Olpash's bluster for what it was: a schemer's ploy. But Kor spoke from the heart. "No longer will I bear with your mutterings, my people. No longer will I be a king for you to humble when it pleases you. You must be led, and follow with one heart, if we are to survive the time that faces us. And I will no longer keep the vigil you have heretofore required of me. I have ventured to Mahela's realm and returned, and that is proving enough for anyone. Even a Seal king."

Some few hundred still faces turned toward him, eyes on him, no sound from any of them, not even a murmur, not even from Olpash.

Tassida had come in while he spoke, and stood at his side, by his right hand. And seeing her, I had risen to stand at his left.

"The Fanged Horse Folk will raid us for what little we have left," Kor said, speaking to his people, ignoring

Olpash. "And likely the Otter River Clan will make war on us as well. But we will withstand them all."

His face, battered, lean from hardship, his eyes, keen and weary and hard, the eyes of a war leader—he was a king. I had forgotten how he could be a king to die for, to walk through fire for.

He drew his sword, and as if at one with him Tass and I drew ours.

"We will withstand them all, and Mahela's hell, and whatever evils may befall. Together." Kor spoke so fiercely, I knew he held back tears.

He raised his blade high above his head. We two, his comrades, raised ours and touched them to his. And where the three swords crossed, starform, there blazed out a light fit to dim the rising sun, white as starlight and dartling, giving off spears of white sheen. The stones in the pommels shone as well, red and sun-yellow and amaranthine. Faces gaped up, pallid. Olpash staggered back and sank down, missing his seat, falling to the stone floor.

"We three together make a multitude," Kor said.

Swordlight flared once so brightly that people hid their faces with their hands. Even Kor narrowed his eyes, and I blinked. Then light dimmed, and shakily I lowered my blade like the others and sheathed her.

Fear showed in the eyes of the Seal people, but also wonder and a hesitant hope. They went out to their many tasks, mending their broken boats and building new coracles for fishing in, trying to gather some sort of food to subsist on meanwhile. And they went the more readily now that they had much to talk of. Tassida watched them with a small frown.

"Your folk are like great children, Kor," she said softly. "I love them as if they were my own children. They think we have come to save them from whatever threatens them. They dream that not even Mahela can harm them so long as they shelter under your sword."

He let out his breath between his teeth, turning away from both of us. "Just so they do what we say," he muttered, and he strode out. I was left looking at Tassida.

"Something is wrong," I said to her, "and I do not know the name of it." She nodded, but she gave me no answer.

I found my arrows and bow and went up through the blue pines to hunt meat for the horses and for Kor's people. By my mother's bones, but it was good to be back in a place of sunlight and trees and sweet air again. The tiny nodding lilies of many colors were struggling up in the cracks of the rocks, amidst moss and ferns, their stems so slender they made my heart ache. Looking at them, I walked for a goodly distance before I missed birdsong. Then I stopped and listened. I heard nothing but choughs and sorrowdoves. The day was chill for springtime, but more birds should have been singing. . . . And I had seen no game, or any sign of game. And already I was tired.

I went on nevertheless, much farther, and at last I found a small herd of wild pigs, foul, fierce creatures, and shot more than I could well carry. I set two on my shoulders and dragged the others. By the time I came back to Seal Hold it was nearly dark, and I was ready to fall and dripping with sweat even in the chill. Kor's folk made much of me, as if I had saved their lives, forsooth! The pigs were butchered, and the offal went to the horses.

"Game is scarce," I told Kor.

"So my people say." His voice sounded dead.

I ate little, and left the hearth hall early, found my chamber and fell asleep at once, I was so spent. When I awoke in the morning Tassida lay beside me.

"Where is your knife?" I teased her.

"I have had no need of it. You were too tired."

Had she forgiven me? I could scarcely tell. But I kissed

her, held her close to me for a while, and then we went out, for there was much to be done.

Kor had gathered his people on the windy, rocky brow of the headland, and he was dividing them into groups: the old men and boys who must go fish in the remaining boats, the matrons and children who could cook and gather and nurse Istas, the youths who must prepare for war. He himself would drill them.

"Dan, if you could bring in more game . . . I hate to send you off by yourself, but I can spare no one to go with you."

I nodded.

"And make us some babies, Dannoc," some youth from the crowd called, "to increase our number."

A quick splash of laughter—even Winewa smiled. But Kor did not smile. And conscious of Tassida, I may have winced.

"Tass," Kor said.

He put her in charge of the maidens and younger women, to teach them the ways of weapons. A murmur of dismay rose from the grayheads at that. Young women of the Otter and Red Hart fought and hunted beside their men, but not those of the Seal, forsooth! Still, they turned away, and there would have been no more said had not Olpash, always on the lookout for advantage, thrust himself forward.

"My king, we are the people of Sedna here, not raiders!" he declaimed, puffing out his massive chest. "Our maidens have been gently reared!"

"And they will be far less gently killed or captured, unless we manage to hold Pajlat off."

"No true king of the Seal Kindred would devise such means! Or bear such an uncouth weapon." Olpash's voice deepened, because for once he was speaking truth as he saw it. "Or fail to keep vigil."

Kor stepped toward him with flashing eyes, and though

Olpash held his ground the onlookers, every Seal of them, shrank back.

"No more vigils, Olpash," said Kor softly, with a softness fit to chill the marrow, for there was fury leashed in that low voice. "No more cowards' games. If you wish to fight me, you must do it in daylight, here, in the clearing, where everyone can see. Now. Or else hold your peace henceforth."

The man shook where he stood, his heavy chin jerking, more from rage than from fear, I thought. He did not give way.

"You are a mighty fighter, Olpash. The Seal Kindred will have need of you when the raiders come." Tone belied the sense of what he was saying—Kor was forcing himself to be fair, but hatred darkened the words, anger lurked dark like a storm just below the horizon. "We must be as one, that fell day. Draw your knife now, or never more against me."

The watching folk had gone deathly silent. Olpash did not move except to quake with wrath.

"Is it peace, then? Or have you neglected to sharpen your blade? I would have sworn you had it ready."

Olpash snatched out the blackstone weapon. "By Sedna's memory, I will fight you," he cried wildly, "to show you for what you are. Though I bear no chance against you and your demon helpers."

"The devourers?" Kor laughed aloud, though it was not a good laugh. Too much bitterness in him for that. "Or do you refer to Dan and Tass, here?"

"Great knives that shine . . ." Olpash spoke between clenched teeth, already crouched for the combat, his short stone blade at the ready.

"But of course I will put off my 'uncouth weapon.' " Kor turned his back on Olpash to show his contempt and came over to me, speaking to Zaneb, then giving her to me to hold—the sword sullenly bore the touch of my hand, since he had willed it. Kor drew his own blackstone blade. A murmur sounded among the crowd of his people, more dismay in it than excitement, for these were gentle folk. I also was dismayed.

"Kor, you are not yet strong. Be careful!"

"That one first came against me when I was a lad of thirteen, and far weaker than I am now." Fury plain and open now, no longer held in check, and at the sound of his voice all his people froze to silence, all heard. "I outwitted him then, and many times thereafter. I do not fear him now."

With a stone knife in hand he went to combat Olpash.

"This is ill," I muttered to Tassida, though I scarcely knew why. Surely a king must protect his kingship. Olpash had been a threat for years, and never more so than now, when all of Kor's folk had to walk as one if they were to survive. Time was when I would have urged him toward this very course. But holding Zaneb in my hands, watching Kor walk catlike away from me, I felt the sense of something deeply wrong.

"Ill enough," Tass softly agreed, though perhaps her reasons were her own. "If it should go against him—"

"Honor be damned, I will aid him, with Alar if need be." Ass though he was, I thought savagely.

At a span of ten paces from Olpash he stopped and stood straddle-legged, proudly erect, head high, letting Olpash make the attack.

"Fool!" I whispered to Tass. "Arrogant fool!"

The man very nearly toppled him with his bearlike rush. Olpash was no slackard as a fighter, far faster than I would have expected of him. A jabbing upward knife stroke speared straight toward Kor's gut at the juncture of the ribs. I could almost feel it in my own clenched body, I almost cried aloud. But lithe as a seal, as if he could yet swim where the rest of us merely plodded and trod, Kor had slipped aside. His knife, trailing him almost absently, a winking black bubble in his wake, slashed across Olpash's upper arm and left a long streak of red.

A roar went up. First blood to Kor.

I think I have never seen a man so enraged as was Olpash that day. He fought with crushing force. And there is no fairness in such combat—they strove with fists, feet, even with teeth—I would not have cared to face him. He ranted aloud, swearing mighty oaths by Sedna and Sakeema and Mahela, shouting—but soon Olpash had little time to shout. He panted instead. Kor was making a fool of him, and the onlookers had ceased to roar.

Kor was cool—no, cold, full of hate, full of the icy anger that is more fearsome than any rage. I do not know how many times he let Olpash rush him—ten, twenty, more. And as many times he slashed him, eluding him in as many different ways. It was a combat of speed, whirlwind strokes that blurred the sight until at last Olpash had weakened and slowed somewhat from sheer bloodshed. And still Kor stood in front of him and baited him. Olpash reeled, his mouth hanging slack, the folds of his face wet with sweat, staring stupidly with pain and exhaustion, and still in a blundering way he charged. But Kor's face was calm and mocking.

"Blood of Sakeema, Kor," I shouted suddenly, "have done!" I felt sickened, and nearly ready to aid Olpash instead of Kor, and I half hoped—

But no. Kor moved in to strike at his enemy in earnest, and though Olpash scarcely seemed to know anymore where he was or what he was doing, still his strong legs bore him up. Kor felled him, finally, as the woodcutter fells a thick tree or as sea hunters kill a whale, with many blows. Upward jabs to the gut, sideward blows that forced the knife between the ribs. With one hand he held off Olpash's weapon, not even looking at it. Nor, I noted, did he look long at the man's contorted face . . . Olpash was dead, I think, before he finally toppled to the ground. But

Kor crouched beside him to slit his throat, then stayed there as if he would never move again.

I had cared nothing for Olpash, but such a nameless heartache was in me that I did not move. I stood where I was, with Zaneb in my hand, and it was Tass who went over to Kor, put her arms around him and helped or urged him to his feet. As he got up, I saw that his cold wrath had left him. He was shaken, trembling and pale.

His people, silent, stared at him in some sort of expectation. Somewhere a widow sobbed.

"This contentious fool has cost us much," Kor said, utter weariness in his voice. "And the day that must be spent to lay him to rest is the least of it." He turned his back in dismissal, walking slowly over to me.

I silently gave him back his sword. Only after his people had scattered toward their work or gone off in anxious clusters did I speak.

"What has become of mercy?" I demanded, keeping my voice low.

Tassida still kept her arms around him, steadying him. She loved him too, I knew, as I had always known she must—how could she not love him? But I did not take time for jealousy. Worse trouble was in me.

"Tell me of mercy, Dan." Kor leveled a stare at me, his tone as hard as his gaze. But I was not to be put off.

"You, who let me live when I was a murderer, now you have killed this one—"

"Who has so often tried to kill me."

"—who for so long you let live! You, who taught me the meaning of mercy. And you took pleasure in it. Kor, you have changed so, I scarcely know you."

"Must there be no pleasure in duty? I did as a king must do."

A king. I had known a king, once, my father, who had changed. A chill as of death, Mahela's touch, crawled through me, and I felt like backing away.

"What has happened?" I whispered. "Have you let a devourer into you?"

"Slit me open and find out!" He laughed with no mirth. "No, Dan. But I have let myself into a devourer. The many times in the one chill night. Mahela has happened."

Some of the Seal folk had caught wind of conflict, as folk will. A few of them had gathered at a small distance, listening, watching while pretending not to watch. I did not care, angry, afraid, betrayed as I felt. He was . . . not Sakeema. He was . . . not even Kor.

"Will you kill me next, then?" I challenged, my voice rising to hold at bay my fear.

You speak of mercy, Dan. Show some. Must you rail at me before my folk? What has become of mindbond?

Mindspeak, he meant—or had he meant that? I stood stricken, unable to answer him either aloud or mind-speaking. I had not mindspoken him much of late, I had not wanted to, and now I felt as if I could not. I stood in horror of him. A devourer took the heart, but mind was left, mind could yet call me. . . .

I turned away from him and fled to the forest. Only because I did not care to admit that I was fleeing did I take my arrows and bow, telling myself I was off in search of game.

Chapter Eighteen

Istas died three days later. Like Olpash, she was laid in a deep cave beneath the headland: bathed and scented with oil and herbs, then clothed and taken down the cliffside amidst weeping and left in the darkness. There was no feast held for the passing of her spirit. There had been none, either, for Olpash. In his case, it had been said that he died in disgrace, that he deserved none. Once the first shock was past, Kor's folk admired their king, most of them, for what he had done. Here was a strong ruler, a savior. No feast for Olpash. But it could not be said that Istas had died in disgrace—no elder of the tribe was more loved. Truth had to be faced that there was no food for feasting, and all my hunting had brought down only a few netted doves and some marmots snared atop the scree.

The evening of that day, after Istas had been left in the abode of the dead, after the meager meal had been eaten and most folk were abed, I was wandering and found Kor standing in a passageway, his face hidden in the collar of Tassida's tunic, weeping, or having wept, her arms around him. I was glad of it, for I had known Kor would be in need of comfort, and I had not felt able to give it to him. I turned away without speaking and left them.

Later, Tass came and lay with me, not for the first time

217

since we had taken up abode in Seal Hold. Silent and proud, as always, she came to me, young warrior that she was. No flirtation in Tass, no giggling behind soft hands, no teasing. Gravely she gave herself to me. Ai, Tass . . . Those days were both a bliss and a misery to me. Bliss, when I held her. As long as the night lasted and we were together, I knew that we would love one another forever. Truly forever. I had never felt that of any other woman.

But daytimes, often as not, she would greet me coolly. She would pass me as if she scarcely knew me, avoiding my eyes.

"Why, Tass?" I asked her softly in the dark hour before dawn, when she rose silently to leave me again. "Are you ashamed? Tarry awhile, come to the morning meal with me."

I could not see her, but I heard unease in her voice as she whispered, "I cannot."

"Why?" I reached for her hand, not finding it in the darkness.

"It is not fitting. All around us, nothing but dying."

I understood, I had seen that misery. It was not only Istas. Everyone in Seal Hold was in mourning for someone. And there would be war, and more dying—every day the youths and young women trained for war. It was a springtime full of dying. Wildflowers everywhere, so dainty, seemingly so frail, but few birds flying, few creatures afoot, scarcely a deer anywhere, scarcely a fawn. Few nests, no birdsong.

"We will defy it," I said fiercely. But even as I spoke a scream shattered my words, a woman's scream that must still echo somewhere, the terrible sorrow of it. I scrambled up and fumbled on some clothing—Tass was already gone, the Hold in a babble, scream after scream sounding, then sobbing. When I blundered out I saw the mother with empty arms. Another child had vanished in the night.

There was nothing I could do or say. These were not my

people after all, and I felt the stranger among them. I went out and netted cormorants for the horses, watched numbly as they rent the scrawny birds, more feathers to them than flesh. The steeds were growing thin. It must be better elsewhere, I told myself. It must be better in the Red Hart Demesne. I longed to be there, to see how my people fared, to talk with my brother Tyee.

Misery only increased as the days went by, because of Kor.

This stranger, my bond brother, what was wrong with him? The first few days back at Seal Hold, harsh and grim as he had been, he had at least seemed to care. Now even that dark caring had left him. He moved through his days like someone dead at heart, like one of Mahela's pet persons going to pay court. He ate little, never smiled, and seldom spoke, though I spoke to him sometimes, trying to rouse him, exhorting him. To no avail. He scarcely replied to me, whether I joked, prodded, or lashed out at him in anger. As days went by, he did less, and often sat idle in the dim hearth hall, staring, his face hardened into a mask.

"What ails him?" I appealed to Tass.

"He is mourning Istas. Time will bring him back to us," Tass said, but so slowly that I knew she was not at all sure, that the silent, angry stranger frightened her as much as he did me.

And except for Tass—and her only at nighttime—I did not know anything anymore. I did not know what to do about Kor, or about the dying everywhere. I did not know what I was about, why I stayed at Seal Hold when I longed to be back in the deer meadows and hemlock forests of my people. I no longer knew who Kor was, that I should follow him, since he was not Sakeema. . . . All I knew was that Tass was with me, in her way, and she had said that we three ought to stay together.

So I floundered on through that coldest of all springs, until the day the storm broke.

I saw it first, from an outlook far up the spruce steeps, a dense black line of cloud pushing over the western horizon. It was dawn of another gray day, the men below were just getting the coracles into the water—enough were finally mended or built anew, now, that at last the fishermen were bringing in fish worth mentioning. I hailed them with a loud whistle, swung my arms like a madman when they looked at me, gesturing them to stay. They waited by their boats, and I ran or slid down to them, told them what I had seen. These were the old men and the striplings, and though the boys merely looked excited, the faces of the elders turned bleak and gray as the day. They questioned me, they peered anxiously out over the sea—no storm was yet to be seen from their low vantage on the beach.

"It sounds just like the last one," one of them declared. "Black as Mahela's heart, and no warning."

"Not even the thrushes to sing it in."

"That last black storm, Dannoc, it came on so fast that we could not make shore once we had sighted it, even though we were out no farther than—" The man pointed. "—than yon bobbing gull."

"I hate to play the coward's part," said another, sounding not at all certain, "and we need the fish—"

"Ai, we could stay ashore all day, and it could sail by and make proper fools of us."

"Or we could go out," said the one who had spoken first, "and it could strike and shatter us."

A youngster gave a shout: the first finger of black was edging above the horizon. All the men took a step back from it, their faces ashen.

"Let's get the boats up the headland," I snapped. "You," I ordered the stripling, "go tell Korridun."

He stared back at me, looking more frightened of Kor than he had been of the storm.

"Very well, I'll go tell him myself!" I swung one of the leather-covered boats onto my back and head, then ran as best I could under the burden, taking it up the steep cliffside trail, across the windy brow of the headland and right into the Hold, into the feasting hall, where I set it down. There, at least, lay one coracle the waves would not smash.

Kor was sitting in the shadows, his face blank.

"One of those hellish storms of Mahela's making is coming this way," I told him. "Like a black hand reaching over the sea's edge."

His glance shifted toward me for a moment, then away. He said nothing. He did not move.

"Can we bring in the horses, think you?"

"It's no use," he muttered. "No one can withstand Mahela's hand."

"We can at least try!"

"She is stronger," he said dully. "It is no use trying."

I glared at him and strode out. Tass and the young women were on the clearing, drilling. I shouted at them, "Storm coming!"

They looked up and gasped. Cloud was curling across the sky like black smoke. Already lightning could be seen.

"Gather the children, get them into the Hold!" I ordered. "Some of you help the men bring the boats up!"

The women scattered, at the run, in all directions. Coracles were coming up over the edge of the cliff, the men, young men now as well as the old, struggling under them. I ran to help.

"Take them right into the Hold, into the hearth hall!"

A hand grasped my arm from behind, flung me around with surprising force. Blinking, I faced Kor, and his eyes were ablaze with rage.

"What, are you taking the place of Olpash, now? I will give the orders among my own people!"

Men hurried past us without looking at us, bringing up the boats.

"Then give them!" I shot back. "But no, you would rather sit in a twilight place—"

Wind struck, swaying us both. Beyond us, everyone was running for the Hold. And I stood shouting at Kor, a torrent and a tempest of anger pouring out of me—I had not known it was in me, so much black anger, sudden as the storm, louder and more furious than the wind.

"You defeated King! All the great things I had thought of you, and now you have given up! You coward, fleeing Mahela's realm like a kicked cur! No mercy in you for a petty mortal enemy, no, but you did not kill her, the great glutton who eats us all, even when she lay sleeping under your hand!"

"What, slay the only woman who has ever preferred me to you?" Kor gave a low, hard laugh, more dangerous than a shout. "Jealous still, Dan? Still wishing you had taken her?"

He had nearly passed into nothingness, bedding her. An image flickered like lightning through my mind of how he had looked after coming back from the Mountains of Doom, bruised face, bleak eyes—it agonized me, and made me cruel.

"Coward! Could not wait to flee! You left your own mother there, whom we had come to save, and my—my father, there, in that deathly place, forever! You betrayer—" I broke off, sobbing with fury, but Kor was as cold as Mahela's chill sea.

"I should have left you there as well."

I struck out at him with my fist, but someone caught hold of my arm—it was Tass. I shook her off, raging at Kor.

"Thrice a betrayer, then! And you would have done it, if it were not for Kela!"

"Yes!" Heat, now, and words like a sword's edge. "I would have. To survive."

Words not spoken merely to hurt me, but fire true—I

could sense that, a truth that stunned me. That at the time had hurt him to the heart. But he had built his barriers now, and found himself a hard shield. Tass was trying to speak to me—I could not hear her.

"If you were not so pitiful, I would kill you, Kor!" I could not believe what I was saying, but anger was shattering my heart, words flying like wildfire spark. "Betrayer, you—you limp thing, flattened to the sand by a storm! You wretch! Creeping into your dim den, licking your wounds! No use, you say, Mahela is stronger! Do you not have the courage to defy Mahela, old cormorant, old glutton woman? You, the great Rad Korridun, noble king, full of wisdom and mercy! Korridun, who comes back from the dead! What is the good of you? Survive, you say! The whole mortal world is dying around us, and will you not lift a hand to save it?"

I had broken through his flinty shield. His face was contorted, mouth curled in rage and a terrible sorrow. "I am not Sakeema!" he cried.

"I know that now!"

I spent all my anger and bitterness in that last, and in half a breathspan I would have called it back if I could have, for it hit him hard—I could see that by the way he became suddenly very still as the storm loomed over us, lightning flaring. Tassida stood beside us, a hand on either of us, trying to coax us into the Hold. But we were not moving. Rumble of thunder, and far below us I could hear the roaring of the surf.

"All the time we were seals together," Kor said softly, so softly I could scarcely hear him above the wash of wind, "all the time we were in the sea, and in Mahela's realm, and storm-beaten on the way back, I was heartsore, Dan, fearing you would be bound by your sea-maiden lover and would never again be able to speak aloud. When you left the sea and spoke and came with me again as my comrade, it was—it was the only right thing happening in the world. And now I wish you had been made mute."

My heart hurt so, I would have said nothing more. Tassida stood with one arm across my shoulders, one across Kor's. "Leave it," she urged. "Come in, before you are swept away." And I would have been glad enough to go with her. But Kor could be as cruel as I.

"Go ahead, Dan," he said, his voice very low. "Take her to your chamber. Tass, the only woman I have ever loved. Or perhaps, if the Hold is too crowded for your sport, you could entice her back to her hut near the Greenstones. You could whisper her name and wish you could see her face—"

He had been there. Inside my mind.

Time seemed to flow together for me. A year was gone as if it had never been. I was a wounded youth again, bereft, betrayed, maddened by the one who stood before me.

"Draw!" I commanded, my voice grating. "Draw your weapon!" My hand grasped at the pommel of my own sword.

"Gladly!" Kor reached for his. Tassida stepped between us and pushed us apart so that we staggered backward.

"No!" she cried, her beautiful face full of horror. But then she stared, turning from one of us to the other, and then she began to laugh.

Our swords would not obey us.

Kor and I stood struggling with the stubborn hilts, red-faced and enraged, grimacing with rage. The weapons would not let themselves be drawn from the scabbards. Tass stood laughing, too loud a laugh, too shrill, as if the strain had been too great for her, and she started to say what Kor and I both knew and would not admit. The words came out choked by her frantic laughter.

"They will not strike—the ones you love—"

Kor glanced at her, a single angry look, and something

passed between them. Her laughter left her within a breath—
terror took its place, opening her dark eyes wide with
terror, pulling her lovely boyish face taut with a terrible
fear. Without a word she turned and ran to the ruined
lodge where Calimir awaited her. I heard the hoofbeats as
she rode the gelding away at the hard gallop, leaving us,
as she had sworn she would never leave us again. She
would be back, I thought. She had always come back to us
before.

"What did you do to her?" I shouted at Kor.

"I mindspoke her." Stonily. I could imagine what he
had called her, but the mindspeaking itself was worse, to
one like Tass.

"Son of a whore! You piss-proud, jealous worm! You
might as kindly have raped her, and had it done with!" I
lunged at him.

He met me without so much as a side step. The clash
sent us both thudding down, sprawling beneath a black
sky. We grappled, bruising each other against rocks, slipping on moss. A lashing rain had started down, the wind
howled like a demon dream, and I was intent on hurting
my bond brother—atop him, cuffing the side of his face,
fervid. In the next moment he had his hands to my throat,
pushing me back, and his knee caught me in the gut.

In no way can it be said that I thrashed Kor that day—he
gave as good as he got, blast him. Whatever advantage of
weight and rage I had, I met something just as strong and
desperate in him. . . . He blackened both my eyes. He
nearly broke my arm. I freed myself with a swinging fist,
blow fit to fell a horse had it landed—he ducked beneath
it. Frustration only angered me the more. He rammed his
head into my ribs. Pain only angered me the more.

No combat of speed and wit, this one, not much like
Kor's fight with Olpash. We could not keep our footing,
we slithered about like undersea creatures, Kor and I, as
wind screamed and the rain streamed down. We strained

against each other, and cursed each other by names unthought-of before the day, and all seemed dimmed and blurred by storm, or perhaps by sweat and blood and tears drowned in storm. . . . I remember my elbow, my fist thudding into Kor's face. I wanted to punish him—I thought I wanted to kill him, but why then did I not draw the stone hunting knife at my belt? Was honor such a great thing to a madman, that I would not draw because he wore none? He had worn none since the day Olpash died.

I had Kor down, I was jerking his head back by his forelock of sodden brown hair, and instead of kneeing me in the gut again he reached across me and drew the stone knife from its sheath, held it before my crazed eyes, gravely offering it to me.

"Slice me open," he challenged, "and see what my insides are made of."

"Do it yourself!" I snapped. I banged his head against the rock, then got up, reaching for his torn tunic to drag him up after me—he scrambled away and got to his feet before I could touch him. At the crest of the headland he stood, under a sky gone mad, gripping the knife and glaring at me.

"Go ahead!" I called across the small distance, over the raging of the storm. "Stick it into yourself! Poor thing, you!" I was panting with passion and the rigors of the fight, and if there were tears on my face it did not matter, he would not see them, I was awash with rain. "Go ahead!" I urged. "Where is your own knife? You have put it away somewhere? Are you afraid of what you might do to yourself with it, wretch that you have become?"

He stood too still—for a moment I was truly afraid. Then with a wordless yell of fury he coiled and threw the thing at me. Or by me—it flew far wide.

Out of the black mouth of the storm above us came the sound of a woman's wild laughter, fit for a cormorant if the ugly things could laugh. I gaped upward into a sky nearly as dark as nightfall. Glimmer and ripple of gray amidst the gloom—devourers there, snaking with the wind.

"Sakeema!" I shouted toward the sky, the name half a blasphemous curse, half a plea. "The whole world is coming apart in shards, and can you do nothing?" My voice had gone so high that like a stripling's it cracked.

Kor stood before me, and with a blow of his curled fist he struck my nose, hard, breaking it. Blood splattered down—even the pouring rain could not wash away all of it.

"If you have thought I was a god, it was your own folly!" he screamed at me. Truly screamed, his face was twisted awry, he was sobbing. "I have told you a hundred times, I am not—our savior."

I stood and let the blood thicken on my face, too weary any longer to strike back at him. Weariness not of body. After a moment I turned away, went and found my knife, sheathed it. Devourers circled overhead. I cared nothing for them.

"I am not Sakeema," Kor said. That same utter weariness in him now, deadening his voice—he was done with weeping. I faced him.

"Then I had better go find him and awaken him, wherever he sleeps." Curse my betraying voice, that needs must shake. "For no one less can save us now. Even the peeping frogs, gone. The whole world sucked toward Mahela's maw."

No longer would I lament and plead, "Sakeema, come back to me." I would go to him, seek him until I had found him, shake him into wakefulness, cudgel him awake if need be.

As for Kor—I had to leave him. To survive.

I started toward the makeshift pen where Talu was kept, then stopped and looked around for Kor. He had sunk down on the rocky brow of the headland and lay there on his back, legs together and arms outspread, straight and still, facing the glare of green lightning in the sky.

"Get into the Hold," I called to him.

He did not answer. I walked over to him, and his eyes stared up at me, stubborn, unblinking.

"Get into the Hold," I told him. "Mahela's minions are out here."

"I don't care," he said.

"Some others care!"

"So drag me there if you like." His face, like the rest of him, lay very hard and still. Only a distant smoldering showed in his eyes. Then he closed them as if to rest. "Go away. I am tired."

I stood, angry again, wanting to jerk him to his feet and shake him, wanting to drag him into the Hold as he had said, my hands trembling with the force of my desire to make him care, make him be Kor again, and a hero—and knowing full well, as he knew also, that if I touched him I would stay with him.

Sharply I turned away from him and strode toward Talu.

The fanged mares were wild with fear of the storm, thunder fit to crack stone, lightning close as sparrowflight overhead. They were lathered like the sea, crashing around the narrow pen. I could not constrain Talu to stand for me—I caught hold of her as she spun by, and only by reckless risk was I able to get on her and out of the ruined lodge where she was kept. Then in great leaps she fled like the wild thing she was, and I clung to her thin mane. No sort of headstall on her—there had not been time for that, or time to fetch my bow, or a deerskin to sleep in, or food, or gear of any kind. If I had stayed a moment longer, time to see Kor's face once more, I would not have been able to leave, perhaps not ever.

Talu bore me off eastward, any trail that would take her inland and away from the black storm of Mahela's sending. Panicked, up slopes so steep that her hooves slithered and clawed, over perilous rocks, past—laughter, and a grinning face in the lightning glare. Ytan was there, standing in the storm on the mountainside, laughing at me like a demon double of myself as Talu carried me by him. I shivered as if I had seen my own pale corpse in that green-tinged flesh. And Talu swept like a pounding tempest up the crags, and I closed my eyes—I was helpless, a nuisance clinging to her back, a gnat tangled in her mane. Sky was as vast as the sea, and storm filled the sky, and I was nothing.

Sakeema help me, I had left my bond brother lying under the lash of the storm.

Chapter Nineteen

Talu carried me until she was as spent as the day. Hard to remember that it was day, it seemed so dark. . . . When she slowed her pace and I stumbled off her at last, I was far up the flanks of the mountains, though I did not know just where. There was no food, nor did I try to set snares, for my mind was in a tempest worse than Mahela's storm. I sat through the night without a fire, keeping vigil as if for someone dead.

Cold. . . . I remembered the vigil on the Greenstones, for I felt nearly as cold as I had been then. And nearly as wet. Talu had carried me out of the rain, but a chill wind was blowing, and everything was sodden, for this was the region of cascades, where fogs and spring dew drenched the nights. Still, I might have been able to make a fire had I used skill and tried, but I did not try. I sat shivering, my back against cold rock, thinking back to yet another vigil, when I had sat through a night and held Kor while he slept, afraid to let go of him lest he turn dead again. He had died for my sake, and folk said I had wept him back to life. . . .

A hunchbacked moon swam above the spires of the firs. Off to the westward somewhere, thunder still rumbled. Within my mind I seemed again to see Kor lying on the headland, arms outstretched as if he were staked there for torture, under the greenish lightning, and I threw back my head and howled aloud in sorrow.

On toward dawn the tempest inside me slowed its whirling somewhat and I was able to think. Nor was I entirely startled when a gray, shimmering shadow moved in the night. Eyes glowed red. The wolf sat just at the limit of sight and looked at me, tongue lolling as if it had run hard.

"Old friend, wild brother," I whispered, "I am in need of warmth. Let me borrow some from your fur. Come here to me, please."

The wolf came closer, but not close enough. It sat down a small distance beyond my feet, near the edge of my rocky ledge, then turned around three times and lay down, curling so that the graysheen flow of its tail covered its nose. Wary eyes watched me, and I did not dare draw near. I sat trembling and thinking.

Dawn was a long time in reaching over the mountains. Somewhere, I knew, the sun shone as yellow as a catamount's eye, but I could not see it. Eastward the sky turned from black to gray, and then a lighter gloom. And that was all.

"I should go back," I said to the wolf.

Head still flattened to the ground, it stared up at me with a look I could not comprehend. Something in that stare seemed to remember back to Sakeema's time, both warm and distant.

"I should go back," I repeated. "Kor needs me more now than ever."

A snorting noise, and the hollow clap of hoof on rock. Talu plodded along the ledge toward me, pink innards of something she had been eating trailing from her mouth. I got up in protest as she stood over me.

"I don't know what to do," I told her.

She stared back flatly, chewing. The gray-pink length of gut slipped slowly up into her mouth and vanished. I had seen Calimir do the same, sometimes, with a stalk of something green. I looked into her large, blank eye, into the blue-tinged depths of it, as if into a abyss.

"I am Kor's friend," I told her desperately. "More than friend. His bond brother. He needs me. . . ." And I knew with a pang, though I would not say it, that I wanted to be with him. More than anything I wanted that, except this: that I wanted my world to be well.

"But if I stay with him there in Seal Hold, then what hope is there for any of us?"

The wolf got up, shook its fur into place, tilted its head and eyed me in some sort of expectation. Anguished, I held my hand to my mouth, bit on my knuckles.

"Sakeema give me strength . . . I must go back."

I dragged myself onto Talu, turned her toward the west, and closed my eyes, for going down this sort of terrain was even worse than coming up it. Easier to shut my eyes. They were swollen almost shut, anyway. Sometimes I opened them just a slit to look, then regretted it. Once I saw a graysheen flash. Off to one side, the wolf was trotting along with us.

It would take all day, I knew, to come to Seal Hold. I let my body rock to the jouncing of Talu's stiff-legged walk, hanging on, putting thought aside for the time. No use, now, thinking of the choice I would soon have to make: whether I was going back to stay, or only to say a decent farewell. . . .

Talu's head came up, jarring me alert. Her ears pricked forward, she blew through her nostrils and started into a pounding trot over scree. I was too startled to try to stop her. For at the same moment I had felt—

Kor! I was so taken aback, I mindspoke him as of old.

Dan! Brother, I am here.

On Sora, he cantered around the hip of the mountain, meeting me at the edge of the scree. The two fanged mares stopped, head to head, whickering, and Kor and I sat on them in a foolish, staring trance.

He was sight enough to make anyone stare. His face was bruised and cut, a long, scraping cut running along one temple. The eye on that side was swollen almost shut. Worse than the bruises was the struggling look about him, the way he carried himself, as if he were burdened almost beyond bearing. But he was no longer utterly defeated, and no longer out of his mind with anger at me. Kor, my bond brother still, he was there.

"You are back," I whispered.

"Great Sakeema," he exclaimed at the same time, "your face!"

"No worse than yours," I retorted. Only that quip kept me from weeping. I felt so weak with relief and sorrow that I had to lean forward and brace my hands against Talu's crest.

"It's far worse! You're all blood." He slid off Sora, came over to stand by my knee. "Body of Sedna," he murmured in awe, "I've broken your nose."

"So you've changed my good looks," I grumbled. "No more easy maidens for me." I was shaking, and trying to hide it.

"Deep scats, Dan, you are an ass."

I blundered off the horse and embraced him, staggering, trying not to lean against him. "You're another," I told him fervently.

"You think I don't know it? Here, sit down before you fall down."

He had brought food. Not much, but as much as Seal Hold could spare in those worst of all times: some bits of cold fish, last year's dried berries, a handful of precious oats. I sat under a massive blue pine and ate. My shaking stopped, though I think I drew strength more from his presence than from the meager food. He slung a pair of cedar bark bags off Sora while I ate, stripped the gear off the mare, and turned her loose to hunt snakes in the scree with Talu. He gathered some deadwood for a fire, scraped clear a space for it, and made a ring of stones. There would be no hurry, I saw, about leaving this place among the blue pines. Kor brought cones and punkwood, set to work with his firebow. When smoke had turned to sparks and flame, finally, he sat beside me.

"I should have brought you dry clothing," he said.

"No need." The food, the warmth of the fire, the warmth of his words were enough. We watched in silence as the flames took hold. I had been riding longer than I thought—already day was drawing on toward nightfall.

"You were right about Olpash," Kor said after a while in a low voice. "His face troubles my sleep."

"No need, Kor!"

"I would like to try to understand what happened."

"About Olpash?" There was more, I knew, far more, but better to grapple with one thing at a time. "It was not wrong, Kor, that you killed him. Kings must protect their power from schemers. It was only—wrong for you."

"Wrong for Sakeema?"

"Blasphemy!" I teased. "No. Wrong for you. Kor. My friend. Bond brother." I reached out toward him. Fingertips met, and despite hunger, despite the world's desperation, despite the dark hand of Mahela looming in the distance, a deep sense of strength and well-being followed. I smiled. But Kor's eyes were misted.

"Dan, do you know how long it's been? Since your handbonded me willingly?"

Since that long night in Tincherel. Nothing had been the same since the sea had so roughly flung us back to the land. "My own folly," I said. "I felt—betrayed."

"By me?"

"By Sakeema."

"But—"

"Don't say it."

"That I am not Sakeema? You knew it by then."

"I felt betrayed, even so. Kor, I have never laid much claim to good sense."

He sighed and spoke very softly. "No holding back for you, Dan. Nothing by halves."

"That is what my father used to say." Thoughts of Tyonoc, still trapped in Mahela's realm, sent a sharp pang through me. Kor must have felt it, for he turned his head.

"I know we said were going to save him somehow. Dan, I did all that I could."

"It was my quest. How did I come to lay it all on you, or on the god? It was I who failed."

Ai, the harsh touch of truth. I had not wanted to know such truth. Less painful, I had thought, to blame Kor. The more fool, I. There was no misery worse, for me, than blaming Kor.

"Saying we failed means little under the finger of Mahela," Kor mused. "She is as mighty as death or the sea. She always wins."

We talked for a long time, as day shaded into dusk and twilight deepened into nightfall. Tall pines sheltered us, long needles shadowed against the bluedark sky. Somewhere an owl calling. Gray wolf came and lay near our feet. Kor got up to tend the fire, sat by me again, and talk went on. Our voices, very low, not for fear that anyone would hear us, but because we needed to be quiet, calm, soft with each other—neither of us wanted to hurt the other ever again. Tears on our faces sometimes, silent, shining in the firelight. Long pauses sometimes as we gathered courage. It took courage to speak of some things. Of Istas, lying dead, and Kor's grief, how I had failed to comfort him. Of too much dying, all around us. Of Tassida. Most of all, it took courage to speak of Tassida.

I—I could not help it, Dan. That night out by the Greenstones. Your love for her, so ardent—it awakened me.

Sometime, unawares, the weary murmur of our voices had slipped into mindspeak. Better understood, some things, in mindspeak.

But you have not ceased to love her, I ventured. Best to face that now.

No. I love her well. Still—it must be love of a different sort, Dan. Yours—so passionate . . .

He let his thoughts trail off into silence, and I waited, almost able to sense how he braced himself. He had once said that my passions assaulted him with the force of a four-day storm.

I have never felt such love, Dan.

You—felt. I understood. In our minds, he was telling me what was nearly unspeakable.

I felt all that you did.

In your body.

Yes.

Silence for perhaps the span of ten breaths—except that I could scarcely draw my breath. The darkness of night seemed to press down on me.

Never—never before, Dan. Or since. Only—that once with you and Tass.

"You frighten me," I whispered aloud.

Yes. It frightened me, also. And made me wretched.

There was no answer to that. Misery upon misery had been his: Istas dying and Tass my lover and the whole deadly matter of Mahela weighing upon him. Small wonder that he, a mortal king, had given way beneath the strain. . . . A mortal king who had died three times, who healed, and mindspoke, and felt the passions of the people around him? I struggled against fear, my chest heavy with it.

So I struck out at you, he thought to me, ashamed. *And at Tass.*

Fear much like mine had been hers, had driven her off, sent her fleeing, when he had mindspoken her in his rage.

"What did you say to her?" I asked in a tight voice.

Kor shook his head. "I do not want to tell you. Something vicious. The substance of it was, Go away."

He got up, kicked at the fire, and strode off into the benighted forest. I stayed where I was, hearkening, and the wolf raised its head and listened with me. We could hear Kor crashing about. After a time he returned with pine boughs to pile on the fire. Flames leaped up. I could see him again, bruises and all, and he could see my face. He settled himself beside me again and leveled a long look at me.

"There is no devourer in me, Dan," he said abruptly.

"Of course, I know! That needs no saying."

"But you are afraid."

"Not any longer." I thought I was not.

"Then why are we speaking aloud?"

"Because . . ." I fingered my cut lip. "Blast," I muttered.

In rueful amusement he said, "You are more like Tassida than you know."

It was true. I had not been afraid of him when I had thought he was a god who could never wrong me. But since I had seen he was but a poor, floundering mortal . . . Three times a mortal loved one had turned against me, and it was like dying: once would have been too often.

"You are afraid of coming too close to me."

"I—I scarcely know you, Kor, you are so changed! You are . . ." I could no longer say defeated. I knew his courage. But somehow Mahela's touch lay on him yet. "You are darkened in a way I cannot understand."

"Dan," he said intensely, "if only you could feel what I feel—"

It had nearly happened, that night in Mahela's domain. "That frightens me worst of all," I whispered.

Why? If you felt what is in me, if you truly felt all that is in me, knew what—what I have undergone, what has made me be the way I have become, then you would see, you would be sure of me again.

"You want me to—to enter into your being?" Spoken words were clumsy, but stubbornly I kept to them until I saw my path clearly.

"Yes. Will you try it? Dan?"

I swallowed at my fear, knowing that things would never again be right between us until I braved it. "Very well," I said. "But how?"

"That is for you to say. Dan, you showed me the way to my sword, to handbond. You taught me mindspeak."

"But this—this other thing," I protested, "you have been doing it half your life."

"Since I went to the Mountains of Doom the first time. Now you have been there, too. Dan, I know—you came close, that night when I lay with Mahela and nearly drowned in her."

Terror, just remembering. I swallowed again. "Handbond came first," I muttered.

His hand met mine, the sword scars met. We passed the grip, warm, steadying. Strength as of four heroes, mine, and I felt I would need it all. "Don't let go," I told Kor.

"Dan, is it such an ordeal? Don't do it, then."

"Hush. Keep the handbond." He had once died in torment for my sake—it would be my shame if I could not do this thing for him. I closed my eyes, centering myself. Courage . . .

Mindbond came next.

Very true, Dan.

Closeness. I heard his mood in his words, hopeful in the midst of despair but trying not to hope overmuch. I felt, as I often did, his presence as a bodiless thing, as if his mind lay against mine. But still that thin barrier, like a skin . . .

I had to risk.

Kor's grip, warm, constant—I took strength from it, then ventured. I was no longer aware that my eyes were closed, for I had none. Or if I could not see, it was because I was all inward. Handbond still with me, as I knew well enough, but I no longer felt it. I was a swimming, flying thing, a spirit, swimming in sky or flying in sea—no, more. I was sky, I was sea, the indeeps of me as

endless as the sea, formless, melting into—other, as tears
melt into the sea. I knew my name, it was Dan. And I
knew the name of the place where I was, the warm sea. It
was Kor. And I also was fluid, warm, we were as one, and
other was so much a part of me, I could no longer
tell—the boundary, there was none. And I felt—

Something so vast I could not name it.

Then terror. My own terror, my very own.

It struck like a graymaw, tossed me as a seal tosses a
salmon, tore me so that I seemed to feel blood splattering,
I wanted to scream but I had no mouth. Fleeing, I was
fleeing in terror because I had no skin, no mouth, no edge.
Because I had been almost, for an instant, someone else. I
seemed to remember a bloody dead body, mangled—my
own. I had died, and I did not want to die, ever—

Arm around my shoulders, hand gripping mine. Eyes
again, open to see a bruised and well-beloved face. I could
scream now. Perhaps I already had, for Kor looked frightened. I let my head sag to the warm cloth at his shoulder
and sobbed. Kor held me tightly, as if he could somehow
stop my shaking.

"Failed," I moaned.

*Dan, I am so sorry! I should never have asked it of you.
Hush.*

I didn't think it could be so hard for you.

I do everything the hard way, Kor.

I raised my head to look at him, already knowing: I had
thought this was a thing I had needed to do for him, and
had failed to do. But it was all his gift to me. What he had
given me in that half a moment before I fled . . .

Grave dark eyes the color of the sea met mine. Burdened he might be, but there was something in him that
could never be defeated.

"You scamp," I told him huskily.

I was not the only one who could love forever. Love
without end, boundless as the sea.

"You forgot," Kor whispered. "Heartbond came first of all."

No need for handbond any longer. Strength enough in me, now, for any hundred heroes. Both arms around his shoulders, I embraced him.

I dried my face with my hands. Together we sat in silence as the fire blackened into embers. Dying, like our world, falling ashmeal into nothingness . . . In the morning Kor would go back to lead his people, and I, on a fool's quest, seeking a sleeping god.

We must have slept, for we were both exhausted.

I awoke to gray daylight, full of fog. Alone. Kor was gone, leaving me gear and food. I readied my horse in silence, remembering a vivid dream: Kor had mindspoken me in my sleep, telling me he would be steadfast and await my return, bidding me gentle journey, sparing us both the impossible parting, leaving us both with a better farewell to remember.

Heartbond came first. . . . The words pulsed in me like heart's blood as I rode eastward, toward the far slopes of the mountains, toward the unknown place where the sleeping god might lie.

Glossary

afterlings: followers, usually on foot.

afterwit: hindsight.

amaranth: a healing flower, disappeared when Sakeema was killed.

awk: leftward.

blackstone: obsidian.

brownsheen: copper-colored.

brume: dense, gray fog.

cachalot: sperm whale.

carrageen: a dark purplish seaweed.

chough: a small, insolent crow.

comity: innate courtesy.

craking rail: a short-billed landrail of drab plumage, shy habits, and excruciating vocal abilities.

dreamwit: a visionary person, a mystic.

dryland: the opposite of ocean. Refers to any land above water, not necessarily arid.

dulse: an edible seaweed.

erne: a sea eagle.

eye of sky: the dispassionate gaze of the nameless god.

fire true: true enough to be sworn to by putting one's hand in fire.

fogwater: condensation.

fry: recently hatched salmon just emerging from the gravel, the length of the first joint of a man's index finger.

fulmar: a stiff-winged, gliding seabird.

gair fowl: the great auk, a sort of northern penguin.

gannet: a large, white seabird.

glimmerstones: agates.

graymaw: a shark.

graysheen: silver-colored.

greendeep: ocean.

grilse: salmon returning from the sea to their native river; "summer salmon."

gudgeon: a rather stupid-looking freshwater fish.

gutknot: navel.

highmountain: alpine (as, highmountain meadow).

indeeps: penetralia.

inwit: instinct.

jannock: unleavened oatmeal bread.

king: a tribal ruler of either sex.

kittiwake: a small, short-legged, gentle-faced gull.

lappet: a breechclout.

lovelocks: curling tendrils of hair.

merkin: a woman's pubic hair.

moonstuff: silver.

moon-mad: temporarily passionate or out of control, with emotions running high, as if influenced, like tides, by the phase of the moon.

nagsback: a shallow mountain pass.

noggin's worth: a little.

orichalc: a hard, golden bronze.

parr: young salmon still in the brown freshwater stage.

peal: salmon returning from the sea to their native river, turning from silver to red.

pickthank: a flatterer.

rampick: a tree whose top is dead or broken off by wind.

roughlands: the shadowlands.

scantling: a toddler, a very young specimen of whatever species.

scarrow: high, thin cloud.

scarrow-fog: a thin haze high in the sky that lets the sun show as a white spot.

scooning: skipping over the surface of water as a flat stone does when properly thrown.

shadowlands: the arid high plains beyond the mountains, the steppes or shortgrass prairie.

slowcome: a slow-witted person or one who is slow to act, sometimes with a sexual connotation.

smellfungus: a grumbler.

smolt: salmon in the final freshwater stage, turning from brown to silver.

smurr: drizzle.

snow mote: snowflake.

stone-boiled: cooked in liquid into which hot stones are dropped to heat it.

stoup's worth: a lot.

sunstuff: gold.

swordmaster: maker, namer, and wielder of his or her sword.

sylkies: undersea folk who can take the form of humans or seals.

thunder cones: volcanoes.

tongueshot: the distance a voice will carry.

troating: bleating, as of a deer in rut.

tumblestone: a rock washed smooth by the action of water.

wanhope: a person who continues to hope against all common sense.

whimbrel: a brown wading bird, related to dowitchers, godwits, curlews, willets, and snipe.

whurr: to burst from cover with a loud flapping of wings, as a partridge or a grouse.

witch wind: hot wind that blows down from the landward side of mountains.